vacation

# vacation

## matthew costello

thomas dunne books
st. martin's press ☙ new york

THOMAS DUNNE BOOKS.
An imprint of St. Martin's Press.

VACATION. Copyright © 2011 by Matthew J. Costello. All rights reserved. Printed in the United States of America. For information, address St. Martin's Press, 175 Fifth Avenue, New York, N.Y. 10010.

www.thomasdunnebooks.com
www.stmartins.com

Book design by Anna Gorovoy

Library of Congress Cataloging-in-Publication Data

Costello, Matthew J. (Matthew John), 1948–
     Vacation / Matthew J. Costello.
          p. cm.
     ISBN 978-0-312-68007-7 (hardback)
     1. Police—Fiction.   2. Family vacations—Fiction.   3. Cannibalism—Fiction.
     4. New York (State)—Fiction.   I. Title.
     PS3553.O7632V33 2011
     813'.54—dc22

                                                            2011024813

ISBN 978-0-312-68007-7

First Edition: October 2011

10  9  8  7  6  5  4  3  2  1

*Dedicated to Brendan Deneen and Vince Mitchell,*
*who simply wouldn't let this Vacation end . . .*

six weeks before

# 76th Precinct, Union Street, Brooklyn

"They gotta be fuckin' kidding," Rodriguez said.

Jack Murphy looked at his partner. Rodriguez was holding the latest in protection offered to the cops who did the precinct's dirty work: a rigid Kevlar body shield that also covered the back and sides of the neck.

"As if I'd *ever* let one of those animals get anywhere near my neck." Rodriguez grinned. "How about something a bit stiffer and lower to protect the crown jewels?"

The night desk sergeant, Miller, walked into the locker room.

"Rodriguez, you *will* wear it. You too, Murphy."

Jack turned to the sergeant. "Did I say I wouldn't? I'm for all the protection I can get."

"Even if it makes you look like a fuckin' turtle?" Rodriguez asked. "Once a stupid mick, always a stupid mick."

Jack waited until Miller left the room. "Wear it, don't wear it. But Rodriguez—do you have to advertise to the world, to the damn desk sergeant, what you're going to do?"

Jack liked David Rodriguez as a partner. Plenty of experience, but with enough of a rebellious streak that he hadn't been able to get transferred from this precinct to someplace better.

Though these days, where exactly was better? Did "better" even exist?

"So fire me. I'm an honest cop." Rodriguez slammed his locker shut and twirled the combination lock.

Billy Thompson walked in. A rookie, barely weeks on the job, and looking as if he didn't know what the hell to do with his eyeballs.

"Hey," Jack said.

Thompson nodded, then as if remembering to respond: "Oh, hey."

Rodriguez took a few steps closer as if smelling fresh meat. "Bad night last night, Billy boy?"

The rookie started working his locker. "Yeah. Pretty bad."

"Where's your fucking partner?"

Rodriguez looked over at Jack, probably loving that he had an audience for this.

*Which is why I should walk the hell out of here,* Jack thought. *As if things weren't bad enough.*

"He'll be here," Thompson said. "Just running late."

"Could be, amigo. Could be. But sometimes, you know, one bad night out there on the streets, rolling and strolling with the Can Heads, is enough." Rodriguez slapped the shaken rookie on his shoulder. "Not to worry, hm? There's always some other young fool who wants to be part of what's left of New York's Finest."

Jack gave Rodriguez a head tilt in the direction of the door out of the locker room. Hopefully giving his partner the message: *give the fucking kid a break.*

Rodriguez hesitated, then followed Jack out. Just past the door, he laughed.

"I mean, *c'mon* Jack. What do you think these kids *should* hear? That the old days of the boys in blue are still here? 'To serve and protect.' Only what's there to protect with the Can Heads raging—each one looking to take a nice big—"

Jack shook his head. "I got it, Rodriguez. Okay? I've been doing this as long as you have."

"Fair enough, compadre. Fair enough. Let's hope for a nice quiet night and some leftover spaghetti, hm?"

"Right."


Some nights it could be quiet.

Some nights, Jack could sit at a desk, shuffle overdue reports, act busy, and there would be no calls. Of course, his partner remembered the days when two cops like them would take the patrol car out just to see what was happening. Catch a few petty dirtbags, get your arrest numbers up.

It wasn't all that long ago, but by the time Jack joined, those days had ended.

Nobody went out if they didn't have to.

Video had some of the precinct covered—at least the part deemed the Safe Zone, the area protected by twelve-foot-high fences and electrified razor ribbon. Thing was, those safe parts were growing smaller and smaller.

In parts of the five boroughs they had disappeared completely, all the zones turned red. The number of fully-staffed precincts had been whittled down to a handful.

Manhattan still maintained most of its precincts, though even there, Red Zones dotted lower Manhattan, and giant areas north of Central Park had been totally written off.

And the Bronx? The Yankees and everyone else human were long gone.

It was work keeping the Can Heads out.

And Jack told himself—tried to convince himself—that this was important work.

As every politician never lost a chance to say, this is war.

Us versus them.

Those who tried to live normal human lives.

And then the others, the Can Heads.

When the Great Drought hit, when water became like gold . . . when the food riots touched every continent . . . when sheer hunger made whole governments collapse, something else happened.

Some switch got thrown. There were so many explanations, so many theories, and no agreement.

No one knew what had happened.

Had it been a secret experiment gone wrong, a secret superfood created, consumed, designed to end the plague of shortages? And if so, did that food actually carry a new virus that played with the genetic code and undo millions of years of evolution?

And what did he think?

*Above my pay grade*, Jack thought. *They just need people like me, and Rodriguez, and Thompson, to make sure the Can Heads stay away.*

And every day, every night, that got harder and harder.


His eyes had shut sometime in the middle of the night.

Cops weren't supposed to sleep; this wasn't like the Fire Department. They still maintained that code of "on duty—to serve and protect."

That meant awake.

Still, it was quiet and he had slept.

The phone on his desk rang, shrill in the middle of the night. Cell service had largely disappeared save for the few satellites services and those that could afford them. Landlines had also grown increasingly undependable—cables cut, telephone poles down. When lines in the supposedly safe areas got damaged, no team would go out to work on them, at least when it was dark.

The desk phone gave out a sharp trilling noise. He saw the time. 2:12 A.M. Christie.

"Hey," she said.

"Up late again?" he said.

"Just checking on you."

Jack laughed. "You know if *I* had a nice warm bed to sleep in, that's what I'd be doing instead of—"

"It's so quiet here. Hate it when you do nights."

"Only a few more days. You should sleep." A pause. "I would."

"Yes."

Jack's tone did little to take the edge off Christie's voice. She worried. But more than that, she kept at him about their need to get away from this, to leave the city.

The chats often turned into arguments. Their relationship another casualty of this new world.

Get away? Another job? Go where? Do *what*?

Supposedly there were opportunities if you traveled deep enough into the country. Factories where things still got made, plants where they struggled to process and stretch the thin food resources.

Jack had resigned himself to this life.

The money wasn't bad. Sooner or later, he might get posted to Manhattan, a desk job. Just had to hang the hell in there.

But Christie didn't buy any of it.

"Quiet tonight?" she asked.

"So far. Fingers crossed."

A longer pause this time. "Okay. Be safe."

"Always do the best I can. Now you—"

A little laugh from his wife. "I'm going, I'm going." She took a breath. "Good night."

"Good night," Jack said, feeling terribly alone when the line went dead.

He hit the keyboard of the ancient computer on his desk, a true dinosaur, and began scrolling through the still-empty fields of information that had to be filled out.


An hour later.

The screen in front of Jack had long turned into a sleepy blur as he lost the fight to keep his eyes open.

*A few minutes* . . . he had told himself.

Everyone did it. As they waited—or hoped that the morning would come without anything happening. But then the alarm began ringing. A door slammed. Jack's eyes opened. Instantly awake.

He looked up at the precinct map on the station-house wall. One spot glowed bright red.

Rodriguez was already suited up. "Breakthrough, Jackie. Red Hook. Same fuckin' building as last week."

Jack stood up, and started for the locker room with Rodriguez at his shoulder.

"Same building? Jeezus." Jack said.

"Yeah. Sorry man."

Jack knew the building well. Most of the old Red Hook section of Brooklyn had been fenced off. A few government warehouses sat there, not much else. But there were still a few apartment buildings with people in them, fortified with some security and really the only option for the poor slobs who lived in them.

Nowhere else to put them. And they didn't have much of a voice in any decision about their fate.

And last week . . .

It had been a mess. A blocked tunnel, part of the water and sewage system that had been shut down for security's sake, had been opened. No one saw, no one noticed, until the Can Heads began clawing their way in, rising up from the ground inside the building's fence.

The Can Heads had been minutes away from getting inside the building. And all those residents sat, waiting—some with guns, some not—all knowing that if the building came under a full-blown Can Head attack, it would take a shitload of cops to save them.

An *army* of cops.

That night, they got there in time. Killed the few Can Heads who had gotten out. Blew the tunnel opening, sealing it.

Jack clipped on the protective vest and leggings, and then the new Kevlar shield designed to keep the lower head and neck safe.

In case one got too close, jumped on you, and dug its teeth in.

"We got any support from the neighbors? Maybe the Six-three? Been quiet over there. Maybe they'd like some fun."

"Not tonight. They had two incidents already." Miller just shook his head. "Captain says you two are all on your own."

And Jack guessed that the Six-three's captain didn't want to leave his precinct low on firepower. Could be the start of a busy night.

You never knew.

Either way, it would be just him and Rodriguez facing whatever the hell was going on in the Van Hove Apartments.

"All set?" Rodriguez asked.

Jack nodded.

Rodriguez clapped a hand on Jack's back. "Good. I'll drive. Now let's go kill some Can Heads."

# 2

# Red Hook

As they navigated the passable streets of Brooklyn, following a maze of detours made by the security fence, Jack thought of the call from Christie.

When she had called, everything had been quiet.

Now, just past three A.M., they were driving through empty streets. Dead streets, heading to a godforsaken place where—incredibly enough—people lived.

Rodriguez dug out a cigarette. The smoke soon filled the interior even with his window cracked. Sometimes Rodriguez would ask Jack if he minded. Tonight he didn't.

Certain open spots were lit by massive tungsten lamps; other streets were islands of darkness, the high-intensity lamps never installed at all or smashed by the Can Heads.

They liked the dark.

From the outside, their squad car didn't look all that different than one from a decade ago. Still almost like a normal patrol car, white with blue markings.

But if you looked closer, you could spot the differences.

All the windows were fitted with shatterproof triple-plate glass. And the exposed undercarriage was covered with a solid steel plate designed to protect the car from any explosions or attempts to sabotage it. A second layer of bullet-resistant metal covered the car's exterior—though it wasn't too often that bullets were the problem.

Its Achilles' heel? Had to be the wheels. As puncture proof as they could be, the army-grade, hybrid steel-belted tires could still be rendered useless.

Trick was to keep the thing moving.

Being stopped, giving Can Heads time to figure a way in . . . that could be real bad.

"Damn quiet," Rodriguez said.

Of course, nobody would be out, everyone trusting the locks on their doors more than the lamps or the police or the grid of fences to stand between them and the Can Heads.

If there was one thing everyone knew, the Can Heads—whatever made them like that, whatever goddamn switch had been thrown—never gave up.

Not when so nearby, so close, there was fresh meat.

"Always quiet, isn't it?" Jack said.

"Yeah. Just don't like it to be so damn quiet when we've been called."

Jack didn't say anything.

Instead, he looked at the backseat. A powerful arsenal accompanied them. Two M-16 machine guns, army-issue that had become the go-to automatic weapon for police. Beside it, a shotgun and an open case with a foam "egg carton" filled with a variety of explosives, flares and smoke bombs.

They both carried a Glock 22—a cop favorite—and a Smith & Wesson .40, small but accurate.

The rule on a call like this was, scope out the situation and then do what you could on your own. Backup might be available, but only if absolutely necessary.

Once they left the vehicle, they had to bring all the firepower they thought they'd need. Because if you travelled light, getting back to the car, to its portable armory, might be a moot point.

Rodriguez cut the car to the left, heading down a narrow street. No lights. Perfect for a trap, but it was the most direct way to the main entrance of the building.

Rodriguez turned on the squad car's twin light bars on the roof. The narrow street became bathed in brilliant white light.

Jack saw a lone rat scramble away.

Even they were a rarity.

*What a fucking world*, Jack thought.

Then they left the narrow street, a turn to the right and the building entrance lay ahead.

"Okay. Looks quiet."

"Yeah," Jack answered. In addition to a Safe Zone's own protective fence, this building—like most apartment buildings—had its own security fence, complete with a guard and video monitoring.

Except most of the guards weren't worth much.

Terrified rummies, cowering in the shatterproof glass booths, peeing into a bottle, waiting until dawn when some other hapless guard relieved them.

Rodriguez pulled the car up to the gate. He flashed his ID. The guard rubbed his grizzled cheek at the same time as his handheld scanner recognized the ID as genuine.

The man inside the booth communicated with them via a speaker.

In some apartment complexes, there had been cases of finding these guys dead inside their booths. Somehow a Can Head would get in and enjoy feasting on something from the bottom end of the evolutionary spectrum.

And every security guard knew those stories.

"Where's the problem?" Rodriguez asked.

The guard coughed, a crackle over the speaker.

"A tenant—fourth floor. Said he saw a new hole outside. Another breakthrough. H-he thought they might have gotten into the building. Sounded scared."

*I bet,* Jack thought.

Rodriguez: "Christ. In the fucking building? Motherfucker."

Jack knew that it could simply be a case of someone who had too much home-brewed alcohol. The real stuff was hard to come by, and home brew could have weird side effects. A bottle or two and suddenly you start seeing Can Heads all over the fucking place.

"Where the hell is it?" Rodriguez asked.

"The opening? Ah . . . way in the back. And the . . . the . . . tenant's name is Tomkins. Guy lives alone. Fourth floor. Four-G."

Jack leaned forward.

"Can we get back there with the car?" Rodriguez said.

The guard looked as if he didn't know the layout.

"Close. Over there. See those spaces over there? That's about as close as you can get."

Rodriguez turned to look at Jack, his expression saying, *We're fucked. We got to get out and fucking* walk *to the opening?* And if there was indeed an opening, they'd have to go hunt for whatever made it.

Rodriguez's eyes said it all.

*Lucky us.*

Back to the guard. "Okay. Thanks. You hear anything more while we're in there, you let us know. You got that, chief?"

The guard nodded.

Rodriguez pulled the car forward as the guard threw a switch. The gate opened, the wall of wire rolling away as they entered the apartment grounds.

Jack looked at his watch.

3:45.

Only about three hours away from finishing his shift.

*Shit*, he thought.

For all the good that would do.

"What do you want?" he asked Rodriguez.

"The usual. Maybe a few incendiaries, in case there *is* a hole. We start by sealing that."

Jack noticed that his partner had already discarded their new lower head/neck covering, an item that had given him the look of a medieval Asian warrior.

"You forgetting something?" Jack said.

"No. I prefer mobility, amigo."


Out of the car.

Jack knelt down and scanned the opening in the fence while Rodriguez kept up a steady 360-degree scan of the surrounding area.

Jack pulled back on the opening.

"I dunno," he said. "Barely enough room for someone to wiggle through. Motion sensors should have turned on the big floods. If they even work."

He looked up at his partner, who kept looking all around, the M-16 held in ready position.

"What you thinking, Jacko? Anything come through here?"

"Someone cut a goddamn hole. I dunno, and—"

"Right. Shit. I hear you. All right, we go talk to the tenant. The eagle eyes who saw something."

Jack stood back up, shifting his own gun into a ready position.

"Yeah. Maybe we got lucky. False alarm. Some dog."

Rodriguez looked right at Jack and laughed.

"Yeah. You think there are still *dogs* in this neighborhood?"

"Well, that hole—"

"Dream on, brother," Rodriguez said. "Dogs. Shit. Just walking around." Another big laugh. "Like the good old days? Dream the fuck on."

They headed to the front door of the building.

3

# Inside the Apartments

They took the stairs.

Way too many stories about elevators that just stopped. And then you were truly trapped. All boxed up and waiting for whatever would work its way down the steel cables to you.

Because whatever the Can Heads were, they weren't completely mindless. They could still think a bit, even when they looked and acted like crazed rabid animals desperate for food.

Only in this case, food meant other people. The ones who hadn't turned cannibal.

Did they turn on themselves?

Undoubtedly. Hungry enough, they certainly would.

But like any other predator, it was much more efficient for them to hunt weaker prey. Humans.

Jack and Rodriguez took the steps slowly, ears cocked for any sounds from the hallways.

"Seems all quiet," Rodriguez said.

"Hmm?" Jack said.

Rodriguez turned to him. "See, Jacko? That new stuff around your head. Cuts down on your hearing. Not the best idea."

Jack pushed the armored flap away from his right ear. "I hear fine. You were just whispering."

"Riiiight."

Past the third-floor entrance door, and up one more flight. The steps littered with trash. Kids probably still came here to screw or ingest whatever they could find in hopes that it might get them high. Maybe doing drugs was all the more exciting with the thought that there were dangerous things out there.

These teenagers had grown up with the idea of Can Heads for more than half their lives.

Just part of the wonderful landscape.

Yeah, different world from the one your parents grew up in.

That's for fucking sure.

"Here we are," Rodriguez said.

As the senior partner, he'd set up their recon plan.

"Okay, after we're in, you lay back here. Just watch the hallway, the other apartments, 'kay?"

"Sure."

"I'll go talk to our Mr. Tomkins and see what the hell it is he thought he saw. Did the big lights go on outside, then go off? Where did he see them go? Maybe we can be out of here in ten minutes. Shit, maybe even stop for a beer on the way back."

A local dive, The Hook, stayed open 24/7. Right near the 63rd Precinct, its customers were cops and those who didn't really have any good place to hide for the night.

Sucking down beers and shots on a stool rather than facing the streets.

"Maybe."

Rodriguez hesitated at the door to the hallway.

"What? You are *so* whipped. Don't want the smell of a brewski on your breath for wifey?" He shook his head. "Better you than me."

Jack grinned. He doubted there were too many women on the planet who could live with Rodriguez.

Rodriguez grabbed the doorknob.

"Okay. Here we go."

They walked into the hallway.


Jack stayed twenty feet back from Rodriguez as he went to the apartment door.

The door moved as he knocked. Just an inch. It was open.

Jack kept looking to the rear, down to the other end of the dingy hallway for any signs of movement. Everyone was probably safely locked down and asleep for the night.

After the knock, no reaction.

Rodriguez looked back at Jack and gave a shrug.

Now a small push while at the same time pressing the doorbell.

The bell gave out a raspy shriek, way too loud, as if they had put the ringer on the wrong side of the door.

"Shit. I'm going in," Rodriguez said.

Rodriguez kicked at the open door, the noise loud, the door banging open. Jack didn't like making noise. He kept looking around.

Always fucking bad, he thought. Not knowing if something was about to happen.

Rodriguez took a few steps inside. Then: "Hello?"

Back to Jack.

Gesturing. Two fingers to his eyes. A freaking army move. *I go, you stay back*.

Like they were in a goddamn war zone. Police as army.

The ear bud in Jack's left ear was silent. The two-way radios were so damn unreliable. No one from the station house asking how things were going. Everyone dozing. Though Miller undoubtedly had their audio on a speaker somewhere.

Very low.

Wouldn't want to wake anyone up.

If he could pick them up at all.

Jack took another look behind him and then started moving closer to the open door. If it all looked cool, he'd follow his partner in.

He got to the doorway.

Rodriguez, louder now to an apparently empty apartment. "Hello? Anyone the hell here?"

Nervous.

Not just me, Jack knew. Rodriguez, too. Jack quickly turned around to check the hallway. Then he took a step inside, looking left and right.

His partner was right—the neck protector made head movement hard. And hearing? That sucked, too.

But—

It didn't cover the front of Jack's face.

So he could smell.

Then, Rodriguez: "Oh, shit. God. We got—"

Jack took a deep sniff, hoping that whatever scent he just inhaled had been more in his mind than anything else.

The smell was metallic. A smell of decay and blood, so powerful here.

"Rodriguez, hold on there," Jack said. "We better—"

He shifted on his feet. Rodriguez shouted back, "Motherfucking guy has been shredded, Jack. Christ, come in here."

Then the sound of movement, steps, feet hurrying. Jack tried to imagine the likely layout. A small kitchen, a dining area to the side, a bathroom down a hallway, bedroom to the left.

The front door behind him slammed.

Stupidly, he turned to see what even his muffled ears already knew had just fucking happened.

Gunfire. The sound of Rodriguez's gun blasting away. But only a few bursts and then the blasts abruptly ended. Jack's hand went to his chest and the control for his two-way radio, his lifeline with the station house.

"Officer down!"

He raised his gun just as two of them appeared in the hallway.

Sometimes you saw Can Heads and they didn't look any worse than homeless guys from decades ago, wearing their tattered clothes, eyes bulging out of drunken sockets, mouths open, teeth brownish, rotten.

These were not like that.

Thin, wiry, the two of them human animals, barely wearing shredded clothes, which made them look even more crazed.

Their eyes opened wide as they looked at Jack, close to being on all fours as they raced toward him.

"Command!" Jack yelled. Then: "Shit!"

There was a response in his ear bud, mostly static and then drowned out by his own gun, now shooting an erratic spray of bullets at the two creatures.

Enough bullets that the Can Heads flew past him, their bodies ripped open.

Nothing from Rodriguez, and as much as Jack didn't want to . . . as much as he wanted to get the hell out of there, he ran deeper into the apartment.

A few steps. His handgun out now, too.

Jack passed a short hallway on his left, then the entrance to the kitchen, and arrived at the small living room.

He started firing crazily even before he knew what he was seeing, blinking as he took in the scene. Four Can Heads down on the carpeted floor, the rug turned a wet, bronze red, like the floor of a charnel house. They squatted around Rodriguez, his body armor roughly peeled away in jagged chunks.

*Way too fucking late,* Jack thought.

In the moments between the last blast of Rodriguez's gun and now, the Can Heads had made quick work of Jack's partner. Gaping holes sprouted in his midsection, his upper legs, and a massive one by his neck.

And yet—

And yet . . .

Fuck. The poor bastard was still alive.

Jack watched Rodriguez's near-dead eyes land on him. Begging. Hoping.

Not a thought. No question what to do. Jack moved his S&W handgun over toward Rodriguez, aimed, and fired twice.

And then the Can Heads could do no more harm to Rodriguez.

Which is when the Can Heads leapt up from their feast and made a mad rush for Jack.

Jack was on automatic now. Job straightforward. The reward clear.

Kill them before they kill you.

Can Heads coming right at him, inches away, he began firing, holding the M-16's trigger down so it just kept spitting out bullets. His handgun—only a few shells left.

And they fell.

One down, then another Can Head climbing over it, still trying to get at Jack, and Jack made that one's head explode. Would they turn on themselves, take the easy pickings, or keep coming at him?

He thought of Christie. Then Simon, Kate.

And he knew that, unlike his partner, there'd be no one to spare him.

No one to help end *his* horror.

In that moment, the other two had gone to either side of Jack; he looked both ways, trying to decide which posed the biggest danger.

All in seconds.

Choosing the one on the left, he tried to aim his handgun but suddenly felt that Can Head's arm shoot out and its claw hand grab his throat. But the hand slid off the protective covering, and Jack both fired and awkwardly jabbed the thing with his pistol.

Then he wheeled to face the last Can Head.

His handgun clicked. Empty. And not a chance of being reloaded. He backed up against a wall of the living room. Now only one gun to keep the Can Head at bay.

Still a chance to get out of this.

Unless there were more of them, already drawn by the noise, the gunfire . . .

The machine gun jammed. Or maybe it was out of ammo too. How long had he been madly firing, his finger locked on the trigger?

The thoughts again.

Christie, Kate, Simon.

The neck protector reduced the sound around him. The grunts, the near-human sounds they made. The Can Head nearly hopping toward him seemed to flash on the fact that the gun had stopped firing.

The thing opened its animal-like mouth, screamed, and leapt forward boldly.

Jack stood his ground.

Not from bravery on his part.

He stood his ground. There was nothing else he could do.

The Can Head grabbed at Jack's face but Jack turned away, the clawing fingers only inches away, now pawing at his armored body.

Those protective layers needed to be peeled away.

If he was to be eaten.

Another squeeze of the trigger. Still jammed.

The tugs threatening to rip Jack's arms and his legs right out of their sockets.

The Can Head held Jack's right leg fast. Armor roughly peeled off. Then it bit down hard.

Jack screamed, kicking at it with his other leg, pounding the useless gun against the thing's head.

The pain—a white heat that made the apartment vanish.

Instinctively, he pulled the useless trigger again.

And now the gun responded with the oh-so-beautiful *rat-a-tat-tat* burp of fire.

"Fuck you," Jack said, pressing the automatic rifle's muzzle right against the head of the thing eating him. He watched the head explode into a fireworks display of bone and blood and smoke.

A look over his shoulder.

More could come.

He hacked out the words: "Command!"

He locked his eyes on the door and hallway outside.

Telling himself amidst the pain and blindness of his seeping wound, *Can't pass out . . . have to stay awake . . . there may be more of them . . .*

But the white electric light of the apartment, of blood and bullets and bodies, gave way to a blackness that Jack, for once, could do nothing about.

## 4

# Kings County Hospital

Jack woke up to the sound of someone's voice, speaking low, but still it made him open his eyes.

He saw Captain Brandt talking to a nurse, hushed tones, unaware that they had already awakened the patient.

"Thank you," Brandt said to the nurse. Then he looked over at Jack. A big smile, and he came to the bedside.

"Jack. Sorry. Did I wake you?"

Jack forced a small smile. "All I do is sleep, so it doesn't take much, Captain."

Brandt's hand went out as if to pat Jack, then hesitated, as if any spot on Jack's battered body might hold a painful wound hidden under dressing and bedclothes.

"Looking good, Jack. They say your recovery is going great. They even have your rehab scheduled."

"Terrific. Can't wait."

Jack regretted the sarcasm as soon as the words passed his lips.

*Least I'm alive,* he thought. *No room for any bullshit sarcasm when you're alive and your partner was turned into roadkill.*

Too easy to beat himself up these sleepy days in the hospital. Replaying the way things went down, what he could have done different.

*Maybe I should have been the point man*, Jack thought.

*Maybe I would have seen the trap faster.*

*We'd both be alive.*

"Did they say when rehab would start?" Jack said.

Brandt pulled up a chair and sat close to the head of the bed. Jack gave the bed controls a push and elevated his head a bit.

"Work begins tomorrow. In bed. Then depending on how the leg does, you'll start the real work with physical therapy."

"Guess I won't be running any time soon."

Captain Brandt hesitated. He probably knew the prognosis better than Jack. "Running? Might be a while for that." Brandt took a breath, then dared some honesty. "Think your running days may be down the road a bit."

*Down the road a bit.*

As in never.

Jack nodded as best he could.

Then: "I'll run. Might be a bit lopsided. Might have a bit of limp. But I'll run."

Captain smiled back.

"I bet you will."

Running.

It was about more than just exercise. Things happened fast out on the streets. Fast. And running, as if some primal ability resurrected from our cave and jungle days, could be the difference between life and death.

"You're eating well?"

Another nod. Both of them avoiding talk of that day. The first time Brandt visited, Jack had been so doped up, the captain had been a blur, drifting in and out of focus, the sound of his voice echoing from miles away.

Today was better.

That was good.

Today, Jack wanted to ask a few questions.

"Captain, I wanted to thank the guys who got me. I mean, I was gone. How long before—"

Brandt patted Jack's shoulder.

"Jack, we can review everything later. I don't think now's the time."

Jack couldn't stop thinking about it, remembering. The smells, the Can Heads all over the place. Rodriguez. And somehow he had been able to stop them.

That part—stopping them—no, that still didn't seem real.

But he had done it.

"Any more trouble there? That building?"

Brandt smiled. "Trouble everywhere these days, Jack."

Even though Jack got a regular and powerful cocktail of pain-killers, he could still see things . . . notice things.

Now, he locked on his captain's eyes. He saw Brandt look left, as if the question might be dodged. He blinked.

More of Red Hook abandoned? The circle of Safe Zones tightening?

"Can't we leave this for later?"

Jack nodded. He couldn't demand that his captain talk about it.

The doctors must have told Brandt: no shop talk.

A nurse walked in, smiled at the two of them, looked at Jack's drip, and then walked out again.

Jack locked his eyes right on Brandt's.

"You heard my radio?"

"Yeah. No response when we pinged you back." Brandt took a breath. "The guys didn't know what they'd find. Pretty surprised. You alive, and a whole lot of dead Can Heads."

"And Rodriguez."

A nod. "Yes. Rodriguez dead, too."

"I . . . I . . ."

"Jack. Easy. Let it rest. For now, hm?"

Now Jack looked away.

*Suppose I should be grateful.*

*To be fucking alive.*

He didn't feel that way.

*Are we losing this fucking war?*

"I guess . . . I should just say thanks."

Brandt nodded, shrugging.

Finally: "Captain, I know I can't be out in the streets for a while. But I'd like to get back as soon as possible. Maybe some desk work. You'll need all the officers you can—"

Brandt shook his head.

"Jack, how long has it been since you've had any time away from the job?"

"I don't need any time. Soon as my leg is good, in a few weeks, I can—"

"You need a break, Jack. Let psych service see you. Get some counseling. You can't just shrug this off. You have a lot of time coming."

Jack arched his back up, raising his head off the pillow as much as he could.

"I don't *need* any damn time."

The nurse came into the room again.

"Officer, your family is downstairs, coming up now."

Another smile from her, but it quickly evaporated as she sensed the tension in the room.

Brandt pushed his chair back and stood up.

"Yeah. I want you to take the time. Talk to your wife. A break. A vacation."

Jack opened his mouth, but he knew Brandt well enough to know that an order was an order.

"Talk to Christie. Get away. The Can Heads will be here when you come back." Another pause. "I *need* people like you, Jack."

A boy's voice echoed from the hospital hallway.

His son, Simon.

Brandt started for the door.

"Get better, Jack."

Then he turned and left.

5

# Christie

Christie watched Simon run ahead, down the hospital hallway, Kate walking tentatively beside her. She had worried how they both would react, seeing their dad in a hospital bed.

She and Jack had agreed to tell them only that he'd had an accident at work.

Their strong daddy took a nasty fall.

"Simon," she said. Then louder, "Wait."

Simon stopped. She looked down at Kate, who was three years older than her brother. Christie wondered whether her daughter suspected something more than an accident. There was no way, even in a protected area of Staten Island, that they could keep things from either of their children.

The times Kate tried to ask questions about his job, Jack changed the subject.

Eventually she stopped asking questions.

With Simon stopped, Christie saw Jack's captain come out of the room. He smiled as she came close.

"Christie. I think . . . he's coming along," he said quietly.

"Captain, that's good. I—"

"But, can I have a word with you?"

Christie looked down at the two kids. "Sure. Simon, Kate, you go in to your dad. Just don't make a lot of noise. I'll be right there."

Simon bolted into the room. After a brief hesitation, Kate followed.

"I just wanted to tell you . . ." Brandt said. "I mean, I told Jack that he needs to take some time off. He's not happy about that."

Kate nodded. "I'm not surprised."

"Right. He talked about desk duty. Something like that. I told him to do his rehab. Get better. Take some time off."

Christie nodded.

"I said he needed to take a vacation. He has it coming."

Christie pushed her hair off her forehead. "Do people still take those?"

"Yes. And he needs to. Maybe the family needs it. Look . . ."

Brandt reached into his back pocket and pulled out a glossy brochure.

"Look at this. Been posted in the precincts. It may be something he needs. You all need."

Christie took the brochure, and stood there for a few minutes reading it.


"Where's your mom?" Jack asked.

Kate stood rail straight, a few feet from the bed. Simon showed no such reticence, leaning right on the crisp white bedclothes, his eyes searching his dad's.

"She's talking to some man," Simon said.

"Captain Brandt," Kate added.

"You kids okay?" Jack said, smiling. "Getting homework done? Helping Mom?"

"I don't like homework," Simon said.

"When are you coming home?" Kate asked.

"Soon. Just need my leg to get better."

"Mom said you had an accident."

Kate. Eyes locked on. Face impassive.

*My daughter isn't buying any of this*, Jack thought.

"Yeah. Took a bad fall out on patrol."

He waited for Kate to say something more. Like: Are you sure it wasn't some of those people? The ones the other kids talk about.

The people who eat people.

But whether it was seeing Jack in the bed or the fact that Simon was here, Kate didn't go any further.

"Can I see it?"

Jack looked down to Simon, his arm on the bed and chin resting on a hand, studying Jack as if he were a museum display.

"See what, Simon?"

"Your leg. Where you hurt it."

Jack laughed. "I'm afraid they have it wrapped up in a lot of bandages. Nothing to see."

"They feed you here?" Simon asked.

"That's a dumb question," Kate shot out.

Jack gave her a look; she could be so quick to dump on Simon. Normal for a brother and sister, he guessed. Still, it always sounded harsh to him.

"Yes. Hospital food. Nothing you'd like."

Funny, Jack thought, food was never far from anyone's thoughts. All the synthetic nutrient substitutes, the soy-based products, the pretend PB&J sandwiches couldn't hide the fact that food—the way it used to be—was hard to come by. For some, impossible.

Most of what was once common had turned into rarities.

And then Christie walked in.

Christie turned around and saw Simon poking at the balloons on the windowsill.

Kate looked down at the bed.

She saw Jack look at the kids and nod.

Back to Christie.

"So, what did Brandt tell you?"

She had her fingers interlocked with Jack's. Jack wasn't normally one for handholding, the random unexpected kiss. Not his style. She accepted that.

Just like she had accepted how strange life had become for both of them.

She gave his hand a gentle squeeze.

"To make sure you did your exercises. Get to physical therapy. He likes you, Jack. Wants you back as soon as you're better."

"And what else? What's that in your back pocket? The department's guide to dealing with recovering disgruntled spouses?" He took a breath. "Psych information?"

She reached into her pocket and took out the brochure.

"Psych is part of your rehab. You know that. But this . . ."

She handed it to Jack. For a minute, he thought it was a joke.

Jack read from the front of the brochure: "'Paterville Family Camp. The place for a secure and safe family vacation in the beautiful Adirondacks!'"

He laughed. "You're kidding me. 'Safe and secure'?"

"Captain Brandt says you should—*we* should take a vacation. Get away from the city. Things aren't so bad up there."

"Says who?"

"Can you listen? It says: 'Families visiting Paterville Family Camp will have the luxury of staying in one of our traditional log cabins, all with breathtaking views overlooking our crystalline lake.' Crystal-line . . . that's good. Gotta love a crystalline lake."

She watched Jack flip open the folded brochure. The first inner page was all about security.

"Look," she said. "See—it's reached only by one road, has two fences, an inner one, and then an outer electrified fence with twenty-four/seven guards."

"Show me a place these days that *doesn't* have fences."

"And look—tons to do. Swimming, boats, hiking, fireworks."

"Cookouts?"

"I knew you'd ask that. Families eat communally, and the camp has been able to grow its own produce. Has a mini-farm right on the property."

"Really? No blight or drought? They should tell the damn govern-ment how they pulled off that trick."

He glanced at the kids.

*Tone it down,* he told himself.

Christie felt her forced smile and cheerful attitude fading. Jack could be a rock when his mind was made up. Probably what made him such a good cop. But as a father, a husband . . .

She leaned close. "Look at your kids. Tell me, have they even *seen* a lake, a real lake for swimming? Walked on a trail, seen a mountain, gone to a beach? None of it. This could be their chance, Jack. A week away from this—"

She stifled the word *goddamned.*

"—world to have a few days in summer like kids and families used to. They deserve that. You do. I do."

Jack looked up from the brochure that he had found so amusing.

He waited. Part of his process. No quick answers out of Jack. He'd think things through and then think some more.

"Okay—here's what I'll do. I'll see how the Highway Authority program has been working. Adirondacks, that's way up there, Christie. *Way* up there."

She gave his hand another squeeze.

"I'll check it out. And, if it's legit, we'll talk about it again."

Now Christie leaned forward. She gave Jack a kiss, his lips dry and cracked. She stayed close to his face.

"Thank you." Then a look back. "For them."

Jack reached up with his right hand and brushed some stray blond hair away from her face.

"A vacation, hm? I guess . . . that really would be something."

To seal the deal, Christie gave him another kiss.

And then it was time for them to leave.

one day before

# 6

## Recovery

Jack raised his left leg slowly, feeling the dead pull of a massive weight working hard to pull the leg down.

From the start, he had quickly ignored the cautious advice of his physical therapy team, and pushed his rehab work. And his undamaged leg . . . he would push it to the limit.

*If I have only one good leg, it'll have to get as strong as it can be.*

*I may not run again. But one way or the other, I'll be able to move.*

The leg reached its full horizontal extension, and then he resisted the always present temptation to rush lowering it. That thought, that *urge* only promoted him to make the descent even slower, even more torturous.

Until it was time to work with the other leg.

The damaged leg, the bum leg. The bad leg.

Weeks after the attack, the bandages had finally come off.

And now, though he could still see the indentation where he had lost some muscle mass, it didn't look too bad. Nothing that would scare anyone, even his kids, who had been so curious about what the leg would look like when all the surgeries were done and the bandages finally came off for good.

"See," he said to Kate and Simon, "not so bad."

But he quickly looked at their eyes, and that had told him the truth of the situation.

They weren't used to seeing their dad wounded or damaged in any way. He was never anything less than their protector. Whatever their idea of police work was in this world, they always saw him as the best and the strongest.

Now? With his leg so obviously damaged, their eyes said—what?

Fear?

Worry?

And that drove his rehabilitation.

Besides working the machines they had installed in his basement, Jack started walking again, way ahead of schedule. He ignored the pull of the healed, tight skin, and the pain that was always there.

And if it didn't go away, fair enough. He'd deal with it.

He walked around their community on Staten Island, past rows of neat and boring suburban houses, all encircled by a fence.

Everywhere, fences.

Even here, far from the "real" boroughs of New York.

Gradually, he was able to suppress the urge to limp, and the need to always favor the right leg.

Despite the warning of the surgeon, Dr. Kleiner, and his rehabilitation team, he didn't slip backward. The wounded leg grew stronger. The shock of each step grew less.

His walks grew and grew, and eventually, until when he returned home, he started to see a flicker of worry in Christie's eyes. Concern. Why are you out there so long? Why are you away for hours?

The few times they had talked about it hadn't gone well.

Now he just did what he did. They didn't talk about it.

While his family simply watched.

He looked at his right leg. The padded bar pressed against his lower shin.

He'd begin slowly, with only a few pounds of weight.

And then, with each slow up-and-down movement, he'd add more weight, staring at his damaged leg, wishing it stronger, better.

He took a breath, and began to raise the bar.


Jack heard Christie's steps coming down the stairs.

He let his right leg slide off the bar. Not bad, he thought. Not anywhere as strong as the left leg, but all things considered . . .

He grabbed a towel dangling from the weight machine and turned to Christie.

"How's it going?" she said.

They had fought over that question during those first weeks. How are you? How's the leg? Are the dreams over? Did you sleep through the night?

They'd had fights.

He wished she would stop asking.

Until he realized that Christie was scared and worried. He forced himself not to react.

Now, with weeks of rehab behind him, he could hear her question, and answer it. No problem.

"Good." He smiled. "In fact, I'm pretty damn impressed. All things considered, my leg seems to be doing really well."

She took a few steps closer.

The exposed lightbulb caught her face. "That's good. Real good. Though at the risk of sounding critical—"

Jack rubbed his face, mopping up the beads of sweat. The floor around him was dotted with the drops.

"It stinks down here. You really need a hot shower, my friend."

Jack laughed. The rough patches they had gone through were fading. He never told her everything about that night. He knew—and she knew—he never would.

The attack. Rodriguez. Shooting him because it had to be done. Then, being stuck here, working his ass off to get better, to get back to being a cop.

"I hear you, boss. I'll hit the showers ASAP."

Christie took another step closer to his machine. Only then did Jack notice that she had her hair pinned back. It always made her look like the teenager he'd dated in Bay Ridge.

"You done doing the school-thing with the kids?"

"You mean trying to teach them? Not sure I'm much of a teacher. Think we should reconsider some of the families getting together, getting our kids together—"

He started shaking his head before she finished.

"No. It's better they stay here. Better that than bounce around to other people's houses."

"You mean trapped here."

He heard the edge in her voice. It was an edge that he had grown used to. Perhaps it was his recuperation, perhaps the world she was forced to live in, perhaps it was his paranoia. Whatever, it was getting too easy for them to snap at each other.

"I'm sorry," she said. "I just wish we could think about it."

He took a breath.

"Okay. I'll think about it."

"Right. Sure."

Then a shrug, and he watched her walk up and out of the basement.

Jack let the weights drop with a loud clang to the base of the machine. And he sat there, sweating in the shadows. Thinking . . .

He knew he looked at things differently than most people. Most people could block out the realities of this new world that they lived in.

With enough fences, enough guards, enough safe sectors, life could almost seem normal.

But even some safe sectors in the city's outer borough were no longer safe. Chunks of infrastructure—water, electricity, government—fell apart. Power failures, sabotage to the city's water supply.

Chaos—always close, always one attack away.

The pressure from the Can Heads always there, always mounting.

Jack got up and moved through the hallway to the door that led to the basement and the adjoining garage. Like most houses, the door to the basement had been reinforced. Double locks, and on the interior side, metal plating. Every house was vulnerable.

Not so different from when he grew up in Brooklyn, and their house suddenly had rats. His father saw the telltale signs—the small caches of food that the rats dug out off the basement shelves and planted behind furniture, the electrical wires chewed through.

Then his dad found a sea of their pellet-sized scat under a radiator, revealing that a tribe of rats, with their lousy vision but incredible gnawing teeth, had found a new home.

And his father, a veteran of twenty years as a street cop, took on the rats.

Rat traps with the poison appeared. Any opening to the outside, the slightest crack, was lined with a thick wire mesh that would dig into any rat even as they elongated their flexible bodies to sneak in.

Dead bodies appeared both in and out of the house. One went undiscovered until everyone got a whiff of the overwhelming stench.

Now on the job like his old man, years later, Jack had smelled far worse.

But he'd thought of his dad and his rat-fighting when he moved to Staten Island with Christie and the two then toddlers.

Every crack sealed.

Doors reinforced.

Motion detector lights and alarms. Nothing expensive, but all good, reliable stuff.

Backup generator. Everyone had one these days.

Double locks everywhere. Metal panels that could be closed tight over the first-floor windows at night.

And weapons?

There were the weapons under lock and key that Christie knew about. Then there were the weapons she *didn't* know about.

Jack had thought through a variety of scenarios, and safely secreted around the house other supplies of ammo and guns.

Not unlike the rats and their caches.

# 7

# Preparations

Jack unlocked the trunk of the Ford Explorer.

It was five years old, and he maintained it himself and had as much confidence in it as he would in something brand new. Maybe more.

He'd done all the modifications—expensive and time-consuming—himself. The standard safety glass had all been replaced with reinforced shock-absorbent windshields and side windows, the same glass they once used in the armored cars of the well-heeled in São Paulo.

São Paulo? Gone years ago.

A layer of sheet metal covered all the vehicle's side panels and undercarriage. The hood got a double layer of the same steel. The SUV would be better than a Humvee in an accident.

Or an attack.

Tires were a problem. Even the best tires could be ripped and gouged and turned into a useless piece of spinning rubber.

But the latest steel-belted battle tires used on the NYPD's patrol vehicles were layers thick. A puncture, even a good-sized one, couldn't come close to deflating them. Jack made sure he carried two spares.

He unlocked the compartment hidden under the mat of the luggage area, revealing the cases containing guns and ammo. Two S&W .40 pistols, a pair of Glock 22s, and—in two pieces—an M16. Beside the guns, a foam "egg shell" held three compact C-4 explosives— "door-busters" the cops called them, all fitted with timers.

He shook his head.

If Christie saw all this, she would freak. Was it just paranoia? Or was bringing all this firepower borne of years of being on the streets, while the Can Heads kept on coming?

He'd wear his service revolver on his ankle as well. Christie had grown used to that.

"Just like your father," she had told him. "You feel undressed without your gun."

He'd smile at that.

And carefully not say anything in response.

Undressed? No. More like unprotected.

He slowly shut the back hatch door, gently, so no loud thump filtered upstairs.

Jack tried to do a good job of acting enthused about the trip. His family deserved that.

He walked to the side of the car—near the front, just below the engine—and knelt down. The SUV had been driven around for a few days, and he wanted to see if the most recent alterations he'd made to the underchassis looked completely intact.

He dug a small flashlight out of his back pocket.

The right leg at the knee sent out a painful burst as it hit the stone floor.

Ignoring it, he craned down and looked under the car.

*Why do I keep looking at this?* he thought.

Checking it day after day.

As much as he didn't want to accept it, he knew the answer.

His hand felt the reinforced underside of the car, the steel plate that ran from bumper to bumper, installed with the help of his cop friend Tim, who lived nearby. Jack then helped Tim do the same thing to his decade-old Land Rover.

But this new addition?

Nobody knew about that.

Positioned mid-car, in the center, it looked like a meter-long protrusion an inch and a half below the rest of the steel plate on the undercarriage.

The protrusion was lined with reinforced steel as well; it was also a compartment. Nobody would notice it. Not unless they did what he was doing now, sliding under the vehicle, a flashlight between his teeth.

And inside the meter-long compartment? Two rows of a mix of pentolite and RDX explosives. Compact and powerful. The NYPD used them to blow up and seal the holes made by Can Heads in their relentless desire to get under barriers.

He looked at the metal tube with its shielded wiring streaming from the compartment and to the front, up to just below the dashboard.

Did he look at this every day because he needed to comprehend what his fear—what installing this really meant? Was that why?

He slid out from under the car. Stood up. Opened the driver's door and crouched down.

Jack aimed the light at a place to the right of the SUV's steering column. The light showed the two-step switch that he had installed. There would be no chance of accidentally triggering it.

No, to make the switch active, he'd have to turn and open a protective cap a full 360 degrees. Only then would the detonation switch become active and be revealed.

And then—a single flick would send an electrical charge down to the compartment and explosives . . . and blow the car to pieces.

He straightened up, and sat back in the passenger seat.

Such a crazy precaution. Insane, really. But as long as no one knew, there'd be no harm.

Right?

His paranoia would be his alone.

And in what scenario would he actually throw that switch?

Despite his tendency to imagine the what-ifs, the possibilities, the dangers in detail—

Part of his job, to be sure.

—for this, he didn't allow himself to go there.


"So where were you?"

"Just puttering with the car."

"That car gets more attention than me."

Christie's tone was light—but Jack heard a dig anyway.

Then she said: "The kids are crazy excited, you know. I have them packing."

He nodded.

"And it'll be great. For them. For you. For us."

"I know," Jack said.

Then: "Think I'll take that shower now."

# 8

# Home

"I'll have some more," Jack said.

Christie passed him a bowl. The mixture of soy and a synthetic protein had been flavored to supposedly resemble chili.

It only reminded Jack that there were no beans here, no meat.

It was filling. And that was about it.

"I don't like it," Simon said. He stuck out his tongue and tried to continue talking. "It makes my tongue feel hot."

Christie laughed. "Okay, maybe a bit too spicy."

"Not for me," Jack said.

He noticed that Kate had barely touched hers. "Not hungry?"

"For this?" Kate said. "Can I go, like, read or listen to music or something? This stuff makes me sick."

"Kate."

The girl looked at her dad.

"Yes?"

"Something wrong?"

"Shelly's having her party when I'm away!"

Jack shook his head. "Not sure we agreed that you could even go to that. I mean, a party—"

"Let's cancel birthdays, too."

Finally, Christie jumped in. "So, you'd rather stay and go to her party than this vacation?"

Kate looked as if she was actually weighing the choice.

"Maybe. No. I don't know. I can't even remember what parties are like."

She turned back to her plate and took a forkful of the pretend chili. "This tastes *weird.*"

*Doesn't everything these days?* Jack thought.

Real food, real fruit, vegetables, or even more rare, meat—when available—were incredibly expensive. The fact that the Paterville Camp offered regular meals, with food fresh from their own protected farm area, seemed nothing short of miraculous.

The kids couldn't wait. For that, and the swimming, the boats, the fireworks, the mountains.

Like going to a different planet.

And despite his fears, Jack started to feel as if this was something he should look forward to.

It wasn't just something the family needed.

*I need this, too.*


Jack waited until the kids left the table.

"Maybe this trip *is* a good thing."

Christie turned to him. "Good to hear you say that."

"Yeah. You may be right. Getting away. Having fun. Doing things together."

She smiled. "Good. That will make for a less grumpy driver."

He smiled back.

For a moment, the only cloud in the kitchen was his secret.

What he had done to the car.

But that would stay a secret.

on the road

# 9

# Leaving

Jack leaned back from the dining room table, where his ancient laptop sat with a printer on the floor. Ink needed to be conserved; printing was rarely done.

Christie stood in front of the refrigerator, packing food and drinks for their ride.

An eight-hour trip lay ahead, maybe more with the checkpoints along the way.

Jack turned back to the computer screen. He entered his password for the NYPD secure site and navigated his way to an innocuously titled tab labeled ROAD REPORTS. Sometimes there'd be a connection, torturously slow, sometimes he'd get nothing.

Today he got lucky.

A screen appeared, showing a map of the metropolitan area.

A section of the Long Island Expressway glowed red. Another red spot flashed in Williamsburg, where the Brooklyn-Queens Expressway passed the Brooklyn Bridge on its way toward Queens.

And up in the Bronx, lots of red spots.

Par for the course for the Bronx.

All the hot spots were clickable, and Jack could see the details of whatever the incident was. But these would be no normal accident reports, no tractor trailers overturned and spilling diesel on the highway, no five-car pileups as commuters raced home.

No, this folder only carried reports of road incidents carried out by Can Heads.

And those could make for interesting reading.

Once, Can Heads had rolled barrels on the Belt Parkway after a fence breakthrough. The cars hit by those barrels became flaming traps; the people within turned into the pickings for the crazed Can Heads, who dug the screaming humans out.

Jack had seen video of that one. Stomach churning didn't begin to convey it.

Human barbecue.

Or the Saw Mill River Parkway attack near Van Cortlandt Park. Though the walkway over the highway near Van Cortlandt Park was enclosed by a heavy-duty, prison-gauge steel-mesh fence, somehow a hole had been cut.

And like cavemen attempting to leverage boulders down to stop a lumbering mastodon, Can Heads had tossed down rocks and then leaped—some to their own deaths—onto the roofs of the careening cars.

Road safety. Shit.

Did that expression even have any meaning at all anymore?

In Staten Island, lots of places still looked peaceful. Living on an island, accessible only by a pair of heavily guarded and fortified bridges, with all the communities with their own security systems, there were hardly any incidents on the island.

Would the Can Heads eventually figure out how to take charge of the ferry, and ram it into the St. George Terminal?

And once they got there, would their contagion spread? Was it even a goddamn contagion?

But that brought to mind another question that bothered Jack.

The holes in fences, the stopping traffic, the breakthroughs.

*Are we losing this war?*

No one talked about that.

Not yet. Not on TV.

And that wasn't surprising. Would anyone want the world to be even more panicked than it already was?

If people thought that the Can Heads were winning—what then?

Jack moved the mouse to scroll the map upward, to where he really needed to look.

He zoomed close to the New York Thruway as it snaked up to Albany. Promoted as New York's safest highway, Jack knew that it had become a vital pipeline for the limited food and supplies that moved back and forth from the ports of New York to the rest of the state.

Who knew *where* they got the money for the ten-foot fences and the armored checkpoints?

A few chopper stations had been built, mini-launching platforms for a response to any problem picked up by the highway's motion detection system or video surveillance.

Then from Albany, the Northway continued the same degree of protective armor.

As expected, these highways showed green all the way clear to Montreal.

But it was the road he'd have to take getting off the highway that concerned Jack.

To get to the Paterville Camp, he would have to travel through some of the smaller towns of the Adirondacks. Most of them—thanks to low populations and the fact that the locals had their own guns to fight back—remained relatively quiet.

Relatively.

Each week would bring the story of another battle between a horde of Can Heads and local townspeople. Each town had its own Home Patrol, a neighborhood watch on steroids. There was some support from the State Troopers, the undermanned National Guard, even volunteer militias.

Still, things could happen.

These roads—watched and guarded, but still very much open and exposed—could be attacked.

And were.

If there was any danger on this road trip, it would come on those stretches of road.

For now, the route they'd need to take—nearly an hour and a half off the highways—looked quiet.

He slid the mouse to the left and right. Western New York. A few spots glowed red, but nothing within a couple hundred miles of Paterville.

*We winning this thing?*

He wished he could believe it.

He clicked on an X in the corner of the screen. The NYPD site vanished.

"Jack, could you give me a hand here?"

He got up and left the quiet shadows of the dining room.

Jack looked down at the freezer chest. Full already, with so-called juice drinks, the synthetic peanut butter and jelly sandwiches—a staple—and some unknown items wrapped in tin foil.

Christie held a few bottles of water, as precious as food.

"Can you help me find some room in here? Maybe move some things around?"

Jack smiled. "Room? Looks packed."

"C'mon. Work your man-magic. Move stuff. I want to keep this water cold for our trip."

Jack crouched down and rearranged things. Like some kid's sliding block puzzle, eventually he made space appear.

"See. I knew you could do it."

"A man of many—"

"Dad! Dad! Tell stupid Simon that *I* get the big bag!"

He turned around to see his kids, each with a hand locked on a purple suitcase. Kate gave it a rough yank that sent Simon spinning, then flying across the kitchen, his hand released.

Jack straightened up, shooting a look at Christie, hoping she would take this one.

"Guess I get the bag," Kate said, shooting a grin at her brother.

But Simon raced back.

"What do you even have in here, dork?"

"Look," Jack started, "we have a lot of—"

Kate unzipped the bag and an assortment of plastic monsters, refugees from decade-old cartoon shows, spilled onto the kitchen floor.

"Hey!" Simon yelled. He gathered up the tumbled creatures while trying to lock a hand on the bag.

Kate, however, continued making jerking motions as the bag went left, then right, then up.

Christie finally took the cue that Jack didn't have a clue how to intervene here.

"All right. *Enough.* Kate, put down the bag. Simon—just freeze."

Simon held his gathered creatures close.

"We have a lot of bags."

"Yes, but I'm the oldest and I—" Kate began.

Christie took the bag. "Really? I need to use this one. You two can use any of the other bags in my closet."

"They're all ugly," Kate said.

"Not big enough," Simon said, looking down at his toys.

Now Jack saw his opening.

"Well, they'll have to do. We leave in an hour. Hate to leave without you."

Kate shook her head and stormed away while Simon stood there, looking confused.

"Si, think you can pick only a few of those toys to bring? We're only gone a week."

Simon nodded and walked away.

Jack turned back to Christie. "Nice peaceful week ahead, hm?"

"Good thing I've already packed for them. Otherwise they'd only have toys and bathing suits."

Jack turned back to the freezer chest and closed the lid. Two snaps on either side locked the top down tight.

"I'll put this in the Explorer."

He picked up the chest and walked out the kitchen door to the car outside.


Jack backed up the SUV slowly.

Not that there was any real danger of a kid racing by on his bike. Kids playing in streets . . . just not something that happened anymore.

Everyone sat quietly, as if they all knew that this trip, this *vacation* was a big thing.

*And it is,* Jack thought.

Now that it was about to begin, he felt good about it. To get away. To a place where there were trees, fresh water, and even—so the brochure promised—fresh food.

Jack edged the car out onto the street.

Nope, nobody out on bikes. Warm summer day. And everyone inside.

Watching old movies. Getting excited if they caught a bit of a TV signal. Mostly boring stuff from the government. The lucky ones had old videogames to play.

*Hiding.*

*Yeah, good thing we're doing this.*

He straightened out the Explorer, and pulled away,

In the rearview mirror he saw Kate and Simon turn to watch their house receding in the distance.

Until he took another curve, and home vanished, and the long trip lay ahead.

# 10

## Outside the Fence

Christie saw Jack look back at the kids as the gate started to roll open and they prepared to leave their fenced-in development.

"Okay. Who can tell me the rules when we're outside the fence?"

"Jack, I don't think—"

"The rules are there for a purpose. So, Simon, Kate, what are they?"

"Window up!" Simon said. Christie had to smile. *This is such a big adventure for him.* She looked at Kate, who rolled her eyes and added, "Doors locked."

"And stay in the car."

"Right—as if I'd ever want to go walking around outside *here*."

"Good," Jack added.

*Such a cop,* Christie thought.

Only then did Jack ease the car outside. And despite everything—the beautiful early-morning sun, the safety of their car, all those rules—Christie had to admit that it felt different.

It always did.

Whenever they were *outside* things looked different. Grass overgrown, the road pockmarked with potholes. Buildings and stores abandoned. No Can Heads here—at least that's what the local police had told Jack.

But could they really know, really be sure? As they pulled away, Christie turned around to smile again at the kids.

*The big adventure begins!*

She looked back to the tall fence with the razor ribbon running along its top as it receded into the distance.

Leaving its protection.

"We're off," Jack said.

He almost sounded happy about it.

Christie had to doubt herself. She had pushed this dream of getting away. Was it a good idea? Would it really be giving something to the kids, something that had vanished in this new world?

Did she need it even more than they did?

Once upon a time she had taught high school English in a school not far from Jack's precinct. But when that sector went red, the school was shuttered. Suddenly there were too many teachers, and not enough students.

Now, like nearly everyone, she homeschooled her kids, and tutored a few neighbor kids in the development. But the neighbors couldn't pay much, and it never had the excitement, the electric feel of a class of kids engaged in a discussion of *Macbeth* or *Slaughterhouse Five*.

Life had contracted.

But she had kept those thoughts to herself.

She reached down and turned on the radio.

———

Christie kept looking at the streets, so desolate, and thinking that she wanted to get on the highway fast.

It felt exposed here, out in the open. Even though she spotted a few people walking the streets and a scattering of open stores, it didn't feel safe.

*I've become so used to where we live,* she thought. *To . . . how we live.*

The song ended, replaced with news.

Jack raised the radio volume.

*"Police Commissioner Edwards again denied reports that some precincts have begun using poison traps against the Can Heads. 'My office has found no evidence of any use of these so-called poison traps.'"*

Christie turned and looked back at the kids. Kate read a book. Simon played with some plastic soldiers, making them climb up his seat belt like it was a mountainside.

Christie lowered the volume.

"Is that true?"

Jack looked at her.

"You mean about the poison traps? Leaving bodies of . . . *whatever* around, laced with poison for the Can Heads?"

"I mean, in your precinct, do you—"

Jack laughed. "And where are we supposed to get these poisoned bodies from?"

"I don't know. You're the police. There are morgues."

Jack hesitated. She didn't talk to him about his work much. She could feel him tighten whenever she asked questions, as if the very act of asking the question could take him back there.

He took a breath, and she regretted asking the question.

"Okay. I've *heard* of it. You find someone dead. Some homeless guy, some . . . nobody. And so they put the body out. Laced with enough deadly zinc phosphate to take out an army of Can Heads."

He took a glance at the back, the kids tuned out. Then to Christie.

"But I never saw it. Never *did* it. So, far as I'm concerned, it's a rumor."

He stopped at a light.

Christie looked away.

Lights. Stopping at a light could be dangerous.

Lots of people just sailed right through them.

Now they waited at this quiet intersection for the red light to give way to green.

All the while, Christie wishing Jack would just *go*.

She chewed her lip. The street felt so empty, so quiet.

Did the buildings hide dark, hollow eyes looking out at her?

Did Jack feel it, too . . . or was that just her imagination?

Even Kate looked up from her book.

The light turned green.

"Almost to the Thruway entrance," Jack said. "Won't be long."

Maybe he had felt it. That fear, waiting at the light.

Somehow that made her feel safer.

He turned the radio volume back up.

"*—Latest reports show leading government scientists remain divided. The senate's panel will continue its hearings for at least two more weeks. The president's press secretary said the administration remains committed to having a new plan to deal with the decade-long Great Drought as well as reversing the so far unexplained blight that has decimated world-wide food production . . .*"

Jack said, "They still have no damn answers."

Christie gave him a look for the escaped "damn." Then she leaned forward and hit one of the radio presets.

"Maybe no news for a while?" Christie said.

Jack nodded and smiled. "No news is . . . probably good news."

Christie smiled back.

When she looked forward, she saw the entrance to the New York State Thruway.

Armed guards flanked a single gated entrance to the highway.

A turret stood nearby, with more guards able to get a 360-degree bird's-eye view of the entrance area.

Jack slowed behind the lone car in front of him.

"Can you get out the papers?" he said.

Christie popped open the glove compartment and brought out a packet. To use any highway, you needed a pass from the Emergency Highway Authority. They had to know where you came from, your destination, how long you would be gone, and a host of other seemingly irrelevant details.

The gate to the highway opened and the car in front pulled away. Jack edged next to the booth as the gate came quickly down again.

Jack knew that Christie had paid all the necessary fees weeks ago, so there should be no problem.

Still, he felt a bit of a chill when the guard, an automatic rifle slung over his shoulder, stepped up to the window.

Odd position for a cop to be in. This slight air of suspicion.

"Hi, folks. How are you doing today?"

Making small talk. A technique. Sometimes Can Heads could look normal, almost act normal. But if you talked to them, if you chatted to a Can Head, you'd *know* damn fast.

Shit, you could even sense it—or even smell it on them, on their clothes, on their breath. You'd see a stray red dollop marking their shirt.

"Going on a vacation, eh?" The guard flipped through the papers.

"Yes," Christie said, smiling. The guard had lowered his head to get a good look inside. "Our first with the kids. We're going to the Paterville Family Camp. In the mountains."

The guard nodded, now looking right at Jack. "I hear it's nice up there."

Jack had trouble engaging in the chitchat, this little routine the highway cop had.

*Could flash my badge,* Jack thought.

Cut this short.

"Have there been any reports?" Jack said. "Any trouble, on the way up?"

The guard laughed as if it was a silly question.

"No. Nothing for weeks. Been real quiet. I think we got them on the run. In this state, at least. And you got a good steel-mesh fence, electrified all the way up there. I wouldn't worry."

The guard scanned the back of the Explorer, checking out the children.

"You have a nice vacation," the guard said, backing away.

He went back to his booth and opened the gate. The two guards to the side, rifles at a 45-degree angle, watched the operation carefully. The gate moved up slowly. Then Jack gave the guard a nod, and pulled onto the entrance ramp.

They were on the Thruway.

Heading north, to the mountains. Their vacation had, Jack felt, really begun.

# 11

# In the Backseat

Simon looked out the window. His parents sat so quietly. Usually they talked.

But now—just sitting *so quiet*.

He turned to look over to his sister. She had her nose in her book. That's what Mom always said, *You always have your nose in a book*.

Simon didn't like to read. Mom tried, and the more she tried the more he hated it.

Kate *loved* it.

He looked out the window. No one else on the highway. So empty, Simon thought. And the fence . . . he knew that a fence surrounded where they lived. He'd seen that *lots*.

But this tall fence with its curled wire at the top seemed much taller.

And every now and then . . . a sign.

Big red letters.

Simon read the words.

WARNING! THIS PROTECTIVE FENCE IS ELECTRIFIED.

The fence was electric. Why was that? Were the bad people on the other side? Is that why it had to be *electrified*?

He wanted to ask his parents.

But instead he just kept looking out the window.

As the car sped down the empty highway, as one sign after the other rushed by, Simon finally picked up his plastic men.

There was danger ahead for his action figures. They'd have to climb, then fight something big and evil.

But Simon didn't know exactly what yet.


"I'm hungry!"

"Can't you . . . shut up?"

Christie reached over and touched Kate's knee. "Kate, no 'shut ups,' please."

Christie watched Simon turn and make a face at his sister.

*Gonna be a long ride*, Christie thought.

"And Simon—no faces."

"Mom, can you please make him *stop?* I want to read my book and not have him whining about food!"

Christie saw Jack raise his head to the rearview mirror. "You guys chill. Want to watch a video?"

Christie knew that was no solution. The two kids never agreed on a video. Sometimes it seemed as if Kate liked being defiant. She still enjoyed the big animated movies from years ago as much as Simon.

*Contrary*, thought Christie. *She just likes being . . . contrary. Must be an age thing, a brother-and-sister thing.*

Some *kind of thing*.

*At least I get to experience what families have always experienced on vacation road trips.*

One of the reasons people always looked forward to coming home.

"Okay, you two. How about food? We have some PB&J in the cooler. And those lemon drinks you like."

"Yuck. I don't like that stuff," Simon said.

As if forced to agree, Kate added: "Me neither. Nothing else?"

"Some of that fruity yogurt too . . . different flavors . . ."

Christie knew that wasn't a crowd-pleaser either. The yogurt had been invented using soy solids. And the supposed fruit? Clumps of color and artificial sweetener.

At least the PB&J used some peanut butter. So they said.

"Go on . . . it's a long trip. Eat a sandwich. And just think of the great food we'll have at the camp. Real food, hm?"

She saw the two of them look out the window, almost at the same moment.

As if looking out at this road, they didn't really believe her. Real food? Something they had at home—what, once a week? Maybe less? The rest of the time it was all the manufactured stuff. Nutritious enough, so they said.

But how long could people eat that and not begin to miss *real* food, *real* taste in a way that almost ached?

"Kate, could you dig out a few sandwiches? A couple of drinks?"

Kate slowly turned away from the window and the highway outside.

She nodded, and then reached into a cooler sitting between her and Simon.

Sandwiches appeared. Then drinks in curved plastic bottles, lots of color.

"Want something, Mom? Dad?"

"No thanks," Jack said too quickly.

Christie shot him a look as if to say this might have been a time for some food solidarity.

*We're in this together.*

"Sure, honey. I'll have one."

Though Christie wasn't hungry.

It didn't taste very good.

She took the sandwich and smiled at Kate. Simon had already unwrapped his sandwich, half of it gone.

Couldn't be too bad.

Christie gave her daughter a pat on the knee.

As if to say, *I depend on you.* And *thanks.*

She turned back to the front and waited just a few seconds before unwrapping her own uninviting sandwich.

Which is when she saw something black, sitting squarely in the center of the far-right lane, just ahead.

# 12

# Rest Stop

Christie turned to him.

"What is it?"

It took only seconds for Jack to recognize the debris on the road: a large, curled piece of black tire tread. He slid over into the left lane.

He looked at the chewed-up tire as he drove by.

"Someone blew a tire."

Nobody said anything for a minute.

Then:

"Someone *blew* a tire?" Christie said. "You make it sound like it's an everyday occurrence."

Jack looked into the backseat to make sure the kids were otherwise engaged.

Which they were.

"Tires blow. Happens."

"*Used* to happen. I did the paperwork for this trip. You're not even *allowed* on this highway unless you have those new reinforced treads. Want to tell me how you blow one of those?"

Jack looked down at the gas gauge, hoping for a distraction, and said, "Going to need a stop soon. Gas is getting low. There's a rest stop in about ten more miles."

Christie leaned close and at the same time lowered her voice.

"You didn't answer me."

He looked at her.

"Okay. There are reinforced tires, and some . . . not so reinforced. We see them in Red Hook. Trucks that have bought them as retreads. They're listed with all the stats that supposedly make them safe. But now and then . . . something happens."

"On its own or with a little help?"

Another look.

"Both."

Another silence.

"So, which do you think this was?"

Jack laughed. "What do I look like—a cop?"

That made Christie laugh.

"Just relax, Christie. Some trucker with inferior tires. He throws on a spare and he's out of here. Leaving that back chunk for us to dodge."

A sign flew by.

NEXT REST STOP 7 MILES.

Then the symbol for gas, and a knife and fork for food.

"Going to stop up here. Fill up before we hit the Northway."

Jack wondered if she was still thinking about the tire. Everything had gone so smoothly, almost as if they were some family from the twentieth century enjoying a simple summer trip up north.

It's true enough, Jack thought. There were cheap "certified" reinforced tires, with the "approved" additional steel and nylon belts.

Normally, even the reinforced tires didn't just blow.

And a trucker doing a long haul on this road . . . why, that would be the last thing he'd want.

Jack took a breath.

He could worry. Or he could let it go. Things happen. And if he didn't get out of his paranoid state of mind—

—if it could even be called paranoia—

—it wouldn't be much of a vacation.

The kids didn't deserve that.

Another sign.

REST STOP AHEAD.


Jack pulled up to a row of gas pumps. He stopped the car but left the engine running.

"Aren't you going to get some gas?" Christie asked.

"Can we get some stuff?" Simon said, eyeing the garish sign that announced a QuikMart inside.

"Hold on," Jack said.

Jack looked at his hands locked on the steering wheel. *What am I doing?* he wondered. Looking around for *what?*

No other cars here getting gas. That wasn't so strange; after all, the highway had been pretty deserted.

And in the parking areas . . .

A sixteen-wheeler way in the back, maybe the driver catching some Z's. Two cars parked on the side, the patrons probably inside the Quik-Mart. Maybe hitting the restrooms.

"Jack? What *is* it?"

He killed the ignition.

He smiled. "Nothing." He pulled the key out and turned toward

Christie and the kids. "Look, I'm going to lock the doors when I get out, okay?"

"Jack, do you really—"

Simon turned again to the QuikMart. "You mean, we can't go in there, Dad? Why not? Looks like—"

Kate leaned close to her brother. "'Cause there are Can Heads inside and they'll eat *you* right up!"

"Kate—" Christie said.

Jack popped open his door. "Locked. Windows up tight. Got it?"

Christie nodded.


*Steady,* Jack told himself.

What the hell kind of vacation would this be if he drove his family crazy? He held the nozzle tight in the tank opening as it guzzled the ever-more-expensive fuel. Amazing, that with fewer people going anywhere, still the OPEC nations could tighten supply and make the once prosperous nations of the West pay and pay.

Just as they would squeeze every last drop of oil out of the deserts, so they would squeeze every devalued dollar and pound and yen from the countries that still desperately depended on their oil.

And while the gas chugged into the tank, Jack kept looking at the rest stop station.

He saw someone sitting at the checkout counter.

But no customers came by to pay for whatever pretend-food items the place sold.

No movement at all.

And the cars remained there.

*Funny,* he thought. *Shouldn't someone have come out by now?*

The gas stopped. Jack looked down at the tank opening and squeezed in a few more bursts. *Should be enough to get us the rest of the way,* he thought. No more stops.

He pulled out the nozzle and placed it back in the tank. He heard Christie's window *whirr* as she lowered it.

"Jack, Simon's gotta pee."

"He always has to pee," Kate said.

The window open, Jack looked around quickly. The whole place was like a still life.

"Okay. Right. You sure he doesn't just want to see what goodies they have for sale?"

"I got to go, Dad."

"All right, all right. Listen, I'll go check out the restrooms. I'll give you a wave and then everyone"—he leaned down so he could see Kate—"and I do mean *everyone* can come in. This will be our only stop before the Paterville Camp. So, make use of it."

Then back to Christie.

"But not until I give you a wave."

"Aye, aye, Captain. We'll wait for the official wave." Christie said.

Jack grinned at her. She had every right to be pissed at him, scaring the kids; instead, she cut the atmosphere with humor.

"Okay. I'm off to take a look."

Jack made a signal with his finger—rolling his finger to indicate that the window should be rolled up.

When Christie had done that, he turned and walked to the Quik-Mart.


Jack pushed the door open.

Couple of cars outside. *Got to be some people in here*, he thought.

But the aisles were absolutely empty.

*Can't all be in the john.*

He saw someone manning the cubicle where people could pay for their sodas, the gas, some smokes.

The man had his head down, as if staring at a newspaper.

Jack spotted the way to the restrooms to the right, a corridor with the universal male/female sign hanging above it.

Jack started walking down an aisle of snacks.

*What the hell do they make this stuff out of?*

Salt was still plentiful. There were new sweeteners that replaced the suddenly, improbably rare high fructose corn syrup. The packages all in screaming colors, as if promising insanely good taste.

As Jack moved down the aisle, he kept looking at the cashier. Not even a look up.

Not like the place was exactly swarming with customers. Not like the guy didn't hear Jack, see Jack.

Once again, he reminded himself to maybe—just maybe—stop being a cop. He was just here to scope out the restrooms for the kids.

No need to engage the guy.

No need to ask him how things have been.

*Quiet on the highway?*

*Business kinda slow these days?*

*These weeks . . . months . . . years . . .*

Feet away. Still, the guy didn't look up.

"Hey. Um, the bathrooms. I mean, do I—" Jack pointed to the corridor to the right "—need a key or something?"

And that's when a different tumbler clicked in Jack's brain.

Guy didn't move. Didn't fucking move.

Jack didn't bother with another greeting.

In a reflex, he bent over, his hand sliding down to unholster the revolver strapped to his left ankle.

No more words as Jack moved around to get a good side view of the cashier so engrossed in his daily news. So engrossed that he couldn't move his head from the paper. Or flip to a new page.

Until Jack got a good side view of the grizzly-bearded man sitting on a stool. Perched on it.

More like *placed* on it.

Because now Jack could see that a good portion of the man's lower body had been chewed down to the bone. A pool of blood, dry and crusty, gathered below the man.

No two-way radio with police backup waiting, this time.

Jack was on his own.

He looked right. No movement. But he could see an open door, leading to a back area—storerooms, maybe—behind the counter.

Jack took a few steps in that direction.

An open door in the back, only a quarter-way open, but enough so that he could see the outside. The brightness of the day, the sun, and even—beyond the tufts of grass overdue for a mow—the fence that girded the rest stop. The tall electric fence topped with curlicues of razor ribbon.

Except he could see that the fence had been cut, a triangle of wire pulled back.

So much for the electricity.

He didn't give that view another look. Not when he imagined that whatever came through that hole could still be here.

He spun around, his eyes darting, looking at the silent aisles, over to the restrooms, and then—as if catching on to the game way too late—to the tinted glass windows facing outside.

"Shit," he said, moving quickly now.

Something smacked into him from the side, sending him flying against a rack of newspapers and magazines. He tumbled awkwardly, falling, and despite his grip—so tight—a metal spoke of the rack jabbed his hand, forcing his fingers to loosen.

His gun slipped away as he fell backward.

Unarmed, as something—and he knew, of course, what it was—jumped on top of him.

He wished time slowed, the way they said it did.

But after so many raids, so many times fighting Can Heads, he knew that was all a bunch of bullshit.

"Mom, I really have to go!"

"You really want to buy some of that junk they sell," Kate said.

"I do not. I—"

"Simon, Kate—can you guys just cool it a minute? Dad will be right back. And we can go in." Christie turned to the QuikMart. She had seen Jack in there a minute ago, but now he wasn't there. Maybe checking out the restrooms? "He'll be right back. Just . . ."

Just what?

*Come on. What are you doing in there?*

Christie waited.

# 13

# The Decision

Jack felt the body on him, then smelled the breath, the mouth close to his head. Classic Can Head strategy. Go for the neck. Like any feral creature, any trained predator.

Immobilize your prey. Bite down.

The attack in Red Hook all over again.

Jack's head turned to the side, meshed in the wire newspaper rack. He could see his gun, so close, but it lay feet away, an impossible distance with this thing on him.

Normal human-body vulnerabilities supposedly didn't apply to them. Too amped up on whatever drove them to feed off their own kind, it was hard to cause any distracting pain when they were at-tacking.

Hard. But maybe not impossible.

Jack shot his right hand up to grab under the chin of the Can Head trying to chomp its way up to his neck.

That served to pin the thing's jaw back a bit, and—for the moment—keep the teeth closed.

Now Jack risked a quick glance to his left.

*Has to be something.*

The Can Head wriggled its head violently left and right to free it-self from Jack's jaw-closing grasp.

A few more twists and it would be free.

Jack's left hand reached out and began to search the area around his pinned body.

He only felt more metal spokes of the rack—but then one piece jiggled a bit. Loose. A bit of the metal frame sprung loose.

Maybe it could be detached.

Jack closed his left hand on it even as he kept his other hand locked on the creature's head, squeezing so tight that his fingers dug into the skin of the Can Head's throat.

He yanked on the metal strut. It moved back and forth, but it still wouldn't come free.

Then, again, now making the piece wriggle, jerk up and down fast until—

It came off.

Jack felt a surge of hope. Now he let the other thoughts in—what might be happening outside. With his family. His kids.

He didn't let himself imagine other possibilities. That there might be more Can Heads in here. That this one was only the first. That the trap was indeed hopeless.

Hand tight on the metal strut, he looked at the Can Head, now rearing back to free itself of Jack's grip.

Jack letting that happen.

'Cause then it would come nice and close.

And as the Can Head reared back, it opened its foul hole of a mouth and dived forward. Jack was ready.

Though the thing's head moved fast, Jack's left hand seemed to match its speed, and his eyes were on *its* eyes, those filmy dull sockets, as he jammed the metal strut straight into one eye. As hard and as deep as he could.

At first, it didn't seem to make any difference.

The Can Head kept coming on its downward, open-mouthed arc.

But when that plunge was completed, the Can Head turned lifeless, falling onto Jack.

He quickly twisted to dump the body off, then pried himself out of the mesh of struts that had helped pin him.

He dived for his gun, grabbing it like it was life itself.

Kneeling then, turning, scanning the room for more of them.

Standing.

*No more here.*

Then outside.

Everything peaceful by the car. Christie, the kids, oblivious.

Christie looked back to the QuikMart.

*Where is he? Just supposed to be checking it out.*

At least the kids had stopped complaining about not getting out.

Then she saw Jack. Walking slowly toward the car.

Too slowly, too apparently casual, she immediately thought.

Then . . .

Something happened.

As Jack got closer he felt Christie's eyes on him. She couldn't have seen anything, all buttoned up in the locked car.

But her eyes . . .

No question, she thought something had happened.

When Jack got to the car, Christie opened the window.

"Bathrooms okay, Officer?"

He forced a smile. He stuck his head in the car window.

"You guys all right?"

Simon nodded. "I still have to go!"

Kate spoke. "We're fine, Dad."

Then, to Christie. "Can I have a word?"

That seemed to spur Simon. "Can't we go in, Dad?"

Jack smiled at Simon. "Your mom and I . . . we have to talk, okay? Can you hang a bit?"

Kate rolled her eyes. "Sure, we'll *hang*."

Christie walked a few steps away from the car.

"What happened?" she sad.

Jack looked away. A breath. "Ran into one of them in there. Broke through the so-called electric fence somehow."

She moved so her eyes were locked on his. "You okay?"

"Yeah. No problem. One less Can Head."

The joke fell flat.

Funny, kids and peeing. Used to be no big fucking deal.

Christie spoke: "So how'd it get in?"

"How the hell do they always get in? Look—I think this . . . *vacation* is a bad idea. We should just—" He stood there, her eyes locked on his. She had wanted this so badly. "We should go home now."

Christie didn't take her eyes off him. And she didn't say anything.

Until she glanced at the car. A quick look, but one meant to tell Jack something.

Then—

"No."

Jack tilted his head. A habit of his when he didn't grasp some edict about life in the house. Like rinsing dishes before they went in the dishwasher.

"What?"

He watched Christie take a breath.

"I don't want to go back. And . . . I don't want them to go back. You said . . . you're okay."

Jack's head tilt turned into a full shake now.

"Right. Sure. But this place is not safe. This goddamn highway."

He spoke quietly, aware that the kids had a window open.

"And I didn't know that before? There's still some TV, Jack. Where do we go that's safe? Can you tell me where the hell that is?"

He had no answer.

She turned away from him and looked at the sky. The wispy morning clouds had all burned off. The sky a clear robin's egg blue now. A few puffy clouds. Beautiful, if you took the time to look up.

Then back to Jack.

"That's the world we live in." She gestured at the deserted rest stop. "*This* is the world we live in."

"Which is why we live in a safe complex that—"

"Safe complex? More gates. Bigger fences. People like you protecting us. Trying to stop them, kill them. Only difference between here and there, Jack, is that maybe we might have better fences. They work—for now. Same world, same fears."

"And what's down there? Down the road? You think the camp will be safe?"

"Could be the same as anywhere else. And this, here . . . we ended up here on the wrong day."

"You can say that again."

"It could have happened at home."

Jack shook his head but the core truth of what she was saying stuck. This *was* the world.

And the unanswered question.

*Is anywhere safe?*

"The kids, you . . . will be safer back home. Mark it off as an adventure."

Christie forced a derisive laugh.

"An adventure? We just go back *home*? And what—we live behind our fence? Sealed in our house, terrified. Is that our life?"

"We don't have to—"

"And the kids? Kate will be an adult before you even know it. Will your fences go with her? Your guns? You want her to huddle in some goddamned—"

For the first time, her voice raised.

Jack realized this must have been simmering for a long time.

"—*complex*? Hiding. Scared."

"There are things to be scared of."

Only now did she stop. Was she close to tears? Was this about fear, but more than just fear of the Can Heads?

Fear of life transformed forever. And would the silences between them only grow?

She pushed stray hairs off her forehead. With the morning haze gone, a cool breeze blew off the highway.

Coming from the north.

"Yes. There are things to be scared of. I guess that's what I'm saying. And I'm scared. For me. For them. You, too."

Jack nodded.

He shook his head at what Christie was saying. Maybe if she had seen how close the attack had been . . .

Would she still think that they should continue with this trip?

*This goddamn vacation . . .*

She didn't move her eyes from his.

One idea became even more clear to him: what Christie feared for them all—about their life—was as great as her fear of the Can Heads.

"So, we go on?" he said.

She nodded.

*Does she know what that might mean?* Jack thought.

Could be, he thought . . . no other incidents ahead. The road north safe and secure. The camp the safest place on earth.

Or maybe not.

Either way, he saw that Christie felt strong enough that she would brave the unknown.

It was *that* important.

"Okay. We'll go on." He laughed. "Have to find someplace up the road for them to pee. They don't go in there."

"An adventure, you said, right?"

"Sure."

Jack didn't say he agreed with Christie. Because he didn't. But he understood.

Now he reached out and took her hand.

"Let's go, then. Simon's gotta pee."

Together they walked back to the car.

# 14

# North

The question came just as they passed the multicity jumble of connecting highways of what was called the Capital Region.

Albany, still the capital of New York State, was considered to have the best defenses of any major city. Families relocated there to take advantage of the superior policing and protection.

The real reason that the Albany-Schenectady area remained safe, Jack guessed, was because no state wanted to risk losing its capital. No one talked too much about the handful of states where that had already happened . . . places like Lansing, Michigan, that had been hanging on by a thread, even before the outbreak.

But here, the intersection of the Thruway and the Northway was heavily patrolled.

Multiple checkpoints, occasional choppers gliding overhead, gleaming tall turrets along the road with expansive views of the area for miles.

The city area compact and all access points secure.

As to what happened in the surrounding areas, the once-farmland rolling north to Cobleskill and beyond?

Who knew?

A question—Simon's question—made Jack smile.

"Dad, are we there yet?"

Classic, he thought. Some things never change. He started to answer but Kate was too quick.

"Right, genius. We're *there*. This car is the camp and—here we are! Want to go swimming?"

"Kate," Christie said. Usually a word from Christie was enough to get Kate to back off her sarcasm.

Simon chose to ignore her.

"Are we, Dad?"

"Well. Look up here."

He tapped the GPS. Service was so intermittent as to be nearly useless. Now it came to life.

"Shows where we are—"

"Which is in a car, driving—duh!"

Christie turned to the back and gave Kate "the look." Not for the first time, Jack though. Things could get interesting as Kate got older.

Wanting freedom in a world where that simply wasn't possible anymore.

"Kate, can you ease up? Please?"

In the rearview mirror, Jack saw his daughter shake her head and then look out the window.

"So, Simon, you see . . . this is where we are. On this map. If I make it all smaller . . ."

Jack touched a button on the side and zoomed out from the screen. "There you go. We stay on this highway for a bit, for another hour or so, until we're in the Adirondack Park."

"Then we're there?"

"Not exactly. Got to take a country road to get to the Paterville Camp. Bet it'll be interesting."

His question answered, Simon nodded.

Interesting? What would it be like when they left the highway? All the reports showing no problems ahead did little to reassure him.

If the Can Heads could break through the Thruway's fence, then what could be happening in the small towns that dotted the way to Paterville?

"You okay?" Christie said to him.

They hadn't talked much since the rest stop. As if letting time go by would somehow make what happened less real.

"Yeah. Fine."

"I can drive."

Jack laughed. "I know you can."

"Don't know why you always need to drive."

Yeah. Why was that? he thought. The need to feel in control?

A cop thing? Something he inherited from his rigid-as-steel father. Someone who didn't believe women should do—or could do— much of anything but cook and clean and raise the kids.

"If I get tired, I'll let you know. I'm good now."

"And your leg. Long time to sit."

"That's fine, too."

That was a lie. Sitting in the driver's seat, in the same position, had produced a growing ache near his wound. He guessed that when he got out of the car, his limp would be back, at least until he loosened the muscles and wrapped up the area again tight with an Ace bandage.

The leg was better. Not perfect, though, and never would be.

Christie reached out and gave his other leg a squeeze, midthigh. Gentle, teasing.

"Good. Just remember, I'm here if you want a break."

"Gotcha, boss."

They drove on.


They passed a sign.

WELCOME TO ADIRONDACK STATE PARK.

Suddenly, the signs turned a rustic brown, themed to show that this region—the shops and towns and homes—was all part of protected land, the great state park.

About as close to wilderness as one could see anywhere near New York City.

But even in this wilderness, Jack saw signs of what had happened. Most of the majestic pines on the side of the road looked untouched, but whole patches of deciduous trees stood leafless, long dead. Almost as if some heatless, smokeless fire had snuffed them out.

Outside, it turned cool enough that he had turned off the AC. Windows open. The sweet smell of pine. The air pungent and cool.

Would the other trees ever come back?

Would whatever killed trees and plants across the country, and led to a blight that decimated the cattle, dairy, and poultry industries worldwide, ever end?

Some trees lived. Some died. Same thing with food crops and livestock.

The world scurried to adjust.

But not fast enough. Certainly not fast enough for the Can Heads, who had their own solution to the problem.

Christie turned to him.

"Smells so good."

She didn't point out the obvious: the disturbing leafless trees looking so eerie.

The kids had their faces at the windows. They certainly didn't see this many trees back at their Staten Island development. And they could even see mountains, still in the distance, but already looking like an amazing backdrop from a film.

"Dad—all those trees. What happened?" Kate asked.

Jack shrugged. "Not sure, honey."

He was tempted to add something, like *Maybe not enough water.* Or the obvious lie, a fire.

But Kate was smart.

Instead: "Something hurt them and not the others. I guess scientists are working on it, right?"

"Yeah, they sure are."

And on all the other things that have happened to the planet.

"They look scary."

Another nod. "Yeah. But look at those pines ahead. Big, hm? And the mountains."

"The mountains are cool!" Simon said, leaning forward to get a better look at the peaks ahead. "Are we going up there?"

Christie turned around. "We go up a little ways. Paterville is on a hill surrounded by mountains."

"Wow. Wish we could go to the top of one."

"Maybe we could drive up," Jack said, unaware if he could even make good on that offer.

Everyone grew quiet, looking at the mountains, distracted from the great stands of dead trees that alternated with the still-towering pines.


Christie kept looking at the mountains.

Except for bare patches, they looked ancient, untouched by time. For the first time since they left home, she felt that they were indeed "away."

That was the whole point, wasn't it? To get the kids away, Jack away . . . her. To leave what had become their daily life with its fears, its walls—what for her felt like a belt, tightening more every day.

Looking at the mountains, she felt something that she recognized was different. Freedom, hope, the idea of possibilities.

Then Kate's voice snapped her out of her mental wandering among the peaks that, though obviously closer, still were so far away.

"Hey, is this near the camp? Looks *weird* here."

"You never saw real mountains before," Christie said.

"Hey—" Jack said.

Christie faced forward.

"There we go. Our exit, three miles ahead."

Exit, Christie thought. Getting off the Northway.

Onto the smaller roads. The smaller towns.

"Good," she said.

Not at all sure she meant it.

Jack slowed, hitting a series of severe speed bumps that signaled the way to the exit checkpoint.

Always checkpoints.

Christie read the bold signs, the letters big.

ATTENTION: YOU ARE NOW LEAVING

THE EMERGENCY HIGHWAY AUTHORITY'S PROTECTION

PLEASE HAVE YOUR TRAVEL DOCUMENTS READY

TO SHOW THE OFFICER ON DUTY

Then, after another speed bump that had the kids laughing from the carnival ride effect, another sign:

BE PREPARED TO HAVE

YOUR VEHICLE EXAMINED BY THE SAFETY OFFICER

YOU WILL BE GIVEN CURRENT ROAD CONDITIONS

AT THAT TIME

Road conditions. As if there was snow, branches down, flooding. The conditions the sign referred to had nothing to down with weather.

Another bump.

Christie scanned the booth ahead. A real metal barrier instead of a simple wooden bar to block cars. Guess the locals might be concerned about New York City riffraff sneaking into their pure, clean mountains. One guard in a booth and another standing to the side with a gun on his shoulder, his eyes locked on the car, scanning it.

Jack pulled up to the booth, opened the window, and looked up at the guard.

A nod and a smile, but the middle-aged man didn't smile back. Could be he was a veteran. There were stories that the Highway Authority had been hiring vets. It took the pressure off the suddenly unemployed combat soldiers in a changed world.

More important, they could keep their cool and knew their way around automatic weapons.

This one didn't look too happy.

Uniform unkempt. A stray stain here and there. Needed a shave. Squinting, narrow eyes in the late afternoon, but open enough so Jack could see they were bloodshot.

"Papers." The guard said it as if measuring out exactly how many words he could use.

Christie passed the papers from the glove compartment.

Jack handed them over.

"Paterville," the guard said. Jack caught the guard looking over to his partner.

"Yeah," Jack said.

This time, Jack didn't engage in any of the small talk. None of the *I hear it's nice . . .* or *never been there.*

The guard looked over the papers.

Then:

"Got to check your vehicle. Mind stepping out?"

*Stepping out?* Jack had read nothing about that. He looked at the guard again—the messy uniform, the grizzled face. Had he read the guy right? Someone who didn't care?

Then the guard added: "Just gotta check your safety precautions. Before we update you on the rest of your trip."

"Okay."

A quick glance at Christie. Nothing needed to be spoken.

Jack popped open the door. As he shut it, he heard Christie lock it behind him.

He walked alongside the guard as he looked over the modifications on the Explorer.

The guard turned to Jack. "Double-walled spun-steel hybrid tires?"

"Yup."

"Set you back a pretty penny." The guard knelt down. "And these things?" He tapped the metal plates in front and rear of each tire. "Good thinking there."

The guard didn't get up. Jack wondered: Does he do an inspection like this with every vehicle that leaves the highway?

*Maybe it's time to flash the badge.*

"But I got to tell you. Even these tires can be brought down."

"Not by a bullet."

"Oh, right. Sure. Not a single bullet. But you ever see those road chains? Two-, three-inch metal spikes, dozens of them on a chain? Could do real damage to even these tires."

"Let's hope I don't run into any of them."

The guard nodded and stood up, the effort of standing revealing that exercise wasn't on his weekly agenda.

"You never know."

The guard continued around to the front of the car. He smiled at the kids.

Or maybe it was a leer at Christie. With his face, it was hard to tell.

"Good front grill protection, and I imagine the body is all—"

"Reinforced steel. Special plate glass. Look, this gonna take much longer?"

The guard cocked his head.

"You in a rush? I'm just trying to do my job, Mr.—" he looked down at the papers "—Murphy. Just making sure you're in good shape to head . . . up there."

"Right."

Jack took a breath and reached into his back pocket. The guard's eyes followed him. Maybe smelling a tip? Did he supplement his income this way?

Jack flipped open the leather case, showing his shield.

"Whoa—NYPD. Guess you *do* know how to make a vehicle safe." He took a few steps closer to Jack. "Imagine you got some weapons, too, hm?"

"A few."

"We're supposed to log any firearms."

The guard held Jack's gaze. "But fuck it. We're in the same business, right? Right!"

*As if . . .*

"Okay, so I want to give you your road briefing . . . *Officer*. You're leaving the highway now. Things will be different."


"See, you take Nine-N to Eighty-six all the way to Paterville. Nice straight drive. And we haven't had reports of any action in weeks."

"Good to hear."

"We know how to shoot up here. Still, you'll bump into a bunch of checkpoints. Places where they'll want you to stop. Ask where you're going. Any latest news, that's how you'll hear."

"And between the towns?"

The guard rubbed his chin.

"That's where you gotta be careful. Don't stop for anything. Keep your eyes open. With this vehicle, you should be in good shape. But it's a no-man's-land between the towns."

"Thanks for the heads-up."

The guard smiled. "In another hour or so, you'll be at Paterville. Now, I hear those folks *really* know security. Good family place. So I heard."

A nod.

"We done here?"

"Sure. Sure we are, Officer."

The guard signaled to his partner. Slowly, the heavy duty barrier began to rise.

"You're on your own now. Drive safe, be safe . . . take care of that lovely family you have in there."

Jack walked back to the driver's side. As soon as he grabbed the handle, Christie popped open the lock.

He slid in and shut the door.

The gate wasn't quite all the way up.

"Dad," Simon said, "can we finally *go*? This is boring."

"Yeah. We're all set," Jack said. "Won't be long now."

The gate fully up, Jack gave the guard another glance, and left the protected world of the Northway for the weaving two-lane back road that would take them to Paterville.

# 15

## The Mountains

"God, it's like . . . everyone just *left*."

Christie watched the deserted motels, bars, and ice cream and hot dog places—boarded up, some with windows and doors smashed, open to the elements—roll by.

Even the kids knew better than to ask if they could stop.

A pair of faded dancing bears advertised the Mountain View Chalet. Chunks of wood missing. For fuel, maybe? One bear with a gaping hole in its head. Target practice. The colors bleached by the elements and the sun.

Then a bar with a sign announcing FOOD SERVED ALL DAY.

The front door missing, all of the windows smashed.

"Guess nobody lives here anymore."

"No tourists, no money."

"Yet Paterville Camp survived."

"Well, if they saw what was coming . . . if they took precautions, Paterville may be the only game in town now."

Then Christie saw a handmade sign, big block letters dripping, on the side of the road.

APPROACHING DINGMAN'S FALLS. Then in smaller letters. BE PRE-PARED TO STOP!

Christie spoke quietly. "Did you know that there'd be so many of these stops?"

Jack shook his head. "Nothing in the brochure about them. No big deal." Then: "Good to know that they're trying to keep their towns safe."

"If you say so."

It was nearly four P.M.

They'd be at the camp soon. Time to wash up. And then sample some of the home-grown food that Paterville offered.

He passed a speed limit sign: 25 MPH. Get cars driving nice and slow through the town.

Just beyond it, a makeshift barrier—a sawhorse with a blinking yellow light at each end.

Jack slowed down.

He leaned over to Christie and whispered.

"God, what is this? *Deliverance*?"

But Simon had unplugged and immediately asked, "What's *deliverance*?"

Christie turned to Simon as one of the locals walked up to the car, a big rifle hung over his shoulder.

"A movie about the mountains, honey." She saw that even Kate had looked up, taking note of the men at the impromptu barrier.

The man by Jack's window made a rolling motion with his hand.

Christie looked at the other men at the barrier. Five of them, all with rifles. As if expecting an invasion.

*Guess they couldn't get into the volunteer fire department.*

"Afternoon, folks."

The man leaned down to get a good look into the car and Christie got an equally good look at him. Eyes filmy. A little drunk.

Good combination, booze and bullets.

The guy did something weird with his mouth, as if removing a wad of gum that had become lodged in his cheek. Maybe shifting an errant tooth back into position.

"Afternoon," Jack said.

Two other men had also come closer now. One of the younger guys seemed to have spotted Kate.

The man at the window tried to widen his eyes. "You folks stopping here, at Dingman's Falls?"

Jack shook his head.

"Just passing through. We're on our way to the Paterville Family Camp."

The man looked away from the window.

"Figured that. Though right here in Dingman's is real nice. Got the falls . . . nice people. Good town. And it's clear. Know what I mean?"

"Clear?" Jack said.

"*Nothing* gets into town. Not past us. Nothing we don't want. None of them . . . Can Heads. Me and the boys—well, you should see some of the trophies *we* got."

Christie saw Jack's hands tighten on the steering wheel. Never a good one for hiding his tension.

"Good to hear. Nice and safe town. Great."

The man nodded. "But I got to tell you. You seem like nice people. So, a bit of advice. Stuff they didn't tell you when you left the big highway. The towns here, they're safe. The people make them safe. But in between, like when you leave Dingman's . . . and head on to Scooter's Mill?"

"The next town?"

A nod.

"Don't stop."

The man was looking right at Kate as if she was the special of the evening at the local greasy spoon.

"Don't stop," he repeated. "Keep your windows up." Back to Jack. "Eyes on the road. Look out for anything *peculiar.*"

"Thanks for the advice."

Jack didn't sound too sincere.

Perhaps the man picked up on that.

"Paterville, hm? Hear it's nice. And pricey. Musta set you back a bundle."

Jack clenched his hands tighter on the steering wheel. He's just about to hit his limit, Christie guessed.

"Yeah. Saved a long time." A breath. "Look, we've been traveling all day."

The man backed up.

"Sure, sure. You wanna get going. Just remember what I said, hm? You seem like nice folk. Wanna see you coming back this way, next week, whenever your *vacation* is done."

"Thanks."

Some of the other men began to move the sawhorse, opening up a lane and a way past this checkpoint and into the town of Dingman's Falls.

Once again, the man made a rolling motion with his hand.

Jack hit a button and the window went up as he slowly cruised past the volunteer guards.

Christie watched the town roll by, dotted with people. A lone boy on a bike. Two men outside a shuttered hardware store, talking, taking due notice as Jack drove by.

"Dingman's Falls," Jack said to her as they left the town.

"Have to make sure we come back real soon, y'hear?"

"Absolutely. Maybe buy a little vacation condo."

Christie laughed. "You could join the local border patrol."

"Get me some *trophies*."

But somehow, the last thing Jack said didn't sound funny.

Trophies. What the hell kind of trophies would they have?

Outside the town, things turned even more surreal. Motel cabins with holes in the roofs, paint flaking off in giant clumps, the color barely holding on, doors smashed in.

Lots of bears on the signs. The Sportsmen's Lodge. The Nite Owl. The Emerald Inn. All those happy bears on the decrepit signs.

The area looked as if it had been hit by bombs, turned into a war zone.

Christie stole a quick glance at the kids, sitting in the back, barely taking notice.

Then to Jack. She had asked to drive. But he kept saying he was fine. A typical male.

*No, I can do it. I can handle it.*

Eight, nine hours of driving.

He had to be tired.

They rolled past more desolation. A neon martini glass that would never again glow an iridescent blue. Carved wooden deer with their limbs chopped off, probably for firewood.

Then just as quickly, another town, another barrier.

If nothing else, now they were closer.

Soon, the road trip would be done. They could get out of the car.

They could actually begin their vacation.

They had begun climbing now as well, winding past dry stream beds that had no sparkling water rippling over the rocks.

The road then began weaving between smaller mountains, and soon some of the high Adirondack peaks were no longer so far away.

Massive, ancient sentinels of stone, eerie with both dead and live trees encircling them.

She said to Jack: "It's beautiful here."

"It is. I almost thought—"

He stopped.

"What?"

"Almost thought places like this had vanished."

She didn't respond to that.

Christie saw an area to pull off the road and park. A sign indicated a trail leading up to one of the nearby mountains. Once probably filled with day hikers.

Now the trail had to be empty. The trail deserted. Nobody would do that these days.

"Here we go," Jack said. "Up ahead."

She turned back to the front.

And saw the sign.

PATERVILLE FAMILY CAMP

3 MILES

She turned back to the kids.

"Simon, Kate . . . almost there."

Everyone looked out the windows, ready to enter the camp.

welcome to paterville camp

# 16

## Greetings

Jack turned onto the small dirt road to the right that led to the camp.

More signs.

WELCOME!

And—

GUESTS—PLEASE PROCEED TO THE WELCOME CENTER JUST AHEAD.

Then, in case anyone forgot why they were here . . .

PATERVILLE FAMILY CAMP—WHERE FAMILIES CAN BE FAMILIES!

The two-lane dirt road was well-maintained, no big ruts or boulders. Any brush at the sides was cut well back.

"I'm excited," Christie said.

"Me, too," Jack said.

He was getting good at saying things he didn't quite believe.

*If only I could ease the hell up.*

What happened at the rest stop could have happened anywhere.

That's what he told himself.

Then, through the thick stands of pine and dead deciduous trees, Jack saw the outer fence of the camp.

No small fence either. Twelve feet, maybe more. Certainly bigger than the one that girded their complex at home. And two turrets, looking less forbidding than those on the highway, painted a dark cocoa brown with a dark pine green roof.

More like little elf cottages than security turrets.

Did they color-coordinate the nice people with their guns inside the elf cottages?

Jack imagined that by now their arrival had been picked up by the camp's cameras and whatever motion-detection systems it had in place. Maybe a license check had already been run.

The turret elves reporting their progress.

"Is this it?" Simon said, leaning forward.

The road curved to the right, then the left.

A sign indicated a speed bump, then another, in the traditional Adirondack colors of brown and green. PREPARE TO SLOW DOWN.

Jack eased off the gas.

"Wow," Simon said.

Wow at what? Jack wondered. The giant fence, the elf turrets, the big sign where log chunks spelled out PATERVILLE FAMILY CAMP, with deer antlers on either side?

*Antlers? Don't tell me they have deer here.*

Weren't deer a thing of the past?

Probably extinct.

A gate opened and, passing the fence, Jack saw a smiling man waiting inside a small booth meters ahead. Only a small candy-cane-striped barrier blocked their way.

Jack stopped the car.

The man's grin broadened as he walked over.

The gate closed behind Jack.

He glanced back quickly at that.

"Go on," Christie said. "Say 'hi.' Find out where we're supposed to go."

Right, Jack thought.

The gate forgotten, he opened his window.

"Welcome to Paterville Camp, folks. And you must be . . . the Murphy family?"

The man radiated his smile evenly over the four of them in the car. Jack smiled back. "That would be us."

"Great. We've been expecting you. Now"—the man leaned close with some papers in his hand—"here's your car tag. Just put that on the dash. And your cabin number. And a map of the Paterville grounds. Your cabin's right here."

"Where's the lake?" Simon blurted.

"Oh, real close. You kids are gonna love it. You need to check in at the Great Lodge to get your keys, arrange credit. And that"—his smile broadened—"is about it."

"Thanks," Jack said.

The man made a small nod and backed away.

"You folks enjoy your stay."

The small candy-striped wooden barrier rose, and Jack pulled away.


"Look! There it is! The lake—just like in the picture!"

Simon announced each discovery as they drove deeper into the grounds.

Ahead, a cluster of rustic cottages, then to the left a small hill led down to a beautiful lake, shimmering in the late afternoon sun. Behind it, mountains, like guards circling the lake.

And not only that, he saw other families. Kids walking around, others sitting on the beach by the lake. Like an image from a past that had long ago vanished.

Amazing, he thought. That such a place could exist.

He came to a circle near the main building, the Great Lodge. In front, parking spaces under a protective overhang, all done in that mix of dark brown timbers and green roofing.

He pulled into a space and killed the engine. "I'll go check in."

"I wanna come," Simon said.

"I don't want to just sit here," Kate said.

"Guess we all go," Christie said. "Let the adventure begin!"

They got out of their car and walked into the lodge.

The Great Lodge's lobby ceiling rose up to a second story. Massive murals of all the animals that once filled this area covered the walls. Guests sat in oversized leather chairs, talking, some reading by lamps with bases made from twisted branches.

To the left, Jack saw the dining hall, its twin doors closed. To the right, a gift store. A registration desk ahead and a corridor past it with a sign that indicated TO ADMINISTRATIVE OFFICES.

One of the women at the desk, dressed casually in a crisp tan shirt with a red kerchief at her neck, looked up and smiled. Jack came forward.

"Hi, I'm—"

But before he got the words out, a short, barrel-chested man with a neatly trimmed mustache came from the nearby corridor.

He was talking to a woman easily a foot taller than him. Dark hair down to her shoulders. A gingham shirt tied at the waist, showing a slice of her midsection. Cutoffs. And in that quick glimpse, legs that went on forever.

Hard not to stare.

The man stopped talking as soon as he saw Jack and his family.

"And then we need— Oh. Hey! Hel-lo!" He looked around at Jack and his family. "The Murphys, right?"

*Guess they were expecting us,* Jack thought.

"Yes."

"Great! Welcome to the Paterville Family Camp!"

The man walked over to them.

"I'm Ed Lowe, camp director and the founder of Paterville."

Jack introduced Christie and the kids, who all shook the man's hand.

Ed seemed to focus on the kids. "You kids are going have so much fun here. So much to do." His eyes went from Simon to Kate. "No matter how old you are." Then to Christie. "And I guarantee some great downtime for the parents. Grown-ups love it as much as the kids."

It was as if the guy was still selling the camp. But his good humor had planted smiles on Christie's and the kids' faces.

"Here you go, Mr. Murphy," the woman behind the desk said. "Your keys. One for each of you. Opens your cabin. They're also your camp IDs, so hold onto them."

The way she said that stuck for a moment. *Hold onto them.*

Looked like despite all the smiles and handshakes, they took their security seriously here.

Jack took the keys. As he did, he noticed the woman standing near Ed watching him.

He had to force himself not to look back.

As if sensing Jack's balancing act, Ed turned to the woman, "Shana, why don't you bring the Murphys' luggage over to their cabin?"

"I can do—" Jack started.

"No. Don't worry. Shana is our jill-of-all-trades here. It's a quiet day—and while she gets your stuff, I can give you folks a quick tour."

Shana came close to Jack. He picked up a whiff of exotic perfume on her. Just a hint. Something you might only smell if you got real close.

Jack felt Christie's eyes on him.

"Car open?" Shana said. "Luggage in the trunk?"

"Yeah," Jack said. "But I—"

"No problemo," Shana said slowly.

Jack handed her the keys.

She started walking away.

Ed moved close. "Now for that tour, hm?"

All eyes seemed to be on their tour director.

But Jack stole a quick glance at Shana as she walked away.

She was looking right back at him.


Standing by the lake, Ed looked up to the sky.

"Hm, it was sunny just minutes ago. Looks like a few clouds slipped over those mountains. Weather can change mighty quickly here."

Jack held Christie's hand.

"I love it," she said.

"The lake? Yeah. Our prize, to be sure. Beautiful, clear water. You can even drink it. And back there—"

He turned around and pointed at the lifeguard stand.

"—always a lifeguard on duty from nine to sunset." To the kids. "No swimming before or after that."

Jack noticed Kate shielding her eyes.

As she checked out the lifeguard.

Time does fly, Jack thought. Something he might need to keep a watch on here.

Ed turned back to them. "Water's cold, though. Fed by those mountains. But on a hot day, it just doesn't get any better." Then, a step closer to Jack, his voice lower: "Same water feeds our wells and underground streams. It's why we can grow things."

"You've had no blight? I saw the trees—"

"Oh, some things won't grow, for sure. But I guess we're isolated enough that a lot of crops still grow here just fine. For now."

"Good."

Ed slapped his hands together. "On with the tour. This way!"

"Down there, got our big playing field. Lot of fun family games, softball, old-fashioned things like sack races. And to the right, a game room—"

"With video games?" Simon asked. "Really?"

"You bet. Oldies but goodies. And Ping-Pong, pool, even that football game, you know, with—"

"Foosball," Jack added.

"Yes, foosball. Now, past there, we have the nature trails. Nothing too big since we need to keep everything and everyone well within the camp's confines. Still, good safe places for a little walk or to explore."

Ed turned around and started walking back to the main lodge.

But Jack had noticed a road up on a hill, past the parking area, nearly hidden by the trees.

"What's over there? By the cars. That road?"

Ed barely tossed a glance back. "Our service road. Maintenance buildings. Laundry. Storage. Landscaping and so on. Nothing fun."

Ed pointed ahead.

"You've seen the Great Lodge. We all eat together in the big dining hall. Sometimes there are special announcements, sometimes we play some games. Like I said, good food and good fun—and good *people*."

Already, Jack thought, the dark streets of Red Hook were starting to look better.

As beautiful as it all was, this was alien terrain for him. And they were caged in.

With this much-too-jolly Ed Lowe as the keeper.

Still, Christie seemed wide-eyed at it. The kids looked like they loved it.

And Jack kept thinking of Ed's assistant. Shana.

Funny how guys work, he thought.

*Probably never see her again.*

*I'm only human. And male.*

"Okay, let's see your digs. Cabin seven. Great view from there. Come on!"


"If I may . . ." Ed took the key from Christie.

He opened the door and they walked in.

The cabin was a picture from a hundred years ago. Homemade furniture, a woven rug, a 1950s-style Formica kitchen table. Small hallway leading to bedrooms.

"No TV at all?" Kate asked.

"Sorry, miss. No stations operating anywhere near us. Get some radio, shortwave and all."

"And no phones?" Christie asked.

*As in: how isolated are we?*

"Well, the workers here like to joke that if we get a good wind off Mt. Hope you can always yell."

Ed laughed.

*What a card.*

"And truth is, Mrs. Murphy, we're kind of self-contained here. Can't say phones would be of much use."

Jack noticed that Kate stood there, scanning the rustic cottage, the lake, the woods—all so unfamiliar to her.

*Should be an interesting week.*

"Well, I guess I'll let you folks settle in. Unpack." Ed looked at his watch. "Whoa, dinner in two hours. Maybe time for a quick swim, eh?"

"Good idea, and thanks."

Ed started out.

Jack turned to Christie, and then with a slight tilt of his head he followed Ed out, catching up a few steps behind him.

"Ed—one more thing."

"Yes? What's that?"

Jack looked around. From this area just outside the cabin, he had a good view of much of the camp, from the lake area to the Great Lodge and all the way to the playing fields.

Even a peek at the service road.

"Just got a question. Didn't want the kids to hear. I mean . . ." Jack looked Ed right in the eyes. "Ever have any problems here?"

"Problems? You mean, like the septic backing up?"

Another joke, but Jack didn't smile this time.

"No. With what's outside the fences. With the Can Heads."

Ed nodded. "Jack, something happen to you folks on the way here?"

"At a rest stop. A break-in. One Can Head. I took care of it."

"That's what you do back home, right? Being a cop and all?"

"Yeah. And I was hoping to get away from that. Which is why I asked."

"You've seen a lot, hm?"

Jack paused before answering.

"Enough."

"Listen, Jack, Paterville has amazing security. Since you're a police officer, you've probably noticed it. And that's only what you can see. The fence is fully electric, and the turrets see everything. We got other things all around—motion detectors at the perimeter, cameras checking the woods outside."

"I imagine you do."

"And yes, they're out there. But that's where they will stay. So, I hope you can forget that stuff that you've dealt with in the city. You and your family can have a real good time here, Jack." Ed put a hand on Jack's shoulder. "You just got to relax and enjoy yourself. We've thought of everything."

Jack nodded.

Then, over Ed's shoulder, halfway to the lodge, he saw Shana watching them. The camp director seemed to notice as well.

"Hey, gotta dash. See you at dinner."

"Sure."

Jack went back inside the cottage.

# 17

## Tom and Sharon

Christie wriggled her toes in the sand. Not quite the beach sand of her childhood summers at the Jersey shore. Grittier, coarser.

But still, after everything—wonderful.

She looked over at Jack.

"You look like the lifeguard."

"Hmm?"

They both sat on the sand, not caring that it would stick to their pants. It felt so good to be here.

"The way you—I don't know—scan the waterfront. No, I got it. You're the sheriff in *Jaws*."

He laughed. A good sound.

"Gonna need a bigger boat."

Christie pointed at a scattering of rowboats and canoes over by the dock to the right of the swimming area.

"That's as big as they get here, I'm afraid." A beat. Then, more seriously: "Gorgeous, isn't it?"

"Oh yeah. Sure."

The sun was slipping behind the mountains. Dusk would come early. The lake captured the last hour of golden sunlight, the water sparkling as if alive with lights. Squealing kids of all ages ran in and out of the icy lake water.

It was cold—Christie had confirmed that.

Simon had been brave, running into the water, then spinning around when fully wet and running out again. It may have been the biggest smile she had ever seen on him.

And that felt good.

And Kate?

Kate went in just up to her calves. She wore a striped one-piece, though she had pleaded to get a bikini. Christie vetoed that.

She wondered if she did that because she knew Jack would have said, quite simply, *take it back.*

Then: "That's some assistant Ed Lowe has, hm?"

Jack nodded. "Yeah. Guess so."

"She seemed to check you out."

Jack turned to Christie and grinned. "Maybe she's part of security."

"Or maybe she's here to keep the dads happy."

Jack laughed.

A little too casual. Jack was a guy. He'd have to be crazy to not have taken in Shana.

*Probably never see her again,* Christie thought.

After all, this was supposed to be their vacation as well. For the two of them.

*And we need it.*

*Something to let us recharge before we go back to life at home.*

Home. She'd like to forget about that life for a while.

"Guess we should head back. Change for dinner."

Jack nodded and stood up.

Christie did as well. She didn't want to leave, but there would be other afternoons, other sunsets, other days ahead filled with the shimmering water and the squeals.

"Kate, Simon, come on!" she shouted.

The kids both turned to her as if her voice came from miles away.

"Can't we stay just a little bit more?"

Simon looked to both of his parents for a reprieve.

Christie noticed Kate seemed a bit distracted. Jack looked as well, following Kate's gaze.

To one of the lifeguard chairs.

*No, she's way too young for that.*

Kate—just out of eighth grade.

She knew her girlfriends talked about boys.

But there was no real socializing.

Kate turned away from the lifeguard chair.

"Mom, there are lifeguards. It's safe. Can I stay?"

Christie hesitated.

"And I can watch Simon, too. You guys always take so long to get ready. Can we stay just a little while longer?"

"I don't need watching," Simon added. Then, as if remembering the point of the argument, added, "*Can* we stay just a little bit more?"

A look from Jack. The decision deferred to her.

"Okay. Fifteen minutes, then back to the cabin for quick showers. I don't think you want to miss dinner."

Simon had already spun around to resume his in-and-out game with the cool water. Kate stood there and put on the dutiful face of she-who-watches-her-brother.

Close to the lifeguard. Nothing to worry about.

"Okay then," Jack said. "Let's go get ready. Remember—fifteen minutes."

Christie looked at the mirror, checking herself in a green polo shirt and capris. Too informal? she wondered. But then again this was a camp. People probably showed up in shorts and T's.

Jack came out of the shower dripping; in minutes, he appeared in the living room in shorts, golf shirt, and sandals. Pretty informal.

Christie was tempted to say something. But here was someone who dressed every day in his blue uniform, every detail in place. If this was Jack relaxing, she'd take it.

"Kids back?"

"No. I'll go and—"

A knock at the door.

"Company?" Jack said.

He opened the door. A man and a woman stood there.

"Hi," the man—tall, strongly built—said. "We're your neighbors. The Blairs. Cabin next door." He stuck out his hand. "Tom."

The woman, short and a bit mousy-looking, did the same with Christie. "Sharon. Hope we're not bothering you or anything . . ."

Christie smiled. "No. Just getting ready for dinner." Then, feeling the oddness of leaving the couple out on the small porch, she said, "Come on in."

The couple came into the cabin.

"Nice," Tom said. "Little different arrangement than ours. You like it?"

"Just fine," Jack said.

Sharon—her dark hair cut into a bob, wearing a summery print dress—turned to Christie. "We've been here for almost a week. We love it. So, if you two have any questions, ask away."

"It's a great place," Tom added. "A real getaway."

"Looks nice so far," Jack said.

"Kids?" Christie asked.

Tom grinned. "Oh, yeah—our two boys. Jim and Sam. The 'ma-niacs,' we call them. They've been running wild in this place, loving it. In fact, we just signed up for two more days. Money's a bit tight, but hell, who knows when we'll be able to come back."

Those words seemed to make Sharon thoughtful.

"So different here. You know?"

"You mean, the lake . . . the mountains?" Christie said.

"The whole *feel* of the place. Everyone just enjoying themselves. Like a world we all thought we lost."

She guessed that Jack was sizing them up.

That's what he did, size people up.

What's their story, their life?

She had told him it was a bad habit.

Maybe with this couple he could let his guard down. People used to have friends.

It would be nice to have some friends.

"Hey," Tom said, as if trying to sound spontaneous, "why don't we all sit together for dinner? Your first meal at the camp."

Sharon added, "They have these big tables. Very homey!"

Christie looked at Jack. Never exactly Mr. Social.

Then the kids burst in through the door. Simon and Kate laugh-ing, Simon racing ahead as Kate tried to catch him.

"Our two," Christie said. "Simon, Kate. Hey, quick showers, guys. Then dinner."

"I'm starving!" Simon said before vanishing into the other bedroom.

"So, see you at dinner?" Tom said, looking from Jack to Christie.

"Sure. It'll be a pleasure," she answered.

The couple smiled. This wasn't something she'd ever do, Christie knew, not back home. Knock on someone's door.

"Great. We'll save you places."

After they left, Jack walked to the window, pulled a curtain aside, and watched the Blairs make their way over to the Grand Lodge.

Then he came close to Christie.

"Meet the neighbors, hm?"

"Seemed nice."

"Yeah. And I guess we can pick their brains about the place."

Simon came out of the bathroom, his still-wet hair sticking up at odd angles.

Christie turned to him.

"Come here, mister."

When the hair had been tamed by a brush, and Kate finally appeared wearing cargo shorts and a collared shirt, looking suddenly very much like her dad, they left the cottage for their first dinner in the Great Lodge.

# 18

# Dinner

Jack took the bowl of food from Tom Blair, and scooped some onto his plate. Looking like a mixture of chili and refried beans, it didn't look bad.

Simon weighed in with his verdict. "What is this stuff? It's good!"

Jack took a taste. Not bad, but—

"Yeah," Tom said, "the food's really not *all* they crack it up to be in the brochure. But it's got taste, and there's plenty of it."

"Tastes better than what we usually make do with," Jack said. "Kate, what do you think?"

Kate kept spooning it in, as if trying to make up her mind. "It's . . . okay."

He turned back to their new Paterville neighbors. Jim and Sam Blair, older than Simon by a year or two, had already finished their plates.

Guess you get hungry up here . . .

"So, you've arranged to stay longer, hm?"

"Yep," Tom said, looking around at the Great Lodge and all the full tables of people scarfing down the Paterville dinner. A small laugh. "Don't think my family would let me leave. They . . . *we* like it here."

Jack noticed a slight hesitation.

"You, though? Had enough of Paterville?"

Tom smiled. "No. It's great."

There was a loud, ear-piercing squeak from the loudspeakers.

Jack turned to see Ed Lowe standing at a podium.

"Hello . . . *campers!*"

Then, as if coached, the families answered Lowe:

"*Hel-lo!*"

"Hope you've had a great day at the camp today. Looks like even better weather tomorrow. Now, I don't want you to keep you from that good camp food, but how about a Paterville welcome to our new-comers!"

"*Hel-lo, newcomers!*"

"Oh, you can do better than that!"

And they did.

Jack caught Christie looking at him, perhaps sensing his discom-fort. Corny wasn't quite the word for it.

Maybe vacations were supposed to be like this.

Jack grinned at Christie.

"And a quick reminder, tonight we have a bonfire down by the lakefront—and tomorrow is the big fireworks show!"

Lowe made a big wave at the tables, and a smile.

"Now back to your eats."

Jack started to turn away—

When he saw Lowe's assistant, Shana, come out from the side, holding papers. She looked at the crowd, no smiles from her.

*Serious woman*, Jack thought.

Tom leaned close from across the wooden table.

"Met Shana? She's . . . something, hm?"

Jack kept watching Lowe and Shana. She handed Lowe the papers. He turned to her and then took a few steps away from the microphone, his back to the diners.

From the other side of the room, a burly man, tall with thick arms and an even thicker neck, came into the room carrying a heavy metal tray and brought it over to a serving area.

Jack turned back to Tom.

"Who's that guy? Big fella."

"That? He's Dunphy. The cook. Or at least the main cook. Brings the food himself."

Lowe noticed Dunphy and left Shana standing to the side while he walked over to the cook.

Jack was looking to see how things ran here, who was in charge. All the little gears that have to fall into place to make something like this work.

Finally, he turned back to the table.

He caught a look from Christie . . . probably thinking that he was ogling Lowe's jill-of-all-trades.

Definitely some of that going on.

Jack smiled. Caught! Then went back to the meal. The stuff, whatever it was, got cold fast and now didn't seem as appetizing.

*Maybe I'll be hungrier tomorrow*, he thought. *After a full day in the mountains.*

The two couples walked out of the lodge together.

Jack and Tom walked together, Christie and Sharon close behind. Kate brought up the rear. Simon ran up to her, with the Blairs' two boys in tow.

"Dad, Mom—we're gonna play hide-and-seek down by the sports field. That okay?"

Jack looked at Christie.

"Um, I guess."

Christie gave it her seal of approval.

"Yes. But stay close. No scouting around."

Tom made a small laugh. "Don't worry, Jack. They do a good job of keeping the kids where they're supposed to be. We let our two just roam around till bedtime. Couldn't be safer."

"Okay, Simon. Come back to the lake for the bonfire before dark," Jack said.

A quick nod, and his son vanished.

He looked back at Kate, who still didn't seem to have embraced this place.

*Hope she settles in.*

"Jack—meet you down there?" Tom said.

Jack looked back at Christie talking with Sharon.

The Blairs seemed like nice enough people.

*Why not*, Jack thought. *After all, this is a vacation.*

Soon they were back at the cabins.


Simon did what Sam and Jim told him to. He folded his arms in front of him, and rested his head against a tree, eyes shut, and counted. But not a normal count.

*One Mississippi . . . two Mississippi . . . three . . .*

Never did that back home. Never played *this* game.

The other two kids hiding while he counted.

He reached twenty and lifted his head from the tree.

A bit of stickiness had attached itself to his arms when he put them against the tree.

*Sap. That's what it's called*, Simon knew.

He looked around for Sam and Jim.

In the time it took him to count, it seemed to have turned darker here. The tall trees blotted out the light from the sky. And though they had led Simon down to this area, telling him how great it was for hiding, now Simon couldn't see where they had come from.

Where was the lake? The cabins? Which way . . . was the way back?

He wanted to call out to them.

Say: *Where are you?*

But that would be giving up the game. Being a baby. These were big kids. Be fun to play with them even though he was a full year younger.

Instead of shouting *where are you?*, he said: "Coming to find you guys!"

Simon took a step in one direction. The leaves and dry pine needles at his feet made a soft crunching sound. Another step.

Was he going back the way they had come, or to where they were hiding, or some other way?

Step . . . step . . . step . . .

He kept turning his head, looking for signs of movement. But all was still here in the woods.

Kate walked out of the back bedroom. "Dad, I'm going to walk down to the lake now."

Jack looked up from a wall map of Paterville and the nearby mountains. A geological map showing elevation, trails risers, the peaks.

"That okay?" he said to Christie.

"Sure. Go on, Kate."

His daughter smiled. Maybe the ice was melting. A good thing. "Back before dark, 'kay?"

"Will do, Dad."

When she shut the door behind her, Christie turned to Jack.

"Guess we're giving them both some room? Feels strange."

"We want them to enjoy this place, right? Some independence . . . might be good."

"My," Christie said with a smile, "what a little bit of vacation does to turn the police officer around. I'm glad."

"Just catch me in a few days."

"Should we head down to the bonfire?"

"You go on. I'll be right there. I need to move the car. It's parked out front, but they say they want all the cars in the back parking lot. Let me do that, and I'll see you there."

Jack grabbed the car keys off a countertop near the kitchen and followed Christie out the door.


Simon froze.

Darker still. And now the air chilled his bare arms and legs. The trees, which had very brown trunks before, had turned gray and dark. The branches overhead didn't look green at all.

*They have to be nearby,* Simon thought.

*They wouldn't just leave me here.*

*Just ditch me.*

More steps—so hard to force his feet to move.

He looked past the shadowy tree trunks and saw . . . something else.

Something shiny.

Maybe part of the camp.

It made him turn in that direction. As he came closer he saw that it was the giant fence, hidden from the camp by the trees. Simon now knew he was very far away from where he was supposed to be.

He started to turn.

Then a voice—deep, rough—said, "Hey, you!"


Jack got up to the Great Lodge and, through a side window, saw all the diners gone, only workers cleaning tables.

Where do they stay? he wondered. Must be another part of the camp where they had staff cabins. Maybe came here for the season, then went back to whatever small towns they came from.

The entry hall glowed invitingly. People sitting on the massive leather couches and chairs, talking, reading.

His car was the only one still parked in the check-in area.

Not much light spilled onto the spaces in front of the lodge entrance.

He dug out his keys.

"Everything okay?"

Someone in the darkness. He hadn't even noticed . . . standing there . . . coming close.

The person took a few steps closer and Jack recognized the smell. That hint of perfume.

Shana.

"Just need to move my car. Y'know, to the parking area."

*Of course she knew,* Jack thought. *She works here.*

"Someone from the lodge would have been more than glad to move it for you, Mr. Murphy."

That sounded too weird. "Jack."

"In fact—Jack—I'd be glad to take it over."

She stuck out a hand. The light backlit Shana so she was all shape, no color.

"That's okay. Want to check some things. I can do it."

"Sure you can."

Odd comment.

A taunt.

"Anything else you need help with tonight . . . Jack?"

"Nope. All good. Bonfire night, right?"

A pause, as if perhaps Shana too realized the absurdity of Jack going from cop to card player.

"Have fun, then. Good night."

"You, too."

The dark shape turned and walked away, not into the entrance hall but down a path to the side.

Jack unlocked the car and got in.

# 19

# Dusk

Christie walked down the path leading to the lakeshore. Twilight, and Kate stood at the water's edge, looking at the now-dark lake.

But it was her position that was interesting.

Only feet away from the lifeguard stand.

One lifeguard was still on duty with twilight bringing a gray and silvery look to the water, the yellow sand now turning dark as well.

The lifeguard, sixteen, maybe seventeen, bronzed by the summer, looked at his watch and jumped down to the sand.

Christie watched the next few moments with a mix of concern, fear, and fascination. Almost as if she was spying.

The lifeguard in a white polo shirt, collar up. Grabbing his back-pack, he looked up and saw Kate.

Christie wanted to whisper, *Move on . . . she's only thirteen.*

But she watched the boy grin, a nod in Kate's direction, and then start up from the beach.

For a moment, Christie remembered what it was like to be young.

The boy walked past Christie, who hoped she wasn't radiating an "I'm the mom" vibe.

Her motherly spying over, she continued down to the water.


Jack got out of the Explorer. The lot sat in the dark with only two tall lights at opposite corners of the sea of cars.

*Guess they don't want people going on any joyrides at night.*

Standing there, he looked at those two lights, the small milky pools each made.

Near the light to the right, he saw the narrow roadway leading up.

The service road.

Jack wondered what the rest of this operation, this camp, was like.

He looked up.

Any security cameras here?

None that he could see, but it would make sense. Didn't every public space have security cameras?

Whatever cameras they had here—if they had any at all—were well hidden.

He slammed the door and went to the back of the SUV.

The electronic key popped open the back.

Now empty, save for blankets, a map book. A New York State Atlas. The Mid-Atlantic Region.

He pushed them aside and lifted up the covering over the storage area.

So dark here.

There was a flashlight in the glove compartment.

But then if they had security cameras here, they might also see.

A chance he'd have to take.

He went and got the light.


Christie walked over to Kate, and smiled.

"You okay?"

"Sure, Mom. Why wouldn't I be okay?"

Conversation with a thirteen-year-old could be tricky. Questions invited questions back. Questions in general—never welcome.

"Good. Nice here, hm?"

"S'okay. I like the lake."

Kate turned back to the water.

"Me, too. We'll get a full day down here tomorrow. Swim, use the boats. I think you'll have fun."

Kate nodded, neither confirming nor denying the possibility.

Christie stood there. She thought of all those years ago, before the Can Heads, when she and Jack first thought about having kids.

When she decided that she wouldn't be a working mom, like her own mother. That she'd leave her teaching job.

She'd raise her kids.

Jack liked the idea as well.

Though there would never be a lot of money, there'd be enough.

And when the great famine started, the worldwide drought—whatever the hell it was that changed things forever—the decision made even more sense. Christie taught the kids—and life closed in.

In a world with Can Heads, being home seemed like the only sensible thing.

Kate turned to her, as if sensing that Christie had drifted.

"Where's Simon? Dad?"

"Guess Simon's still playing with those kids. He'll be here soon. Your dad's parking the car."

Kate nodded.

Together they waited.

"Stop right there, kid."

Simon didn't move. The man's voice sounded mean, the way he barked at him.

Had he done something wrong, was he in trouble?

The man came between Simon and the fence.

Simon couldn't see much, but the man held a gun. He could see that. And he was tall . . . big.

Bigger than Dad, Simon thought.

"I'm sorry," Simon said, not really knowing what he was apologizing for.

The man took another step.

"You're not supposed to be over here. There are no trails over here. You're supposed to stay on the trails, kid."

Simon nodded, then realizing that his head movement wouldn't be seen, he said, "Yes. I—"

Simon wanted to explain about the other kids, the bigger kids who got him to play here, to play hide-and-seek. That brought him here, to this man, to the fence.

He didn't mean to go somewhere he shouldn't.

For a moment, the man didn't say anything.

"Now you just turn around, son. And walk back. That way."

Simon made a pointing gesture somewhere over his shoulder.

"Over that way? There?"

"Yeah. Nice and straight. You'll come to one of the paths. Make a left on it. Keep walking."

"Okay. I'll do that."

Simon wanted to ask, *Will you tell my parents?*

But instead he started to turn, feeling the man with the gun, this guard, looking at him.

He walked as straight as he could.

Step after step.

Nice and straight.

Almost all the light faded here.

And the other kids? Had they run away when they saw the guard? Or had Simon gotten so lost that they had never been around here at all?

He blinked.

Hoping he could tell when he reached the path.

He made promises to himself. Going to stay only on the paths. And maybe he wouldn't play with those bigger kids. He'd stay close to his family, their cabin.

The crunchy covering of the forest changed. A path. Barely able to be seen, but he could feel the smooth flat dirt of a trail.

Simon turned left.


"Hey, where's Jack?"

Tom and Sharon had walked close to Christie, near the warm glow of the bonfire.

"Oh, he's coming, Tom." Then: "Think the kids are okay? It's getting dark . . ."

Tom nodded. "Sure. But I'll go find the hide-and-seekers and bring 'em back alive!"

He walked away.

Christie stood alone with Sharon.

"So, where do you guys live?" Christie asked.

"Yonkers. Know it? Quieter than the city. If you know what I mean. You?"

"Staten Island. Same thing. Quiet. Isolated."

Quiet. A new code word.

Meaning no break-ins. No attacks. With the flames flickering, reflected on the water—that world seemed so far away.

"Good for the kids there. I know that's what's important to Tom."

"Got to think about your kids."

Sharon turned to her. "Well, yes. But they're not my kids."

"Really?"

"Yes. Tom—his wife died a few years back. She died when the drought came. Some illness. They didn't understand."

"Did it have anything to do with what happened? To the crops, the farms?"

"The doctors didn't know. I was her friend. And I, well, I helped him through things. Just a friend. At first. But then . . . we got married." The woman, now seen in an entirely different light by Christie, took a breath. "Seemed to make sense. Now, they're *mine*. They know that. Tom knows that. That's how I feel. They're my kids now."

"Good for you."

Silence. Then: "The boys, your boys—they seem happy."

"I hope so. It's hard. But I try my best."

Tom's voice rang out: "Got them. Safe and sound."

Christie turned to see the two Blair kids walking side by side, and then off on his own, yards away, Simon.

Christie's instincts told her something had happened.

But that could wait for later.


Back at the open trunk, Jack aimed the light at the storage compartment key hole.

He saw something—stray marks around the hole. Small scratches.

All the marks of someone trying to break in.

*I would have seen those marks before.*

Jack turned to look over his shoulder. If there were cameras, they would pick up his light, his bending over the compartment. The hesitation.

But as soon as he had the thought—*someone tried to get in here. Maybe someone* did *get in here*—he pushed it away.

Who knew if the marks had been there, made by his key trying to find its way in.

And if there were cameras?

He hunched over the compartment as he put the key in and unlocked it. The metal cover popped up.

Jack held the flashlight in his hand as he opened the lid.

He tried to shield what lay below with his body.

The armory. His indulgence to his concerns and fear . . . and his paranoia.

He sure as hell couldn't tell where legitimate concern ended and paranoia began.

Everything looked in place. The guns neatly nested in the foam. Boxes of shells on the side. The small, timed explosives. A larger flashlight.

Crazy, he thought, to be traveling with this.

But then he thought, *Crazier not to.*

Then back to his paranoia: If someone had gotten in here, saw this, what would they think?

Or had they only *tried* to get in?

Jack shook his head. No way he could answer that one, no possible way.

He turned around.

Sensing someone looking at him. His flashlight made a random pool of light in front of him.

The sound of the insects, cicadas—so rhythmic, so loud—could drown out a lot of sounds. How did they survive here?

No such summer sounds back home. They were long gone.

He took a breath, then went back to the compartment. All the goodies safe and sound. He shut the lid and heard it snap into locked position. He turned off the flashlight and put it in his back pocket

As he walked away, back to the main area of the camp, he pressed the electronic key and heard a chirp as all the SUV's doors locked.

It was fully dark when he got down to the lake.

## 20

## Night

"What—no marshmallows?"

Jack walked down to Christie and the Blairs. He looked at all the Paterville families gathered by the lakeside. Off to the left, the roaring fire sent glowing embers flying up to a clear night sky. Already, stars could be seen, way more than in the murky skies over Staten Island.

Tom laughed. "Marshmallows. Wouldn't that be sweet."

Jack spotted Simon sitting on the sand close to Christie. Too close, he thought.

Digging in the sand. Not playing with the Blair kids. Jack's antennae went up. Something happen there?

And Kate?

He looked around and spotted her, a dark shape but recognizable to a parent, standing by the fire while some young guys fed the blaze pieces of wood.

"The fire's nice enough," Jack said.

Tom came closer, lowered his voice. "You know, we *could* blow it off. Head back to the cabins. Have a drink?"

"Drink?"

Tom grinned. "Doesn't taste great but packs a wallop."

Didn't sound bad to Jack. He nodded. "Okay. Let me see if Christie and the kids are all okay."

He went over to Christie.

"Tom and I going to go up to the cabin and talk."

"Talk?"

Jack leaned close. "He has something to drink."

As Jack said the words, he thought, *How long has it been since I sat quietly, just talked to another guy? Shared a drink?*

"You okay with that?"

Christie nodded. "Sure. If it's drinkable—save me some?"

Jack laughed. "I will." Back in the day, she liked her glass of white wine. Rare stuff now.

"Yeah," he said. "I will."

Jack was about to add, *If Simon goes near the fire, keep an eye out.*

As if Christie wouldn't watch him like a hawk.

"All right. See you later."

He turned back from the shoreline and joined Tom for the walk to the cabins.


Kate looked at the fire. The red glow painted the bodies of those tending the fire, the boys poking it, feeding in piece after piece of wood.

She stood so close to the blaze that the heat felt as if was toasting her face. The streaming flames reflected in the lake; the water so flat like a black mirror.

She caught one of the guys working the fire look right at her—and he smiled.

The same lifeguard, she thought. The same guy she had seen today. Skin all tanned, his hair bleached blond.

The boys where they lived, the boys her age, seemed so stupid, so immature.

This older boy was different.

She smiled back, and then quickly lowered her eyes down to the fire, right into the heart of the burning wooden coals sparking like reddish-yellow jewels.


"Go on. Take a hit of that."

Jack brought the coffee cup up to his lips, first giving the substance a smell.

Alcohol.

The government hadn't exactly banned the sale of it, but with anything that could be used for food or fuel, booze became both hard to find and amazingly expensive.

"And it's okay to drink this?"

"Been having it every night. Under the stars. It's a beautiful thing."

Tom extended his cup for a toasting clink. Jack knocked his cup into Tom's.

"Down the hatch," he said. The smell: gasoline. The taste: well . . . maybe this was what gasoline tasted like.

"Whoa. Nobody light any matches around us."

"The cook brews it up. Somehow. The kitchen workers can get you a bottle. Supposedly Ed Lowe doesn't know about it. Keeping this place all about family fun and stuff."

Jack took another sip, suddenly less eye-popping than the first.

"I'm guessing . . . a little bit goes a long way?"

"Got that right."

Then, quiet. The sound of singing began to echo from the lake below. The bonfire's glow flickered in and out of the dense trees that shielded the cabins.

Jack turned to Tom. "So, Tom—what do you do?"

He tried to keep the cop-tone out of his voice.

"Do—or did? I used to work at a research center run by NYU in the city. Now I work at one of those government supply centers. Handing out food when we have it. Place is a zoo."

"What kind of research?"

The question seemed to make Tom hesitate.

"Lots of things. You've heard of GM food? Genetically modified? My lab experimented with that a lot. All government funded. Modifying strings of DNA, playing with—oh, I'm just boring you."

"Not at all."

Tom didn't continue.

The sounds rolling up from the lake were undecipherable. Voices, laughs, a squeal. The fire casting a reddish-yellow glow over the water.

"What happened?"

"Hmm?"

"Why did you leave?"

"The government shut the whole thing down. Actually, they cherry-picked a few of the team, brought them to Washington. Think they were disappointed in the rest of us. Like we couldn't stop what was happening."

"Then—this was after?"

Tom looked at Jack. "After? You mean after the world went to hell, after the food started disappearing? Yeah. *After.* But, you know, when the genie is out of the fucking bottle, damn hard to get him back in. Not sure any of us knew what might happen when we started playing with the GM stuff."

Jack wondered if Tom had something do with what happened.

So many theories. Experiments gone wrong. Tinkering with food production.

But already the shared sips of alcohol had lost their zing. Too many questions.

"Now, I just hand out what passes for food these days." Tom said, closing the door on that part of the conversation.

It was something that Jack would like to get back to.

"And you—what's your line of work?"

Jack took another sip. Almost done, and he didn't think he wanted a refill.

"I'm a cop."

"Really? Wow. Could have fooled me. I mean, you don't *seem* like a cop."

*And how exactly are cops supposed to seem?*

And was that comment supposed to be a compliment?

People got funny around cops.

"I'm on vacation. On the down-low, as the kids say."

Tom took a breath. "And how is it out there? On the streets. Getting worse?"

Jack looked away. "Worse? Not getting better. Looks to me . . . like it's spreading."

"Shit."

"Each day, new blocks. Gone. More Can Heads. No new cops."

"You know, there was a theory one of the guys in my lab had. That this was how the dinosaurs ended. Feeding off each other. That's what really wiped them out."

"Really? I could believe it. When you see humans hovering over a body, slicing it into pieces like crazy butchers, bundling the goddamned meat up like—"

Jack suddenly realized that he had gone too deep into the hole. The hole of being a cop. Fighting them.

"Sorry. Get carried away, you know. That's what's good about being here. Shake all that shit off. Get away from all that 'beware your neighbor' paranoia."

"Except not one who has some booze, hm? And this is a good place, Jack. Lot of guards. The gorgeous lake. Enough food. Not a bad place at all." Then: "Glad you guys are our neighbors."

He clinked his glass against Jack's.

"And you're staying a few more days, right?"

"Yeah. No one wants to leave. What the hell do we head back to? No real family for us. Least not around New York. The family would love to just stay here forever."

"You and a lot of people, I guess."

Tom again reached down for the milk bottle filled with the clear liquid.

"Refill?"

Jack was about to say no thanks. Instead, he held out his cup and watched Tom pour.


The cabin was quiet.

Kate and Simon in bed. Windows wide open so a cool breeze blew in. The occasional sounds from the woods.

Christie sniffed, taking in the strong smell of alcohol on Jack's breath, and smiled when he said, "You wouldn't have liked it."

Now he lay in the bed, the background noise in his ears, Christie close, her back to him.

Not feeling sleepy.

Not at all.

He inched a bit closer so that his body pressed against hers.

He put an arm around her and with the precision borne of years together, his hand smoothly cupped her right breast.

He felt himself stir against her. Always a good feeling.

But then Christie turned to him.

"Want some sugar, hm?"

Her face caught the scant light of the room. No moon outside, but the glow from the lights on the paths filtered into the room a bit, outlining her face.

"Could be."

"Maybe that leggy assistant got you going?"

"No, not at all," Jack said, realizing how quickly he said it.

Realizing that he hadn't told Christie about his encounter with her in the parking lot.

Then: "The kids. They're right there. Not sure they're asleep."

"I can be quiet," he said.

He could make out a smile. "But can I? I think we should wait. When they're both out for some activity here or something. Okay?"

When Jack didn't say anything it seemed like a bit more distance between them. Maybe something he hoped being here would change.

He felt Christie reach down and wrap her hand around him.

"Save that big boy for later. All right?"

"He hates waiting."

"I promise it'll be worth the wait."

Christie turned over, her back once again to Jack.

He followed suit, turning away and waiting for sleep to come.


Except sleep didn't come.

Had to be a good hour later, and still he felt awake. Maybe the uncommon feeling of a little alcohol buzz was keeping him up?

Maybe . . . something else.

He lay on his back. He could hear Christie—always such a deep sleeper—as she took in each measured breath.

Deeply asleep.

The noise from outside didn't help either. For a guy from Brooklyn, that was a lot of nature out there. He wished he had ear plugs.

He sat up.

Pointless to just lie there.

Especially when his mind went over the past. His partner, the trap, his wounds.

Maybe a bit of a walk. Some of that cool mountain air.

He slid to the side of the bed, his boat shoes only a few feet away. Shorts and T-shirt idly tossed on a chair in the room.

He snatched them up and then slipped into his shoes.

He walked out to the living room and into the night.

For a moment, he stood on the porch, looking at the camp. All the cabins nice and quiet. No more sounds of singing coming from the lake to compete with the cicadas.

In the moonless night, he could just about see the outline of the mountains that circled the lake.

He took a breath.

Fifteen. Twenty minutes of walking.

Then another try for sleep.

He walked off his porch.

# 21

# The Service Road

Though the day had been hot, the night quickly turned chilly.

Jack rubbed his arms as he stepped outside, holding the porch door behind him so he could close it gently.

He took a breath of the sweet mountain air with just a hint of pine. Another breath. Another smell. Perhaps the decaying mulch of last summer's leaves and needles sitting on the forest floor.

He started down the path that led away from the cottages and the center of the camp.

It wasn't long before he saw somebody.

A man standing near a curved lamppost, the light low, just barely enough to illuminate a spot where three intersecting paths met.

The light caught the man's collared shirt, pants—and the recognizable shape of a gun holstered to his side.

Jack kept walking.

When he got closer, the guard said, "Evening, sir."

Jack kept walking.

"Evening."

"Anything I can help you with?"

The man seemed to stiffen a bit. Perhaps late-night walkers weren't that common at Paterville. The camp quiet, save for the cicadas chattering in the background.

"No thanks. Just getting some air."

The guard nodded as Jack came abreast of him.

"Couldn't sleep."

"Just be careful. Dark spots on the walkways. You could trip."

Jack stopped. "Sure. Will do."

"And sir, of course, stay away from the perimeter. The fence."

Jack smiled at that one. Did anyone need reminding not to wander over there?

"Oh, I will." Jack looked at the path leading toward the Great Lodge.

"See you."

"Night, sir."

Jack continued.

He came upon two more guards. Now he was curious.

The first guard stood at the entrance area of the lodge. Not so strange. Jack avoided talking to him and walked well past him to the right, a direction that led out to the playing fields and the game room.

Guard number three stood near the back of the lodge.

This one smoking a cigarette, which he threw to the ground as Jack approached.

The guard coughed.

His voice seemed a bit slurred. Maybe he'd just had a hit of the cook's home brew?

"Lost, sir? The cottages—"

That word came out a bit wrong.

"—are back that way."

"No. I'm fine. Can't sleep. Walking around."

As if the guard hadn't heard him, he gestured behind Jack. "They're back that way."

Jack nodded. "Thanks."

He turned around, headed back to the front of the lodge.

When he got there, the guard at the front was talking quietly on what had to be a walkie-talkie.

The guard gave him a quick look, and went on talking.

Jack sailed past the Great Lodge entrance and then passed the trail leading back to the cabins. Instead, he started heading down the winding trail to the parking lot.

*Where am I going? And what's with all these guards?*

He didn't understand that. Sure, a guard by the gates, the fence. Armed and dangerous. Yeah, that all made sense. Here, though, all around the property? Seemed like overkill.

A few yards down the path to the parking area, he heard a voice.

"Excuse me, sir. Do you need—"

"No. Need to check something in my car."

*Everyone asking if I need some goddamn help.*

This time Jack didn't stop, didn't even turn around. All the watching and monitoring made him feel penned in.

He kept walking, picking up speed. More guards ahead? he wondered. He guessed he'd find out soon enough.

The parking lot seemed almost intentionally poorly lit. The two scrawny yellow lights left most of the cars in darkness.

He could find his easily enough.

Except he wasn't really going to his car.

Instead, he walked to the back of the lot. To the service road.

And through the trees, twinkling like stars hanging too low in the sky, lights.

Jack moved into the sea of dark cars. He'd probably be as invisible here as the cars were.

He moved slowly through the lot.

He stopped by the service road entrance. Even without any real light here, he could see a sign with large painted letters:

SERVICE ROAD—PATERVILLE CAMP EMPLOYEES ONLY.

Jack walked past the sign.

The dirt road curved up, rutted with big stones that, in the pitch black, made him lose footing, his ankle slipping left and right. One twist sent a spike of pain into his injured right leg.

Not what the doctor recommended, he thought.

*Maybe I should go back.*

But the lights ahead resolved from twinkling stars to big bright lights. Lots of lights.

Then, as he walked up, sounds. Voices talking in the darkness. Employees blowing off some steam?

Until he could make out through the wall of trees a large building. A steady stream of white smoke snaked its way from the roof into the crystal clear night sky.

Must be where they prepared the food.

The voices louder. Laughs. The sound of someone giving an order.

Pretty busy considering how late it was.

The road's angle grew steeper. This service area actually sat on a hill above the main camp.

From up there, you could probably see the whole camp.

He took a deep breath, the effort of the climb made harder by now-steady pain from his leg.

Soon, he'd be on level ground, at this camp within the camp.

"You can stop right there."

Two men came out from the side. Jack hadn't seen them at all. How long had they been watching him? Did they know he was coming? Or did they just hide in the shadows, waiting for the stray visitor?

"Yeah. Right. I'm—"

"Lost? Yeah, you're lost, all right. You're not in the camp anymore, friend. This is a restricted area. Didn't you see the sign?"

The polite "sirs" of the previous guards had vanished.

One of the men took a step onto the path, directly in Jack's way. Big guy, burly arms that his shirt—even with sleeves rolled up tight—was barely able to contain.

"Sorry. Had—"

What? He fished for something that explained all about going places where one wasn't supposed to go.

"—insomnia."

"Restricted area," the man repeated. "You have to leave. Now."

"Okay. Thanks. I will."

Thanks? Stupid thing to say. Thanks . . . for what?

The other guard had also stepped into the clearing of the path, picking up a bit of the scant light.

Jack saw that this guy held an automatic rifle.

So, Paterville never had problems with the Can Heads outside?

Then why the heavy firepower? All the guards?

To keep guests from wandering onto the service road?

How safe *was* this place?

The two men in front of him didn't say anything more, which made the noises from behind them even more pronounced. Laughs, voices, an engine starting.

"G'night, guys. Thanks for watching out for us."

They didn't respond to that.

Jack turned around and started down the hill.

Downhill now—always harder on his leg.

All his exercises couldn't make up for the damage and pain that he'd have to live with for the rest of his life.

To the parking lot.

His eyes better adjusted to the murky blackness, and it seemed brighter.

He'd have to pass more guards on the way back to the cottage. His night walk would probably be a big topic of conversation with Ed Lowe and his team.

*What was that guy up to? Walking around like that?*

The parking lot, an open dirt plain, was at least flat. He had no trouble spotting the path leading back to the center of the camp.

He didn't worry about greeting any of those guards on his return.

But he did worry about Christie; he hoped that he could slip back into the bed, under the cool sheets, his body with its slight sheen of sweat, and fall asleep without her waking.

Without her asking any questions.

In minutes, he was there, back in the cabin as if he had never left. He got into the bed, slowly lowering his head onto the pillow.

And though he had questions—things that confused him, things that he wanted to know more about—he quickly fell asleep.

# 22

# Morning

Christie looked at her watch. Nearly ten A.M.

Not like Jack to sleep in. Though at home, after a rough week, he could sleep well past ten. And after getting wounded, getting up didn't seem as easy for him.

But there was something else . . .

Last night. She had heard him slide out of bed. Thinking he was getting a drink of water. Going to the bathroom. Instead, she heard him slip on clothes and step outside their cabin, so quietly.

She didn't turn over. Didn't say anything. She didn't want to be asking him all the time, *You okay? Everything all right?*

She had drifted off again, only waking when she felt the mattress tilt as he slid in.

Again, she just lay there. Keeping her eyes closed.

*Give him time,* Dr. Kleiner had said at the rehab wing of Kings County Hospital. Time to do the work, time to make his leg stronger.

But time also to get over what had happened.

And that's what she was doing.

She emptied her straw bag filled with beach towels. After a cool night, the sun was already hot.

She looked around at the other families on the lakeshore.


Simon kept digging a massive hole only feet away from Christie's blanket.

Sharon Blair sat nearby in an aluminum beach chair with circus stripes. Floppy hat, oversized shades, lost in a book.

Which was good, since Christie had had enough talk.

*Maybe we've all gotten used to being alone,* she thought. *Independent. Or suspicious.*

Now she was just as glad to sit, listen to the kids squealing in the icy water, and watch the occasional cloud hit a mountain peak.

Simon kept on digging.

While the two Blair boys went in and out of the water as though performing some kind of drill.

"Simon, why don't you go in? Cool off."

Another scoop of sand came out. "I will. Digging now."

Christie made a small laughing sound. Keeping it light.

"That is one big hole."

Christie remembered how at the Jersey shore her dad would always make the joke whenever she dug.

*Digging to China?*

Time to retire that, Christie thought. The thought of those days at the beach, her whole family, didn't bring her any sense of joy.

"You go in later, I'll go in with you, 'kay?"

"Sure," Simon said.

Christie turned back to the water.

Obviously something had happened with Simon and the other two boys. Bit of bullying, perhaps? Teasing? Did he get scared?

Christie guessed he'd eventually tell her.

Eventually kids tell things.

Just have to be patient.

And she wondered: was she also thinking now not just about Simon, but her husband as well?

The dream—so vivid, lifelike, that in his nightmare sleep Jack tossed and turned in the bed.

His family in a car.

The rest stop. And Can Heads surrounding it. First a few. Then more. Circling it, banging on the metal. Probing.

For some reason, he was on the ground, unable to get up. No gun—nothing he could do but watch the scene at the car as a window shattered. The another. The screams of his kids. Christie yelling.

Still he lay on the ground, more Can Heads on top of him, pulling, picking at him. He would be alive to see the horror that would engulf his family.

He moaned in the dream.

Then in the room. Quiet sound at first, then louder, and then—

His eyes opened wide. Taking in the unfamiliar bedroom. The late morning light through the curtains.

The dream lingered, the feelings holding on even as he sat up in bed, hoping to shake off the horror. He cleared his throat.

"'Lo? Anybody home?"

The cabin quiet. He could see the porch door open, with only the screen door shut to keep the outside and the bugs away.

A small tent of a note with his name on it sat on the dresser.

He moved to get out of bed, feeling that familiar jolt of pain that was part of the everyday routine of getting up. Getting up, moving. Doing some stretching in bed.

That would be followed by the pressure of finally placing his right foot on the ground. It always hurt first thing, the first time he stood on it. As if the leg just wanted to be inactive forever and give in to the wound.

No fucking way that was happening.

He walked over to the note and picked it up.

*Down at the beach, sleepyhead. See you there! Xoxo, me.*

Jack put the note down.

"Morning," Jack said to Tom and Sharon as he sat down next to Christie on the beach towel.

Tom made a knocking gesture at his head—obviously also the worse for wear after the cook's moonshine.

"There you are!" Christie said. "Thought we'd have to take drastic measures to get you up for lunch."

"Guess . . . I was tired. All that driving."

He couldn't see her eyes behind her dark sunglasses.

"Yup. Lot of driving. And . . ."

Jack nodded and turned to Simon.

"Morning, Mr. Simon. Tunneling, hm?"

"Hi, Dad."

Christie lowered her glasses a bit, and gave Jack a look up and down. "I see you're in your bathing suit."

He grinned. "Yeah. I mean, it *is* a beach."

"Kind of expected you to wear khakis and"—she leaned close—"strap your 'little friend' onto your ankle."

"Right. Let everyone know I'm a cop."

Truth was, he had looked at his ankle holster and thought of doing just that. Did he go anywhere without a gun these days?

Hardly.

Instead, he had taken the gun and holster and buried it under a pile of his shirts in a bottom drawer of the bedroom dresser.

Not that he felt comfortable now.

"Well, good. Maybe we can all go in the water, then."

Christie made a small nod in Simon's direction.

Jack could see that his son hadn't gotten his suit wet.

He turned back to Christie. "Yeah. Let me toast a bit. Then we all hit that water."

"It's cold," Tom said. "It will wake you up, that's for sure."

"Maybe I'll wait."

"Tonight's the fireworks—sit together for dinner again?"

Jack looked at Christie. Did she like them?

"Um, sure. Great."

"We'll save you places."

Jack looked around at the islands of umbrellas and chairs and blankets.

Then: "Where's Kate?"

"She wanted to go to the game room. Said the sun was too hot."

"She just went off on her own?"

"Er . . . yeah. This is a camp."

Jack tried to gauge why that bothered him. Was it due to those older boys, the lifeguards that he now viewed as human sharks circling an impressionable, just-turned teenager?

Or leftover feelings from last night? The guards, the whole feel of the place at night.

He would have liked to have told Christie about it. But why? Make her nervous? Let his paranoia be her paranoia?

"I think I'll go look in on her."

"Jack—Jesus. She's okay."

"I know. But a look doesn't hurt. Going to be lunch soon."

"In an hour. Can you just—"

But he was already up. Feeling half-naked in his blue bathing suit and a plain black T-shirt.

"I'll be right back."

He turned and headed toward the game room.

He could hear the voices and the music from inside even before he pushed open the screen door.

Place was jumping. Obviously the teen hangout for the kids who didn't want to stay with their obviously too-embarrassing families by the lake.

But not just guests.

He saw three young guys playing pool, one of whom had been on lifeguard duty the previous afternoon.

Kate stood by an old-fashioned pinball machine, all blinking lights and flashing dice. "Viva Vegas," the game was called. An Elvis carica-ture danced above a roulette wheel.

Except Vegas, according to most reports, was as dead as the King himself. A ghost town.

He walked over to Kate.

"Hey, kiddo, how you—"

She spun around quickly as if being caught doing something she shouldn't.

"Dad, what are you *doing here*?" The lasts two words made it seem like a major crime.

Jack became suddenly aware that there was no one over sixteen in the room. Kate seemed to have taken note of that as well.

He tried to smile, even as he felt his ineptness in all this. "Just wanted to see how you were doing."

"What? I'm fine." Then louder. "Fine!"

Their conversation had caught the eyes of other kids. Now it was a show. Kate's voice loud. Jack trying to keep a smile on his face.

"Good. Everything's—" he started.

But Kate turned away from "Viva Vegas," and marched to the door. "Now that you're here, I'm leaving."

In a flash, she was gone. The screen door slapped shut, punctuating the whole scene.

The kids in the room, grinning at it all, had gone back to their games, their conversations.

*Handled that well,* Jack thought.

He left the game room, only steps to the outside, but feeling as if it took forever.

And out.

Standing there. A breeze blowing, taking some of the heat away. The game room a good-sized building. Looked like kayaks and canoes and other beach stuff were stored in the back.

The game fields, deserted on this hot day, were on the left.

But the game building was big enough that it shielded an area behind it. More fields, more storage buildings?

Perhaps not wanting to face his daughter down by the shore, at least not until she cooled off, he walked behind the building.

He saw a path leading to another building, only a little bit smaller, a short walk away. Someone standing outside.

Holding an ax.

Slamming it down on a block of wood.

He recognized the person. Shana. Chopping wood like a pro.

*I should just turn around,* Jack thought.

*Right now.*

But he didn't.

*Thwack!*

A chunk of pine a foot in diameter split into two nearly perfectly equal halves.

Shana hadn't looked up until Jack stood only a few feet away.

Then she stopped. Heavy beads of perspiration on her brow. Before she looked up, Jack took in her bare midriff, which showed a smooth sheen of sweat.

"Looks like they keep you working hard."

She smiled, her eyes directly on Jack.

"I like the exercise," she said. "And besides, I live in back here. It's one of the woodworking cottages. We make a lot of our own stuff . . . use the wood that's all around us. The dead trees."

"Looks like you're good at it."

"I'm good at a lot of things."

Again, her eyes didn't waver. Where was that breeze now?

She had placed the ax head on the ground, the handle held close to her side. Then she made the handle end jut out. "Care to take a whack?"

"I don't think I could—"

She took a step, lifting the ax, handing it to Jack.

"Go on. It's very therapeutic."

She stood closer now, the beads of sweat so close.

Instinctively, he looked over his shoulder. The game building effectively blocked anyone from seeing the two of them. Secluded back here.

"Okay. Here goes."

Shana effortlessly put a fresh block of wood on the tree stump used as a platform for the wood splitting.

He brought the ax back.

"Nice smooth swing, city boy. Keep your eye on where you want the blade to hit. And once it's in motion . . . just let it go."

Jack took a breath. He felt her watching him. But he kept his eyes on the wood chunk in front of him.

Then another breath—and he swung.

Eyes locked on his target spot.

It didn't land smoothly in the middle of the piece. It was an awkward swing, nothing like Shana's.

But Jack was glad to see that the force of the hit was enough to split the wood, sending two unequal pieces flying to either side.

Shana clapped once, then again. "Well done. For a city boy. Little bit of training, and you could be useful around here."

Jack smiled.

He should get back. Christie would have questions about his encounter with Kate.

But Jack had questions. About this place. About Shana.

A few more minutes back here wouldn't hurt.

# 23

## Questions

Jack peered in the window of the front workshop part of the cabin, the windows filmy, making most of what was inside a blur. He could make out a huge saw with planks of wood lying before it.

He turned back to Shana. She had come close, invading space that some would describe as private, a distance being violated.

"So, where'd they recruit you from?" he asked.

A smile. "Recruit? That's what the U.S. Army did. *They* recruited me."

"You served?"

"Oh yeah. Until they started taking the army apart piece by

piece. Who has time to save the world when there's so much to do at home, hm?"

Jack nodded, and as he did, he moved back.

"So, you got a job here? At a camp?"

Shana shook her head as if the idea was silly, black strands flying. "I'm from near here. A little town—a village called Two Rivers. A few miles away, on the other side of Mt. Hope. Nothing there now."

"A local?"

"Everyone who works here is local, Jack."

She said his name as if they were old friends. "Well, nearly every-one. When Ed decided to set this place up, he offered jobs and sanc-tuary to the locals. Some came in to clean, to cook"—a gesture at the filmy windows of the workshop—"to build. A way to be safe."

"They all live here?"

"There are cottages up on the hill, near the camp shops and store-houses. A little community, you might say."

"Some didn't come?"

"Yeah."

"And how did that work out?"

"Oh, a few retreated to the bigger towns. You probably saw them on your way here. With their checkpoints and guns. Some didn't make it. Like those people who stay when a volcano is going to blow. Some vanished. Some, I imagine"—she smiled at the full-circle joke of it— "were *recruited*. Some of the Can Heads in the hills around here used to be our neighbors, friends . . . lovers. Now they just look for a way to get in."

"Not easy with all the guards I saw."

She arched one eyebrow. "Guards? You mean at the gates?"

Jack registered the word she just said. *Gates*. More than one way in and out of this place. For trucks, workers.

Maybe over by the worker's part of the camp, at the end of the ser-vice road?

"Yeah, at night you guys have this place locked down. Guards everywhere."

Shana hesitated. "We like to be safe. And you, Jack? What does a Jack Murphy do? Besides split wood badly."

Another step closer by her; he had the feeling that he was being cornered.

He thought of lying.

"I'm a cop."

She paused now. A small smile played on her face. Had she known that? Did Lowe tell her? Was that exciting to her?

Every cop knew that some women found the whole police thing a turn-on.

Jack tuned that stuff out.

Finally: "NYPD?"

"Yes."

"Then you've seen things, haven't you. I'd love to hear all about what you've seen, Jack. That is, if it's not too upsetting for you."

Jack grinned. Exit time, and an exit line. "Not upsetting at all. But 'fraid I have to dash back to the beach. Can't be missing in action for too long."

"Sure. We can catch up later, city boy."

"Right."

Jack turned and started walking away. Feeling the heat of Shana's eyes on him as he strolled away.


As he reached the beach, he saw Kate on a floating dock out in the water, jumping in.

Christie stood up when he came.

"Pretty good," he said, pointing to their daughter.

"You should have heard her before. Not too pleased with your game room drop-in."

"I know." Then: "Better she's down here. The sun, water. That's what we came for. And is Simon still . . . ?"

"Still playing sand crab. Maybe you can."

"Sure. I'll see if he'll go in with me. Enough sand digging."

"Where were you, by the way?"

Jack kept his gaze on the water. He watched Kate smoothly pull herself out of the water and back into diving position on the platform.

"Oh, I saw another building behind the game room. Didn't know what it was."

"And of course you have to know what *everything* is."

"It was a woodworking shop. Looks like they build a lot of their own stuff. The lamps, those tree-limb chairs."

He wondered if being a cop made him a good liar, made him good at *not* telling things . . .

Or just the opposite.

He let the moment pass and turned to her. "Time to hit the water."

He walked over to Simon.

At first, he held his son's hand in the water. Incredible that they had water here to swim in. Fresh water, like so many things, so scarce. But Simon soon let go as the tiniest of waves rippled against their ankles.

"It's *cold*!" Simon said.

"Sure is. But feel that sun. Gonna feel mighty good to get wet."

To show the way, Jack took a few steps farther in. He looked again at the dive platform, Kate going in and out. As if putting on a show.

A show for . . . ?

He looked behind to see the lifeguard chair. The blond kid staring out at the lake glistening under a midday sun.

Simon squealed. But he also grinned.

"There you go, Simon. Not too bad, eh?"

"It's freezing!"

"But notice that your feet feel fine. You get used to it. Look at your sister."

More steps, and more squeals. The process torturous, but fun. Jack for the first time feeling a bit of what they came here for. To get away, to escape things, to simply enjoy his family.

Simon hit the upper-chest mark well ahead of him.

And then, amazingly, Simon dove into the water and emerged like a human otter, black hair plastered against his head, his eyes flashing.

Jack realized what his son was about to do.

"Simon, don't even think—"

But Simon let go with a volley of splashes, the tables turned, wonderfully, and soon they were both fully wet, swimming, diving, and playing in the cold, clear water.


Jack followed Simon out of the lake, but didn't copy him when Simon threw himself onto the sand, laughing, and basted his body in the fine beach sand.

Christie threw him a towel.

"Thanks."

As he dried himself, he looked around.

Off to the side, away from the main pools of families sitting in the chairs and blankets, he saw Tom Blair, smiling, talking to Ed Lowe.

Ed in jolly mode, Tom probably pleased that his family could stay for a few more days.

Jack worked on his hair, neck, but kept watching the two of them.

Tom walked away and in the moment Lowe turned, he saw Jack looking at the two of them.

A smile from Jack. Nice day at the lake, isn't it?

For a second it looked as though Lowe's grin just evaporated. Then back on again. Like a switch.

Jack nodded at Lowe. He came and sat down by Christie.

"That was great, getting Simon in the water." She laughed. "Of course, now he'll have sand everywhere. Maybe a shower down here before we get back."

Jack nodded. "You see our happy leader?"

"What? You mean talking to Tom Blair?"

"Weird the way he can turn the smile on and off."

"Jack, come on. He's in the—what do they call it?—the hospitality business. What do you think it is?"

"Right. Yeah, he's just being . . . hospitable."

"I don't get why you can't just relax. Let the cop thing go. Christ . . ."

Jack started to defend himself. "I'm just saying . . ."

Kate came over, still annoyed with him, Jack imagined.

"I'm going back to the cottage."

"Okay, honey," Christie said quickly.

*Before I can say anything*, Jack guessed.

He watched Kate walk away.

"Look, Jack. Relax. Okay? I love it here." She took in a deep breath. The clear air. "It's perfect."

"Right."

"Unless you just want to spoil this for everyone."

"No. Don't want to do that. I hear you. Relax mode . . . on."

But he had turned back to Tom, now standing with his wife.

Jack tried to stay seated. Instead, he started to get up.

"Gonna go chat with Tom."

Christie shook her head as he walked over to Tom.

"Hey, Tom."

"Jack. Hi."

"I saw you with Lowe. All set?"

"Oh yeah. I mean, he may have to shift us to another cabin. People request the ones with a view. I said no problem." Tom laughed. "As long as my cash holds out."

There was a flicker of something. A distant look in Tom's eyes. Everything about Tom in that moment—his eyes, the way he stood, the sudden hollowness in his voice—said that there was something unsaid here.

For now, Jack decided not to push him. There'd be time to talk tonight, at the fireworks.

"See you guys at dinner?" Jack said.

"Sure. See you there."

Jack walked back to Christie.

"They all set? To stay?"

"Appears so," he said.

Christie kept her eyes on him. "And something else?"

"What? No. Just they may have to move cabins."

"Why is that?"

"Other reservations. Something about the view."

"Guess it doesn't matter."

She shaded her eyes, still looking at him.

"Nothing else?"

He smiled. An Ed Lowe smile, he thought. "Nothing else."

She nodded. "Good. Just try to remember that you're here. With me, and the kids. And this is *not* the precinct."

"I hear you."

Then quiet.

After a few silent minutes, he stood up. "I'm going back to shower."

"Or to check on Kate?"

He didn't rise to the bait. "See you there."

He walked away.


Christie felt her annoyance with Jack subside.

With her mix of Italian and Latin blood, she could get steamed pretty fast. Early in their relationship, she had worked hard to watch it, control it.

*Was I too hard on him?* she wondered.

What she said seemed reasonable. This was a vacation. They were safe. And he needed to leave his old world behind. At least while they were here.

She pushed the thoughts away, focusing on the sun, the water, the warm sand between her toes.

"Can I go back in?" Simon said, writhing toward her like a sand snake.

"Sure. Another dip will get all that sand off you. Just stay close. Where you can stand—or squirm!"

Simon turned around like an eel and started slithering toward the water.

She let her thoughts fade as she kept her eyes on Simon.

Locked on him, catching every shimmering slash in the water.


Most families had already left the beach for the communal lunch. The beach took on a deserted feel with everyone packing up.

Time to go soon, she knew.

Though Simon still twisted and leaped in the water, oblivious to everything but the fun he was having.

Other kids were swimming, too.

One girl near Simon's age. A little older.

And definitely farther out. A swimmer—she could move her arms in a simulation of the Australian crawl—but awkward, expending too much energy. Stopping to plant her feet.

The water at her chin. Inches away from covering her mouth.

*Where are her parents?* Christie wondered.

She looked up and down the beach, trying to match the remaining people with the girl who, Christie thought, was now too far out in the lake.

She didn't catch any worried eyes locked on the little girl. No parent standing up to issue a command to come back in.

She looked to the lifeguard. Amazingly, his eyes were also averted as he laughed and talked to two girls in bikinis posing to his right.

No one was watching the girl.

Except for Christie.

*Should I tell her to come in a bit?*

No. That would seem crazy.

Still . . .

The girl flailed at the water with her ineffective crawl, then landed. To Christie it seemed that she must have been on her tiptoes to stay above the water. There were no real waves here, just a light, gentle ripple. The tiniest of wakes made by the wind off the mountains.

Tiny water movements.

But perhaps strong enough to push someone a few inches one way or the other.

She gave Simon a quick glance, perfectly fine in his foot or so of water, still in sea-snake mode.

To the girl.

The water closer to her lips.

The girl pushed up a bit, toes probably stretched to their limit, Christie's eyes completely locked on her. The girl attempted to swim. But whether from fatigue or fear, those arm movements seemed to do nothing.

Or worse, they seemed to take the girl those precious few inches into deeper water. The feet, the toes going down again.

Only now they didn't touch sand. The head went under water. The lips covered.

Christie stood up.

She yelled.

One word.

"Help!" She spared a second yell toward the lifeguard, expecting to see him racing into the lake, reaching with those strong, muscled adolescent legs into the water before the sound of Christie's scream faded.

A blurry look, actually, since she could see the guard was still locked in his chat.

Christie started running.

Not sensing anyone else with her. Though surely the parents had looked up, had seen the girl bobbing, her long hair held with a scrunchie that made it look like seaweed on the surface as her head went down.

The girl's hands were above the water.

Then they weren't.

Christie stormed past her son. She didn't remove her sunglasses, her beach coverup.

The sprint—the fastest she had ever run.

Water churning under her legs, slowing her as it got calf high, then a dive, to find the exact spot the girl had disappeared.

A hunt because by now, the girl had indeed vanished.

Christie under the water.

Trying to open her eyes. But the silt, the sediment, made it impossible to see.

She didn't surface. How long can someone be under? How much water could someone gulp before they'd die?

Kicking madly in the four feet of water until she felt something. The feel of skin, and Christie locked her arms around the girl's body. She used her legs to shoot to the surface.

She held the girl like a sack of groceries, racing back to the shore.

The lifeguard was finally there, taking the girl from Christie, who for a second didn't want to release the girl to such an idiot.

But she let the girl go, and the lifeguard moved fast, getting the girl to the shore, pumping her chest with his hands.

Christie's joined the other onlookers.

The girl coughed. She spit out water. Her eyes opened wide as if waking up from a nightmare.

A few in the crowd applauded.

*Applauded.*

A woman that Christie hadn't seen before. Nondescript, with a doughy belly that matched the roundness of her face.

"Thank you," the woman said.

Christie squinted in the sun.

*Lost my sunglasses,* she thought.

"Er, it's okay. I was glad . . . um . . ."

She wanted to say:

*Where the hell were you? Why the* hell *weren't you watching?*

Instead, she said nothing.

She turned back to the girl, to the circle of people around her. The lifeguard grinning as if he had pulled her out of the water.

Even the girl was smiling. So much attention. Such a big adventure.

Eventually, she walked over to her dour-faced mother.

The lifeguard started back to his stand.

"Stay here," she said to Simon. "Out of the water."

She hurried to catch up to the lifeguard, still trailing the two teenagers.

"You weren't watching," she said at his back.

The boy stopped and turned to her.

He didn't say anything for a moment. But he no longer smiled. Then:

"I was watching. I went into the water to save her."

Christie stood her ground. "No. *I* went into the water. *I* was watching. *I* pulled her out."

Then the smile returned.

And the lifeguard, shooting an extra display of grin and teeth at the girls, said, "Whatever."

He turned and walked away.

Christie had only one very clear thought: the lifeguard wasn't intimidated or scared at all.

As if he knew that what just happened didn't affect him at all.

She turned and headed back to her beach towel, to Simon.

And felt—without really knowing—that people were now watching *her.*

Christie stood outside the small beachside shower, a wooden cabinet.

"Simon—you okay in there?"

She could hear him humming, playing in the streams of water.

"Si?"

"Yeah, Mom, I'm fine."

From here, she could still see the beach. Now nearly empty, everyone hurrying to the dining room. The few people who remained must be on a diet, Christie thought.

*A diet. Does anyone diet anymore?*

But then, some people here *did* seem well-fed. Almost fat. Guess if you ate enough of the soy hybrids it would add some pounds.

A voice from behind startled her.

"Your son in there, Mrs. Murphy?"

She turned to see Ed Lowe, smiling, sunglasses hiding his eyes, dressed in khakis and a plaid collared shirt with his name plate and the Paterville logo.

"Yes. He got so sandy."

Lowe's head bobbed, looking like a blind man behind such dark shades.

"I heard what happened down at the beach.'

"Yes."

Christie expected Lowe to thank her for helping the girl. Already she was summoning an appropriately dismissive reply.

But that's not what he said.

"My lifeguard said you were upset."

For a moment, she didn't know what to say.

"I was. I mean, he—"

She heard the shower turn off.

"Jim saved that girl. I just wanted to see what was wrong."

She took a breath. "*I* saved that girl, Mr. Lowe. I—"

"Mom! Mom, I have soap in my eyes!"

She turned away from Lowe. "Turn the water on again, honey. Get your face under there."

"Owww. Okay!"

Back to Lowe.

The smile remained on his face.

"You were saying?"

"*I* pulled that girl out. Your lifeguard was too busy flirting."

A nod from Lowe, but no loss of his smile.

"Boys. They do like to flirt. Still, he did the resuscitation pretty well, no?"

The conversation seemed surreal. Christie didn't know what to say. No apologies? Nothing about getting the lifeguard to look at the water and not the babes?

The shower door opened.

"Thanks, though, for what you did down there. Just wanted to tell you that personally."

Lowe feigned a look down to his watch.

"Whoa—got to do the midday announcements soon. Best get ready."

A look from him down to Simon. A hand patting her son's head. "You, too—don't want to miss lunch."

"Yes," she said, then put her own arm around her son. "C'mon, Simon, let's go get dressed."

"See you there," Lowe said.

Christie nodded, and amid the blazing splotches of sunlight and shade she walked steadily back to the cottage.

## 24

## Dinner

In the afternoon, sitting in the golden sun with Jack, Christie didn't mention anything about her talk with Lowe, about what happened.

It was just good to see him begin to enjoy this.

But later, on the way to dinner, she did tell him about the girl, the rescue—but she cut off any questions, looking at their kids as they walked to the Great Lodge.

"It was just a little strange," she said quietly.

"You saved the girl. What was with her mother?"

"Don't know."

When they got to the same table they sat at the night before, the Blairs were already there.

"Hey, guys," Tom said. "Good day at the beach?"

Christie shot a quick glance at Jack, then: "It was beautiful."

"And tonight . . ." Tom looked at his wife as if this was his gift to her, to the kids. "Fireworks! When was the last time you saw fireworks?"

Simon, holding his knife and fork as though the food couldn't get here fast enough, spoke. "I've never seen fireworks."

Tom laughed. "Then you are in for a treat."

Which is when Christie noticed something. Tom all excited, thrilled. Smiling, happy. His wife, this woman who took over the family, the kids . . . so quiet. Had they had a fight, a disagreement over something?

Not on the same page.

*But then, are Jack and I?*

*Hope we don't look like those two.*

"Meet you down there after eats? Get a good spot up close?"

"Sure," Jack said.

Tom leaned across the table, lowering his voice. "And I'll bring . . . y'know."

The servers arrived with oversized plates of what looked like a stew. And then actual bread. Small brown rolls. A real rarity these days.

Simon grabbed one off the platter before it even touched down. He opened the roll, and spooned some of the stew in.

"I don't think you're supposed to, um, put the stew in the roll," Christie said.

Jack laughed. "Let him eat it the way he wants to." He picked up a roll. "They must grow their own wheat somehow. Or something like wheat. Amazing."

Another family, with a pimply-faced boy, came and sat down at their table with them. Christie said hi, smiled at them.

They nodded and said hi back, but didn't seem interested in any getting-to-know-you chat.

Fine with Christie.

Soon, the whole hall quieted as everyone dug into the food.

Between bites, she looked around. Then to Jack. The room so quiet as everyone ate.

*Hungry people.*

Her back to the podium, she didn't see Lowe arrive, and then was surprised by his booming voice.

"Good evening, Paterville families!"

Like a Sunday congregation, they chanted back. "Good evening!"

"Hope all of you enjoyed this amazing day, and now some great camp food. Got a few special announcements for you . . ."

Christie looked across the table. Kate picked at the stew, studying it.

The examination over, she took a big forkful of it.

"Any families leaving us tonight, be sure to check out with us at registration. We'll make sure all your charges are correct and we even" —he looked over Shana—"have a special good-bye present from all of us at Paterville."

Shana seemed less formidable tonight. Her midsection covered, though the shirt's buttons strained against her breasts.

*That is one mighty . . . distraction for an assistant,* Christie thought.

She resisted the temptation to look over and see if Jack was watching the battle of buttons and boobs.

"Tonight's the big fireworks . . ."

Ed paused for the whistles and clapping.

"Now, enjoy the rest of your meal and we'll see you down at the lakeshore for the big show!"

She and Jack turned back to the table.

The kids had finished their meals. Servers appeared with what looked like an icy sherbet. No ice cream, with dairy being so rare, but ice probably, some sugary flavoring.

Simon grabbed a cherry-red bowl, Kate a lime-colored one.

Christie took a few more bites of the stew.

When the sherbets had also vanished, she smiled at the Blairs and the other family sitting grimly near them. She looked at Jack. "All done?"

Jack nodded, and they got up and headed out of the dining hall.

siege

# 25

## 8:46 P.M.

Night.

Everyone had gathered down at the lakeshore, all the Paterville families waiting for the fireworks to begin.

A guard, Jay Fergus, walked along the perimeter of the fence.

He thought of the kid he had chased the night before. Kids don't get the danger that's out there, he thought.

Fergus had seen that danger up close. Like the night the Can Heads attacked his house where he and his family used to live. Good thing he had stocked up on weapons and ammo.

Still, all that firing, the kids, his wife screaming like a crazy person behind him.

Enough to make anyone a little insane.

The bodies of the Can Heads piling up around the house, as Fergus ran from front to back, holding them off.

Like the fucking Alamo.

A few, he recognized. The old police chief, nearly unrecognizable but still with that jowly face, only with more skin sagging from his neck. His clothes tattered, spattered with red.

Fergus had initially turned down Ed Lowe's offer.

To be penned up in here.

Taking care of guests.

But that night . . .

That night convinced him.

In the end, they got so close that he could barely get rounds off. A few times he had to smash the butt of his gun into their heads, sending teeth and bloody drool flying.

When it was over, Fergus stood on his porch and sobbed.

He walked back into his house a changed man.

His wife said nothing. The two little kids kept crying.

But no one said a fucking thing.

Because he was a changed man.

Now Fergus walked the well-worn trail around the perimeter of the camp. Each night the same damn thing. Soon he'd pass Billy Kemp, another guard moving in the other direction.

Billy usually with the stench of cook's moonshine. The stuff burned like gasoline in your gullet.

The stuff worked for Billy. Cook's booze got the job done.

*Cook.*

To call that fat load, the guy who used to work at—

"'Sup, dude?"

Billy appeared early. Hustling too fast along the perimeter. What good was doing this walk if you didn't actually take the goddamn time to look at the fence?

"Nice and quiet, Billy. You?"

Same routine every night.

Billy burped. A full belly, and a good pint or so of white lightning in his gut.

He slurred the words. "Same here."

Careful, Billy, Fergus thought. How long would Lowe let him go on like this? He might be under the radar now. Couldn't last forever, though.

Drunk guard. Puts us all at risk.

Billy walked past him, his automatic rifle dangling loosely when Fergus knew it should be held at a 45-degree angle. Didn't the asshole ever take any gun safety courses?

Good thing it wasn't Billy who had stumbled upon the kid. Probably would have blown the little shit's head off.

Then he would have made a joke.

*Look, roadkill!*

Fergus kept walking, looking the fence up and down. Unlikely anything would even come close. The outer fence electric, the inner fence taller, with two feet of razor ribbon at its top.

*This camp is a fucking fortress.*

*Nobody gets in*, he thought.

He heard a blast, the fireworks about to begin.


Tom Blair gave Jack a nudge. Everyone's eyes turned upward, waiting.

"Want a swig?"

"My head's still ringing from last night."

"I hear you—stuff can be painful."

Tom took a gulp, then nodded at the beach full of people. "It's like the world is still the same, hm? Families, fireworks . . ."

Jack nodded in the dark. "Yeah. But it isn't."

Christie stood near Sharon, the kids close to the water's edge. Jack enjoyed talking with Tom. Nothing about work. But he didn't think Christie enjoyed the quiet company of his wife, Sharon.

Then, as if reading Jack's mind, as if he had to spoil things . . .

"You check out the security here? I mean, being a cop and all."

"I've looked around. Fence looks secure. Lots of armed guards."

"Seen the cameras?"

"Hm?"

"They're in the trees. All over the camp. I just happened to spot one. Then I saw others. Way up."

That was something Jack should have spotted.

"Guess they're useful."

Another swig for Tom. When he extended the bottle again, Jack took it. Changing his mind, and wanting that burn.

"Sure. They take their security seriously here."

"Looks that way."

Each took another swig.

A few silent moments.

"Come on," Tom said. "Let's get this show started."

And then a single rocketing yellow-white streak flew into the sky and exploded into a dazzling explosion of sparks.

The crowd cheered.


Jay Fergus came to his turnaround point, just in time to see another guard, Jackie Weeks, hitting his. A casual wave in the shadows, as they both turned and started their slow, gradual walk back along the perimeter.

Tedious work. No wonder so many guards drank. Nothing but the bug sounds, the occasional creaking of a tree limb bending if there was a wind.

You had to force yourself to keep your pace slow.

Billy Kemp would be coming back this way as well. The jet fuel in his gut making his walk a snaky thing on the straight path that ran beside the fence.

Fergus looked up.

Fireworks starting for real.

In their glare, he could see Billy stumbling along.

*Christ, what a freakin' mess. Ed Lowe should can his ass.*

*Put him outside. See how he likes it out there.*

And now—closer to Fergus.

A big explosion boomed from the lake.

Then, in the quiet, something new.

A rattling.

From real close.

A rattling. From the fence.

Fergus looked up.

Nothing at first. Not without a flashlight. Flashlight killed your night vision.

Best not to use it.

But on a moonless night it was hard to see anything except when the skies lit up.

His eyes moved up the fence—a big flash of light—and he did see something. A dark shape at the top. Like a sack or a bag? Resting right on top of the tight coiled of razor ribbon.

Thoughts came quickly to Fergus.

Whatever it was should have shorted the outer fence. Made a connection. Shorted the fence out, triggered an alarm.

What the hell was it? He started to reach for his flashlight.

Kemp came stumbling toward Fergus, oblivious. Fucking oblivious. Hand on the flashlight.

But there would be no time to get it out, unclip it from the belt, turn it on, aim it.

A bunch of smaller explosions echoed in the woods. No light from them.

So many things had to happen to get the flashlight on.

None of which could happen. Now. When there simply was no time.

———

A big *ooooh!* erupted from the families.

Jack saw the light of the fireworks reflected in all the faces looking upward.

A breeze blew off the water. Chilling. Gooseflesh rose on Jack's arm. Christie leaned into him. He put his arm around her.

The kids nearby, heads tilted up.

For the next few seconds, Jack just enjoyed the show.


Hand on flashlight.

About as far as Fergus got.

Then, they leaped onto the outer fence—three, then four of them. Tattered clothes, nearly naked, clambering up to what was now clearly the body that had been thrown on top.

A bridge across the razor ribbon.

But what about the thousand volts of electricity?

Nothing, as they made their way up quickly.

Fergus yelled, "Kemp! Look!"

All Kemp did was stop, standing next to the Can Heads nearly at the top of the fence.

Fergus stopped reaching for his flashlight.

He backed up. He started to lower his gun, wondering why it took so long to get it into position, to get the damn safety off, to get his goddamn hand onto the trigger, to begin aiming—all so *fucking* long.

His left hand flew to the walkie-talkie clipped to left shoulder. Even hitting the send button seemed to be the most difficult task.

He pressed hard, and yelled, *"Code Red!"*

They'd know who sent it. They'd know what sector. Back in the service area where they had all the cameras, where they monitored the entire camp, the fences. By now, they should have picked up the shapes on their cameras.

The first Can Heads had reached the top, using the body to slide over and leap down.

One landed right on Kemp, who never saw it coming.

Fergus itched to shoot but now he'd kill Kemp. No doubt.

There were others on the fence. Another two, three, four.

*Christ*, he thought.

What the hell was wrong with the goddamn fence?

He started shooting.

But even as he sprayed the fence, he began pulling back.

With that one thought that drove him to come here, to live in Paterville, to do this:

*I want to stay alive.*


Jack turned his head.

Hearing the noise above the intermittent explosions coming from the sky.

Everyone else would have missed it.

Just another explosion.

He tightened. Gently, he pushed Christie away.

"Jack, what's—"

He listened. *Shots*. Popping noises that he could hear between the firework blasts.

Maybe kids with firecrackers, he thought for a second, taking the most benign thought that his brain offered.

Fireworks. Kids. Leftover firecrackers.

But no. Gunfire had such a distinctive sound.

"C'mon," he said, to Christie at first. Then, almost roughly, he tapped the heads of the kids. "Kids. We gotta go."

Another brilliant flash.

"What? Why are we—"

Other people barely noticed Jack herding his family away from the lakeshore.

No one else had noticed the gunfire.

Only seconds for all this, and then suddenly everyone knew why

Jack was pulling back, why he was guiding his family away, why he was ignoring the people giving him confused looks as he roughly pushed past them.

A giant horn blast sounded that dwarfed even the explosive sounds booming from the lake. Ear-splitting. One blast, then another, and another.

Then a clipped voice as no new fireworks rocketed into the sky. Saying its short sentence, alternating with horn blasts: *"Everyone return to your cabins immediately."*

Jack and his family nearly off the beach.

The voice calm; the horn screaming down at people probably said enough about what was happening.

More blasts, then the voice again. Jack rushed, almost shoving his family back to their cabin as they were suddenly joined by a sea of people, all hurrying.

Some screaming; the panic there so fast.

Jack was tempted to just push people out of the way. To his left, he saw someone stumble to the ground, and get trampled.

He steered Christie and the kids close by the figure on the ground. With one hand he reached down and pulled the woman up.

Her eyes wide. Crazed. She didn't stop to say thank you, but turned and joined everyone madly streaming away.

The lake was hemmed in the one side by the Great Lodge and the cabins, the thick woods to the rear.

No one would go in the direction of the woods.

Everyone funneled onto one of the paths that would get them off the beach, away from the lake, the crazy alarm horns only making their terror worse.


They moved so fucking fast, Fergus thought. Flying over the top.

He watched the two of them on Kemp. Ripping him apart like kids tearing into a present on Christmas morning.

The others began scattering.

Except for a few who noticed Fergus shooting.

He kept backing up even as he sprayed his gun left and right.

Can Heads could take a lot of hits. Like they felt no fucking pain whatsoever.

They'd be on him soon.

He thought help would have arrived, the other guards.

Where the hell were they?

One of his bullets kicked a hole in the skull of a nearby Can Head with no clothes and a beard that made it look like a deranged lion.

"Fuck it," Fergus said.

He turned and started running.

There was an army of Can Heads entering the camp, and there wasn't a goddamn thing Jay Fergus could do alone but find someplace to go, someplace to hide—to stay alive.

As he ran, he became aware that all the sounds he heard before— the bugs, the wind—were now joined by so many others.

The alarm, the screams, and just behind him, so close, the terrible sound of steps chasing, racing after him.

# 26

## 9:11 P.M.

Fergus looked over his shoulder, the sound of the steps as close as mosquitoes buzzing his head on a muggy night.

A quick look back, and then he didn't see what was in front of him as he ran right into a Can Head that had somehow appeared on the trail in front of him.

His slam sent them both falling forward, rolling on the packed dirt and pine needles.

God, he felt them grabbing him, pulling at him, then bites—one, two, three—until he couldn't tell where the pain was coming from anymore.

He prayed that someone would see.

One of the other guards. And not hold back, not flinch—but fire as quick as they could.

To stop this.

He screamed out his agony.

A howl that must have filled the woods.

Then a blessed sound as he heard the repetitive coughing of machine-gun fire.

His prayers answered as bullets hit, and one, somehow, somewhere, made everything instantly black.

Jack hurried his family along. The cabin not far now.

Christie guided Simon, holding his hand. Jack had a firm grip on Kate. Now families started breaking away, bolting, tripping, racing for their own cabins, the horns blaring, so loud, deafening.

At one point he felt Kate stumble on something, but his grip was tight enough to hold her up, near dangling, not even pausing in their forward movement until she regained her footing again and started running.

The horns—you almost couldn't hear the screams with them blaring so loudly.

Or the gunfire.

Jack tried to place the gunfire as he ran.

Where were they fighting?

How the hell did the Can Heads break in?

With goddamned electric fences?

Jack raced up the path to their cabin, Christie right behind. He saw the Blairs get into theirs.

Good, he thought. They're inside.

He got his family into their cabin.

He released Kate, and went around to the windows, then to the front and back doors, shutting and locking them.

The windows. So damn easy to toss a rock at one and gain entry.

Had Lowe and his Paterville team never expected this?

Ever planned for this fucking situation?

Everything shut tight, he ran into the bedroom. Opened a drawer and took out his gun. He grabbed a box of bullets.

Out to the living room.

At least the horns sounded more distant with everything buttoned up. The kids looked up at him, hiding the gun still in its holster.

But Christie saw it.

"Jack."

He walked over to the three of them on the couch.

Perhaps it's the way he held the gun. Not as if he was going to use it. Because he wasn't.

He passed it to Christie.

"Jack, what—"

Then he passed her the box of bullets.

She knew how to shoot. He had made sure of that.

"Where are you going?"

"It's loaded, Christie. And you got more bullets in the box. And here, on the couch"—he looked around the small living room—"is where you stay. You understand? You can see all the windows. The doors. Right from here."

He felt the kids' eyes moving from the gun to his face.

He forced himself to smile.

"Probably nothing. But best to be safe. Just like we've practiced at home."

The drills. The government urging everyone to practice what they would do. To prepare.

Like what to do in case of fire.

Only in this case, what to do in case of cannibals crawling into your house.

Finally, Christie asked the question: "What are you going to do?"

He stood up. "Make sure things are okay out there."

She shook her head. "Jack. You stay here. We need you *here*."

He took a breath. Yes, true, he thought. If you wanted to wait until some of them came.

Waiting could be just the wrong thing to do.

"I'm going to take a look." He paused. "Make sure it stays nice and quiet in Paterville."

"Daddy, stay," Simon said, picking up on his mother's worry.

"I'll be back real soon."

Kate said nothing.

"But you don't have a gun now!" Christie said, her voice sounding exasperated, as if she already knew this was an argument she would lose.

He looked right at her. "Yes, I do. Plenty of guns." A casual shrug of the shoulders. "In the car."

She shook her head.

"If you get there."

He wanted to tell her that if there was something bad going on outside, then one small revolver and a box of bullets would be precious little against a bunch of Can Heads.

That he knew.

But he didn't have to say it.

"We may need those guns." Another smile. "Or not. But I can get them fast."

Did she agree? He didn't know. But he saw her eyes had grown watery. She fought her fear for the kids.

Then another telltale sign. Her right hand closing over the grip of the pistol. She also put the box of bullets down beside her and undid the holster clasp.

"Keep the doors locked. Listen for sounds. And when I come back, I'll knock—*three . . . two . . . one.*"

Christie nodded.

He looked at his kids. Scared. Quiet.

He went to the door, undid the sliding bolt lock, and walked out, not having a clue what he'd see there.

The first thing Jack noticed: nobody outside.

Gunfire came from three, maybe four different areas, so all the guards must be out there, dealing with the Can Heads that had gotten in.

If the fence had gone down, was it back up yet? Or could the Can Heads keep coming in?

Some of the cabins were dark. Maybe the people thinking that if they looked dark, empty, the Can Heads would skip them.

Might work.

Or might be exactly what a deranged Can Head would look for.

He started running full out, arms pumping, and immediately felt the pain in his leg.

*Can't run for a while,* Dr. Kleiner had said. *No running for you.* All that running, the sudden stretching of muscles. *Could set you back, way back.*

Not to mention the pain.

Jack ran as fast as he could.

The Great Lodge looked empty, unprotected. Yep. All the guards dealing with the attack.

Maybe everyone was. Not just the guards. Lowe, Shana, the cooks. Anyone who could use a gun.

He peeled away down the trail that led to the parking lot. The parking lot as dark as ever, with its two spots of light.

Perfect for a trap.

But he didn't hear any gunfire down there.

Got to do this fast, he thought. Get a gun and get the hell out of there.

His left foot hit a rock and he went flying forward. Breaking his fall with his right leg.

Months of rehab loomed when he got out of this.

*When.*

Always the right way to think about it. When. Not fucking "if." "If" could lead to mistakes. "If" led to fear.

He ran between cars, scraping doors, banging into mirrors, hurrying as fast as he could to the Explorer.

It would be so damn easy for one of them to jump out from behind
the shadow of a car.

Not much he could do about that.

He reached his car and used the electronic key to open the rear
door.

He ripped up the mat that covered the metal plate of the storage
compartment.

Now he had to use the key. In the goddamn dark. Get the key in,
turn it, get the thing open.

*What's around here? Anything around here, coming closer, while you
fumble with that key?*

In the wrong way at first, then a little twist and the key slid home.
He unlocked the compartment.


Christie released her hold on the gun.

Kate wanted a hand, and so did Simon. The gun sat on her lap,
almost in a line with the two hands she held.

The horns constant. The warning message, though, had stopped.
The dull, repetitive voice saying, *Please return to your cabins immediately.*

Everyone had done that.

Christie looked at Simon.

"You okay, Si?"

He nodded. Then to Kate, waiting her turn for the question.

"Kate?"

Another nod.

Then Kate said, in a voice that sounded as if it came from miles
away, "Mom . . . are *you* okay?"

The question made Christie's heart break. She was fighting so
hard to hold back the tears, of fear, worry . . . she didn't know what.
The emotions all jumbled.

And Kate asks about *her*?

Christie gave her daughter's hand a squeeze, then a smile. "I'm fine."

Then, feeling that they both wanted more, "Dad will be back soon. They stopped the message. So, things must be okay now. Maybe . . . maybe it was a false alarm."

As soon as she said that, her optimism sounded hollow. "Dad will be back. We'll do what he says. He's a police officer. He knows what he's doing."

The two kids nodded at that.

Because that was one thing they all agreed on.

Then all three of them went quiet again.

Jack grabbed the M-16 automatic rifle, loaded with hollow points.

He stuffed his pockets with boxes of shells. Then he grabbed one of the Glock 22s. Double the kick and killing power of the gun Christie had.

He wished she had it.

Too much kick for her, though she had shot it, before trying the bigger handgun out at the firing range. Laughing as it threw her backward.

*"Got to plant your feet, kiddo."*

*"I see that."*

*"Plant your feet, lock your arm into position. Tense your muscles. Get ready for that kick. Then, eye on the target—"*

*"Squeeze slowly."*

*"Exactly."*

Jack still had other weapons in the compartment, and the timed C4 explosives built for use in the narrow corridors and hallways of city apartment buildings. Blow in a door. Kick a hole in a wall.

No need for them now.

He took an extra flashlight he had there and stuck it in his back pocket.

He slammed the case shut, pulled down the trunk door, and started running back up to the main area of the camp.

The gunfire continued.

This thing wasn't under control.

When he got to the top of the trail, near the left side of the lodge, he saw a guard there.

"Hey, you got weapons? They're in the fucking woods. We can use all the help we can get."

The guy radiated fear like woodstove heat.

"Getting back to my family," Jack said, barely pausing his agonized limping run.

The guy reached out and grabbed Jack's arm.

"You leave the Can Heads out here, and your family and all the families could be fucked. You get that?"

Jack shrugged off the arm. Started to run.

But the words were clear enough. And worse, Jack knew they were true.

Holing up in the cabin was just the wrong thing to do. Not with them still here, using the darkness, the trees, the shadows. Waiting.

"Okay. Where the hell are they?"

The guy pointed to the woods near the field. "Over there, and some have headed up to the service camp. Firing going on there. That's where I'm headed. Other spots down by the main gate."

"And the fence? Is it up, running, or can those things just keep coming?"

"I don't know," the guy said.

Jack looked at the path that led to the field and the thick woods past it. That was the area closest to his family's cabin.

"Okay."

Jack started running, this time in the new direction.

*Jesus. Fucking. Christ.*

*I* have *to do this.*

He moved as fast as he could.

The woods turned into a wall of darkness, a black gloom made by the thickness of the trees, the shadows.

Flashes of gunfire.

But not a lot of it.

Could the Can Heads be winning?

He tried to come up with a plan. Couldn't just run in there. But all he had to draw on was working the city's streets and their massive buildings.

Out of his element here.

He lowered the rifle's muzzle so it pointed straight ahead. He looked at the flashes of gunfire and entered the woods.

Jack moved slowly.

When a Can Head attacked, it moved fast. Some crazy adrenaline-fueled burst of speed that helped them nail a body.

So, moving slowly might actually tip off any guards that he was human.

He walked steadily in the direction of a lone gun spitting out flashes.

Jack saw the guard.

One fucking guard, standing with a group of Can Heads circling him. They moved around the guard, taking steps, tightening the noose they had him in.

They could take a lot of bullets.

And that was another thing: how many bullets did Jack have? Should he have brought more? And when they were gone . . .

Jack saw a Can Head leap forward, taking shots from the guard and dropping to the ground. But the suicide move also allowed the others to accelerate their hunting circle. The guy began literally spinning on his feet, blasting, crazed.

Maybe, at this point, insane.

If Jack was going to help, it better be now.

He slowly tightened his trigger finger. The Can Heads' crouching bodies caught the scant light, making them look like rocks and bushes . . . dark clumps moving.

Jack began firing.

Two of the Can Heads fell immediately.

The others, seeing their simple feral trap fall apart, turned to him.

Jack had planted his back against a tree. It gave him some protection from any rear attack.

The guard had stopped firing.

Stopped—or out of ammo?

Either way, the few Can Heads left surrounded him, ready to leap.

This would all play out in seconds. That's all he had, Jack knew, from so many attacks and battles in the city.

He aimed at one Can Head to his left, firing, kicking it back, maybe not dead. But shifting to the right, and catching that one in the skull, dead center. A head shot always took them out.

Always, that is, except for those freakish moments when they didn't and somehow the thing could *still* move with a chunk of skull and brain matter missing.

This time, though, the Can Head got kicked off his feet. A third hesitated, perhaps smelling death.

Jack fired at it. At the same time, he dug out his Glock.

Anything could happen with an M16. A jam, some malfunction.

Two guns gave him some security.

With all three attackers dead, Jack hurried to the guard, now with one Can Head riding his back, mouth open. Another had locked it-self to the guard's midsection.

Not a job for the rifle. This was up-close work.

Jack took aim at each Can Head, knowing that mere inches sepa-rated a shot that could save the guy's life from one that would just make the Can Head's work easier.

Jack's first shots were tenuous. Not wanting to get too close. But each second brought deeper wounds to the guard.

He adjusted his aim, taking a chance that a sudden jerk of the guard's body would expose him to a killing shot.

The Can Head on the guy's back caught one shell. It fell off the guard as if thrown from a horse.

The guard fell to his knees. Jack fired three shots at the creature digging at the guy's midsection.

It stopped moving.

But as if clamped on, it stayed stuck to the guard.

Jack walked over and crouched down, not knowing whether he'd just saved a dead man.

The guard's eyes were open. He could speak.

"Th-thank you."

Hard to tell about his wounds. Guy could be bleeding out all over the place.

Jack pried the dead Can Head off the man, like undoing a blue crab from a net.

Its claw hands, even the feet with their uncut nails, all dug in.

Then the man was free.

"Can you stand?"

What little light there was caught at least three nasty wounds, all oozing.

But the blood wasn't gushing out; it wasn't pouring onto the forest floor.

With his own gun silenced, Jack could hear gunfire around them.

"Can you *stand*?" Jack asked again.

The man seemed to wobble as he tried to make his legs work to get himself up.

But then, like some amazing feat of science, the guy stood.

"You have some bad wounds." Jack nodded at the woods. "Things still going on in here. Think you can manage to shoot some more of them?" The guy made a face that looked about as unsure as any Jack had ever seen.

"I'll be with you. I have a little experience killing these suckers."

The man nodded.

"Good. Clear this area. Then you can get your wounds tended to. Okay?"

Another nod.

"One thing: remember to reload whenever you can. Got it?"

"Yes."

Jack wanted to get back to his family.

But then from behind the lodge, more gunfire.

*Fuck*, he thought.

The snaps and pops insisting that he go there.

He left the guard and ran as best he could in the direction of the gunfire.


He stopped.

The figures ahead—shadowy. But he could see Lowe, Shana, a few other guards, surrounded.

Christ, had to be ten . . . twelve Can Heads. Circling. That hunting shit they did.

Everyone's guns out, maybe thinking about conserving bullets. Their own panic making them do just the wrong thing—turn to look this way, then that way, feeding their panic, fueling the disorientation.

Only seconds before the Can Heads would pounce. Lowe and his workers would be turned into mincemeat.

Jack took a step—a twig snapped.

One Can Head shot his head around, the sound of the dry stick just able to penetrate its consciousness. One of Lowe's guards fired a gun at another. Then another shot, only this time—a click, the weapon empty.

Another Can Head spun toward Jack as if smelling the new interloper.

*Right*, thought Jack. *I'm here.*

He started firing.

For every shot that hit one of the Can Heads between the eyes, another barely grazed a shoulder, an arm. Now the group of cannibals was equally divided between moving toward Lowe's group, and moving on Jack.

Jack started walking toward them, reminding himself: stay steady, take time to aim. Try to fucking anticipate the Can Heads' next crazy move.

Anticipate.

As if.

The rifle kicked one back on its heels. Another blast removed one's head clear from its shoulders. And still the thing walked another few damn feet before collapsing to the ground.

Jack kept walking into the circle, as if bridging the gap between Lowe's party and his weapons. The closer he got, the better he could aim and shoot.

Only two of the things were left standing; sniffing the air like pigs, snorting, smelling the blood, mad with hunger but also seeing the death around them.

*Got you, fuckers,* Jack thought.

He easily took these two out in their confusion.

And then it was quiet.

Lowe and his people safe.

Jack's guns smoking in each hand like mini-chimneys.

"Yeah," he said. "*That's* what you get for ruining my fucking vacation."

## 27

The alarms stopped.

"It's over," Christie said. "I think you should try and get some sleep."

Kate asked the obvious question.

"Where's Dad?"

"He'll be here. I'm sure he helped." She forced a smile.

"He said he'd be back soon," Simon said.

"And he will. Tell you what. As soon as he's back, I'll send him in. Okay?"

"Okay," Kate said.

Simon looked up. "I want to hear what happened."

"Probably nothing. Only an alarm."

Just saying those words made them sound false.

"Come on—brush your teeth and into bed."

The two kids slid off the couch and walked into their room. With them gone, Christie looked at the door and then walked over to the front windows.

Lights on outside. Everything looked quiet.

Where the hell was he?

She turned away from the window, the locked door, and walked into the kids' room.


Ed Lowe nodded to Shana and the others, who headed to the Lodge.

At the same time, a different kind of siren started coming from the horns all around the camp.

Lowe stood close. "The all clear. Fence back up." He took a breath. "We stopped them."

Jack looked right at him. "Fences back up? Great. So what the fuck happened?"

"I don't know. We've got power back up now. Something— I'll check it out. I'll find out what goddamned happened."

"So much for your security." He turned away to head back to the cabin.

Lowe grabbed Jack's right arm. "Hey, Jack, hold on a second."

Jack shrugged off Lowe's hand.

"I got to get back. My family's waiting."

"Of course, of course. Can I walk with you a bit?"

"Be my guest."

The pain in Jack's leg had come roaring back, now that the adrenaline had faded. All that running.

*Killing my leg*, he thought.

"What you did was amazing, Jack."

"Right."

"Helping us. Taking down those Can Heads. Can't thank you enough."

"Don't mention it."

"You know, we could use someone like you."

Jack shook his head. "Someone like me? What's that? Some cop who came up here to get the hell away? And finds his family at fucking risk?"

His voice rose, the tension of the night hitting him.

He would have liked nothing more than to take Ed Lowe and shake him, grab his shirt and ask him, *How the hell did you let this happen?*

"No. And easy, friend. No need to raise your voice. Just that this *can* be a safe place, Jack. Protected, with guards. But even in safe places, things can happen."

Jack stopped. They were close to the path that led directly to his cabin and he didn't want Lowe following him all the way there.

"Things can *happen*? Is that how the damn fence got knocked out?"

"Hey, Jack—I said easy, huh? No need to yell. We're all friends here, right?"

"How about an answer?"

"You can take the cop out of the city . . . and you still get a cop, right?"

"Lose power to your fence, and—shit—in a place this large, everyone here is suddenly vulnerable. Enough Can Heads outside, waiting. If they had all gotten in, it would have been a bloodbath."

"We have backups. Backup power. Should have kicked in. Redundancies. I'll get to the bottom of—"

Jack shook his head. "Redundancies? Really? Didn't see anything too fucking *redundant* tonight."

"I said things can happen. Whatever shorted out the fence led the backup to overload. Never happened before. Should have been a smooth transition, like a switch being thrown. Don't worry, Jack. I have people looking at it . . . working on it now. Won't happen again."

"How reassuring. Will you call the state police?"

Lowe's face caught the glow from the lamp behind Jack. The fleshy face now smiling. The tight-as-a-drum Lowe from before had been re- placed by this stubby guy with an idiotic grin.

*Welcome, newcomers!*

"Of course I'll call the state police. But they have their hands full out there. They'd come if we needed any help. But it's all over now. They'll swing by tomorrow."

"And who'd you lose?"

Lowe grimaced. "Not too sure yet. But I know of one. A guard. Drunk. Right near that section of fence that went down. One drunk guard who couldn't fire fast enough."

Lowe looked away.

"We're better off without that asshole."


Christie heard the voices and went to the big front window of the cabin.

She saw Ed Lowe standing in a pool of light, talking to Jack.

*Why don't you just come back?* Christie wondered.

*Why do you have to do a goddamn postmortem with Ed Lowe?*

She remained standing at the window.


"Jack, I meant what I said. We could use you here. Your skills— training my guys."

"I have a job, thanks."

"Yeah. Back there. You think your family is really looking forward to going back? How long before things in the city go completely to hell? And the food? What you have to eat there. Is that how you want your family to live?"

"That's life."

"Not here, it isn't. You could be safe. And we have food, *real* food."

Jack looked up at his cabin.

"Look, I said thanks, but no thanks. Gotta go. Just make sure you find out what happened with the fence."

He turned away and walked up to the cabin.

For a few moments, he thought Ed Lowe would stand there and watch him walk all the way back. But Lowe headed back to the lodge.

No longer engaged in a heated conversation, the pain hit Jack full force.

*Need to take some real painkillers tonight.*

Even though he hated the way the Vicodin made him feel in the morning, all cotton balls in his head, so groggy.

Christie opened the door for him and immediately raised her hands, balled into fists as if she was about to beat his chest.

Instead, she backed up, letting him in.

"The kids . . . I said you'd come in. Say good night."

Her voice cold; her eyes on him equally chilly.

She had passed being worried and sailed straight on to really pissed.

"They still up?"

"I'm sure. Guess they want to hear what happened. The cop adventures of their father."

"Yeah. Okay. As soon as I wash off some of this blood."

"Then we talk," she said.

"Fine."


Christie had started by telling him how she expected him to come right back. How scared she was, and how angry.

But then, when she was done, she let him talk.

And she listened as Jack spoke about the fence, the guards, and she quickly knew he was downplaying it.

The failed fence had been a major threat.

And despite Lowe saying *things happen,* he didn't understand how it could have happened.

"So, with all their damn security, the safety of Paterville—"

"Not so safe."

He then told her what Lowe had asked him.

"What? To live here?"

"Yeah."

She looked away. "God. I don't know. I mean after tonight . . . But maybe . . . ?"

Jack didn't say anything.

He got up. Their chat ended. She watched him take a step toward the bedroom.

"Your leg—you messed up your leg. Your doctors won't be happy."

"Me either. Can you grab me a Vicodin? Hate it, but . . . And a glass of water. I need a shower."

While she went to get the pill and the water, Jack limped into the bedroom.


Jack took the pill and held it.

"Thanks," he said.

Christie, in a short nightgown, turned off the lamp on the dresser.

As she did, Jack took a sip of water.

But he put the pill on the end table near his side of the bed.

He had planned on taking the Vicodin. Planned on getting knocked out and sleeping.

But in the shower, his plans changed.

He got under the covers. Windows still shut and locked, outside now all seemed quiet and still, as if nothing had happened.

Christie shut off the light on her side of the bed.

Jack lay there, feeling so achy, the too-soft pillow surrounding his head.

His eyes were shut, but sleep seemed impossibly far away.

He felt Christie's arm around him. Then it tightened, the hug promising, her hand straying. He felt her reach down, encircling him, the feeling electric.

He turned to her, ready so fast, his senses so awake after the madness of the night.

"The kids?"

"Asleep," she said. "Late for them." Then: "Just be quiet."

He felt her slowly slide down, her lips planting kisses. No sounds outside to compete with the gentle noise of her kisses. His hands went to her face, caressing her, and she started to slide back up to kiss him on the lips.

He could feel her body, lean, taut—she put as much time into exercise as he did—position itself over him.

A big kiss, and he felt her on him, straddling him—and suddenly there really was nothing else. Just this shaded room, the bed, the sounds each of them made, the waves of pleasure making the idea of pain seem distant.

He became invulnerable.

At some point he turned her over, a move that had been impossible only weeks ago. He could support his weight with his knees, trying to minimize the pain to his bad leg.

Her legs entwined his.

When her foot moved over his healed wound, he detected no flicker of a reaction from her.

For her, too, everything else had vanished but their lovemaking.

And as he looked at her in the shadows, kissing her hard again, at one point, she took a breath.

And as if welcoming him back from a long trip, she said:

"I love you."

His answer was in his movements, driving deep, another kiss, holding her almost too tight.

Until it was done, and they both fell into the lightest of sleeps.

secrets

# 28

# Morning

Jack woke up, the aches from the night before still hitting him at a dozen different points on his body.

He heard steps . . . expecting Christie to walk in . . . but it was Kate. "Hey, Dad."

"Hey, Kate. Um, where is everybody?"

"Mom took Simon down to the lake. I'm going down, too."

He felt his daughter scrutinizing him.

"You okay, Dad? After last night."

Jack had already decided to minimize the break-in.

"It was nothing. Certainly no worse than what I see every day."

She nodded. Not exactly looking convinced. "Can I get you anything?"

He guessed all was forgiven.

Jack laughed. "No, I'm fine. Thanks, though."

"'Kay. Then, I guess I'll go down to the beach. It's really hot out."

"Great. You go and enjoy."

After slipping on his bathing suit, and a T-shirt, Jack started down to the lake—then stopped. He turned and looked at the Blairs' cabin. Were they okay after last night? Seemed like anyone who was behind a locked door would have been fine—the Can Heads who got in were busy with guards and other camp workers trying to stop them.

Still . . .

He walked back up toward the Blairs' cabin.

Knocked at the door. Quiet. He tried the door knob.

Though he knew that would look odd, what was he going to do? Just walk in?

"Hey, Tom! You guys at home?"

No answer. Must be out enjoying the day, which was indeed gorgeous. Sun filtering through the pine trees, the lake in the distance shimmering.

A bit of paradise.

Last night started to seem more and more like a bad dream. Something that happened in the dark and you forgot by morning.

He started down for the lake again.

Christie turned and, shielding her eyes, looked at Jack walking down to their blanket and the beach chairs. When he caught her looking, he tried to hide the limp.

"Morning!" she said.

"It is, isn't it?"

She turned to give the lake a glance, glistening jewels of light dancing on it.

"Simon is . . . ?"

"In the water. Made some new friends. He's having a ball, Jack."

He could see Kate parked near the lifeguard stand, acting as though she was reading a book.

"Well, with the crackerjack lifeguards here, best keep an eye on him."

"Yeah." She seemed distracted.

He sat down beside her on the blanket.

Then she looked at him again.

"Jack, about last night—"

"Yeah, I enjoyed that. And you?"

"Not that. I mean . . . I did. Of course. It was amazing. But I was thinking about Lowe's offer."

He didn't say anything.

"I mean, look at this place. Maybe you should . . . *we* should consider it."

"After that attack?"

"Is it any worse than your precinct?"

"No. Not really. Still, that was a major fuckup." A little girl digging in the sand close by lifted her head at hearing the dreaded F-bomb.

"Oops," he said. "Anyway, a fence failing? Could have been bad."

"But it wasn't. And as head of security, you could make things better. We'd have sun, this air, the water, food—I mean, I've been thinking . . ."

"Apparently."

"Why would we go back?"

"It's our home."

She took a few seconds to respond to this.

Then: "What kind of home? Fenced in, too, but just rows of houses, scared people, and you tell me that things are getting worse." Another pause. "How long?"

He knew what the rest of the question was.

*How long before it's bad there, too, where we live?*

Jack broke off from her gaze, out to the lake. Simon dived into the cool, clear water. Like a regular kid. Back in the good old days.

"I don't know."

"Jack, tell me you'll think about. That we can talk about it again."

From her tone, he knew it wasn't so much a question.

She was saying something important to him. And he'd have to do just that.

Think about Lowe. And his offer.

"Seen the Blairs?" he said.

"No. Not down here."

He nodded.

"You like Tom?"

"He's okay," Jack answered. "Just good to have someone to talk to who's not a cop."

He saw boats dotting the lake. It all looked picture perfect.

"Maybe we'll do the boats, after lunch."


In the lodge's great dining hall, Jack looked around.

"What's wrong?" Christie said.

"I still don't see the Blairs."

Christie started scanning the room.

"Think they left?"

"Could have been spooked by last night. Still, you'd think they'd leave a note or something."

"Strange . . ."

Ed Lowe came to the microphone. Jack expected him to talk about last night's incident.

Instead, he started immediately with . . .

"Hello, Paterville families!"

As if nothing had happened at all.

# 29

# Afternoon

"Which boat do *you* like, Kate?"

"I like this one!" Simon said, pointing at a rowboat.

"That's just a rowboat," Kate said. Then, definitively, "I like this canoe."

A line of three canoes sat together. Out on the lake, a few other boats went back and forth lazily. No motorboats here.

"Canoe looks good to me," Jack said.

A boat attendant dressed in a Paterville polo shirt and jeans walked over. The name tag read: FREDDY.

"Know what kind of boat you want?" he said.

"One canoe to go."

Freddy nodded and walked back to the middle of the small dock where an umbrella made shade for a chair and storage chest. Jack watched the guy open the chest and start digging through a pile of life preservers.

"Okay," Jack said, turning to Simon and Kate. "A few things about canoes."

"I still like the rowboat."

"Next time. So, canoes tip easily. Shift your weight too fast, stand up—and we all go swimming."

Kate listened intently.

*I'm back to being Dad,* Jack thought.

"That sounds like fun," Simon said.

Jack smiled at him. "Let's not experiment. And where we sit is important, one person in front, one in back, and—"

Simon quickly said, "I call front!"

*Oh, to be a kid.*

"We can—carefully—take turns. But we all get to paddle. Need to, actually, so—"

The attendant returned with three faded orange life preservers.

"Try these," he said.

Kate got hers on fine, but Simon put his on backward, which Jack quickly righted. Both looked a little roomy, but they weren't heading out into the Atlantic.

Jack's was snug. He could barely buckle it.

No matter, he thought.

"The paddles are in the boat," Freddy said.

"Okay crew, let's—"

Freddy put a hand on Jack's shoulder.

"Few rules."

Jack stopped and turned. Rules.

"Yeah."

"No standing or moving around—"

"I was just telling them that."

"Boat tips, any damage—you're responsible."

Jack nodded.

Freddy rubbed his chin. "We close here at five. All boats back by five."

"Doubt we'll be that long."

"And . . ."

A last rule coming. Slipped into the others as if it was just as obvious.

"You see that spot out there, on the right? And also over there, on the left?"

Jack turned and looked. The beach on either side of the lake gave way to brush and trees that ran midway around the lake. But that shoreline girding the lake ended in abrupt rocky faces and gradual cliffs that ran clear to the mountains on the other side of the lake.

"See those rocky points there?"

"Sure do."

"Don't go past there. You get there, you turn around. Got it?"

Jack nearly said aye, aye to the insistent boat boy.

Why? he wondered. Why the hell couldn't they canoe all the way to the other side?

"Okay. Anything else?"

The attendant shook his head.

"Okay kids, guess we're good to go."


Simon kneeled in front, his strokes doing a mix of helping the canoe go forward and then stopping it. Getting that rhythm . . . not easy.

Jack took the middle, applying paddle strokes to either side as needed. Kate took the rear, a spot she seemed happy to have since she could steer and turn the canoe.

Control was good. At least in her universe.

*Mine, too,* Jack thought.

His right leg ached in the position needed to make the boat go.

Sand from the beach ground into his knees, and his scar felt the pressure, the stretching and pulling as he squatted in the middle.

*Let's make this a short voyage,* he thought.

"How am I doing, Dad?"

"Super. Keep those strokes nice and steady, Simon."

He looked back at Kate and gave her a wink.

Jack thought of the last and only time he'd ever canoed. Ten years old, with his parents and his older brother. Only a few years before he'd lose both his mom and dad to cancer.

One of his last good family memories with his older brother, who never came back from the Mideast. He became a name in a box in the *New York Times.* A dead soldier in a war that was long since over.

He remembered the few minutes of instruction from an old man who ran the Irish Alps place they'd stayed in.

The J-stroke. And how to hold the paddle. Even how to right a tipped canoe.

Then, a few hours of exploring the lake. A memory you hold forever.

Maybe like today.

Jack looked up at the icy blue sky.

*Maybe like today.*

The memory of last night faded under the brilliant sun and the gentle sound of his kids paddling.


Jack looked right and left. Rocky cliffs suddenly appeared at both shores. The turnaround point.

He turned back to Kate. "Okay, kiddo, work your magic with the paddle."

Kate smiled, but when she put her paddle in the water, it sent the canoe gliding farther away from the camp.

The boat now arced straight toward the mountain, moving quickly past the turnaround point. Simon had actually gotten into the steady left–right rhythm. The canoe moved sleekly through the glass-flat water—but in the wrong direction.

Again, back to Kate.

He smiled, not wanting to start up with her again.

"Hey there, Captain, think you need to get that paddle in the water out, like so. To steer us back."

He demonstrated the angle she should take.

Jack thought he might try to guide the canoe from the middle. But that could make it rock.

They were pretty damn far away from the beach.

"I'm *trying*, Dad. You mean, like this?"

Her smile evaporated. Her new paddle position only made the canoe zig a bit to the left. The beginning of the cliffs were now well behind them.

"Don't worry. You'll get it."

Jack felt powerless. He couldn't change positions with his daughter, and so far, his instructions had little effect on getting the boat turned around.

"Keep trying, honey."

What was the worse that could happen? A reprimand from the attendant?

A scolding from Ed Lowe?

Canoe rights revoked?

As Jack turned left and right, looking at Kate's attempts to hold the paddle in the water at the correct angle and make the canoe obey, a flash of light, a reflection from the cliff to his right, caught his attention.

He stopped looking at Kate for a moment.

The flash of reflected sunlight vanished.

But he saw something else.

On the cliff. Hard to make out at first.

The kids occupied with rowing. Jack squinting at what he could see through the trees.

It resolved into something almost recognizable: houses, cabins, close to the shore.

But now blackened, timbers exposed.

Fire. Had to be. A whole group of them, like a town at the cliff's edge, burned down. Not a building untouched.

He turned back to the shore, his paranoia there. Knowing, feeling that this was something they were not supposed to see. The burned houses. The charred remains of where people once lived. What happened? Lightning? A wildfire?

He shook his head.

The woods near the houses were untouched.

He thought he saw something at the window of one building. Could have been anything, really. A shape. A branch that fell and got burned.

Sure, he told himself. That's all.

*Why do I think I see what look like arms? The shape of a head. The thing half in and half out of the window.*

*White bones, toasted black.*

He took a breath, then looked at his kids, both oblivious to what he had been studying.

Then to the shore. As if someone there could be watching him.

Then, seemingly booming from the sky above them, a long, deep blast of a horn, aimed right at the lake.

Like the loud moan of a fire alarm in a small town, late at night, rousing the volunteers.

One blast, then another.

Simon's hands went to his ears and he dropped his paddle. He immediately twisted to see where it went. His motion made the boat rock. Instinctively, Jack moved in the other direction to steady the boat.

"My paddle!"

Jack's voice took on a clear, commanding tone: "Simon. Stay seated. We'll get the paddle."

One that he hoped expressed calm. But one that Simon would obey.

The paddle coasted past Kate, any opportunity for an easy recovery gone.

"Dad, I'm—"

"Nice and still, Simon. Just like I showed you."

Then another, longer blast of the warning horn.

Jack looked back at Kate, checking on her. She looked scared, and held her paddle up in the air.

*Good. At least she's not making us go farther into the forbidden zone.*

He looked to the trees at the top of the cliff. Loudspeakers.

Christ, loudspeakers out here? Why? Then the answer came.

"Turn your boat around immediately. You are leaving Paterville property."

A recorded voice. Just triggered by their arrival here? Or did someone send those blasts, the messages?

The message repeated.

"Turn your boat around *now!*"

"Daddy," Kate said, "are we in trouble?"

Jack forced a smile. "Oh, right—big trouble. The canoe police will want to have a chat with us."

That made her face ease a bit.

"My paddle!" Simon said, as if a reminder.

Then another horn blast.

"All right, here's what we're gonna do. Let me just do the paddling here—"

Can that even be done? Jack thought. From the middle of the canoe?

"—and I'll get us over to Simon's paddle. Then we'll figure out how to turn around and get back."

He looked from Simon, then to Kate.

"Okay, then?"

They nodded.

"Here we go."

———

It took longer to get the paddle than it had to canoe all the way out there. But Jack eventually got to it, reached down, and picked it up.

"Here you go. Back in business," he said to Simon. Then to Kate: "Now, I think, if you just do this . . ."

Jack again modeled the angle and position with his paddle.

"And if Simon and I row nice and straight, we should turn around fine. And head back."

He made sure he didn't look back at the cliff edge, the burned out places barely visible behind the bushes and trees.

But the thought: *The horn. They don't want anyone seeing that.*

"Will that horn blow again?" Simon asked.

Jack looked up, back to the shore.

"No. I think they know we got the message."

This time, Kate got the position right.

When the canoe was finally pointed straight at the beach, they began paddling as before, streaming through the water, heading back to the Paterville beach.

Moving quickly away from the secret on the lake.


Jack had expected Ed Lowe to be waiting for them, a reprimand at the ready.

But only the attendant was on the dock.

Freddy waited, arms folded, until they had gingerly stepped out of the canoe and onto the dock.

"I told you," he said, dully, like a parent reminding a kid of some chore forgotten a dozen or more times, "not to go past that point. No one goes past that point."

Jack took the life preservers from the kids and handed them to the attendant.

"Had a little trouble with the steering. Maybe put some damn rudders on these things."

The joke brought nothing. Freddy gathered all three preservers on one arm and started to turn.

"Hey," Jack said.

Still smiling, still keeping it light.

More for his kids than the sullen attendant.

Did this kid even know what was out there?

"What's with the horns? Pretty loud."

Freddy didn't stop. Jack followed him to the storage container.

"They warn you." The kid picked up the lid and tossed in the jackets. "Least they're *supposed* to warn you."

"We heard them, all right."

"Dad, can I go back to the cottage?" Kate said.

"Sure. Take Simon."

In seconds, they had left the dock. The splintery storage container lid slammed down hard.

The attendant moved to his chair. Picked up a clipboard.

*Lot of important paperwork with this job*, Jack thought.

"Looks like there was a fire up there," he said.

He studied the kid, focused on his clipboard.

When the kid didn't respond, Jack took a step closer. "Know anything about that?"

Finally, the kid looked up, his eyes narrowed. Jack could feel the anger there. Freddy didn't like the questions.

"Nope. Never been out that far."

Back to the clipboard.

Jack walked away, catching up with his kids, already back on the beach, knowing that Freddy knew exactly what was on those cliffs.

But something more than that worried Jack.

The look in Freddy's dull eyes.

The anger. Something familiar about it.

The sky remained as blue and crisp as before. A beautiful sky.

But as Jack walked back to the beach, he took no notice of it.

# 30

## 4:55 P.M.

Christie was still in the cottage when Jack came out of the shower.

"I thought you were going with the kids to the game room?"

"They're okay," she said. "Told them we'd meet them there before dinner."

Jack had wrapped one towel in classic fashion around his torso. He used another to dry his hair. "So," he said between drying, "why do I have the feeling that you're waiting for me?"

"Simon told me about the horns. You weren't going to mention that?"

Jack looked at her and nodded. "Yes. We heard horns. I was going to tell you. But later."

"When?"

"When the kids were gone. The whole thing rattled them enough without them seeing us talking about it."

She hesitated a few moments, as if weighing the validity of what Jack had said. "Okay. Probably a good idea. But Jack"—she stood up—"what the hell? Alarms? On a lake?"

"Apparently."

Should he tell her what he had seen? Not yet, he thought. Not until he knew more.

"Alarm horns. I don't get it. Do you? What—"

"Hold that thought—let me get dressed. Then I'll see if the Blairs have surfaced for dinner."

"If they're still here."

He went into the bedroom.


The door to the Blairs' cottage was shut.

Most of the cabins only kept their screen doors shut, letting the cool early evening breeze blow in.

He knocked.

No answer.

Why would they have their door shut?

Kids away playing? Some adult quality time, perhaps?

Sharon Blair didn't look like the most playful of women, though.

He started to turn away when the door opened.

Shana stood there, the mesh of the screen door giving her a shadowy look.

"Yes? Oh, Jack. Hi."

"I was looking for the Blairs."

Shana opened the screen door, held it a second and backed away. Jack took hold of the door as she walked back to the interior of the cabin.

Jack followed her through the living room, back to one of the bedrooms.

To see the bed.

Which had been stripped. Shana shook the pillows out of their cases, letting the pillows fall onto the bare mattress.

"Where are the Blairs?"

"They're not here."

The sheets lay in a pile by one wall. All the drawers of the dresser were open, empty.

Shana scooped up the pillowcases and threw them onto the floor.

"They're gone."

"Really? They said they were staying a few more days."

Shana kicked the pile of sheets and pillowcases away. Now she gave Jack her full attention.

"As you can see, they're *gone*."

"What happened?"

She smiled.

"Happened? I don't know, Jack. Not my department. Maybe problems with their credit. Paterville isn't free."

Her scent, so strong in the small room.

Jack became acutely aware of where they were. Shana closed the row of open drawers with a bump from her body, facing Jack as she did so.

Did Shana normally clean out guestrooms?

He looked at the sheets, left in a pile.

"Did they leave a message? We were kind of friendly."

Shana made a look as though thinking over a thorny question.

"I didn't find any messages. Did you check"—more steps, closer to Jack—"at the lodge?" Another step closer. "The registration desk? I hear—" Mouth open. Full lips.

*Time for me to move this conversation outside,* thought Jack.

"—that people do sometimes leave messages there."

Jack nodded. He began to back out of the room.

Then a thought: Shana wasn't here to clean the room, to get it ready for the next guests.

No. She was here giving it a once-over.

What was the word for a place cops found in this condition?

*Tossed. It's been tossed.*

"Maybe last night spooked them, Jack."

She came closer.

"Certainly didn't spook you, now did it? We all hope—"

She put a hand on his shoulders.

"—that you'll consider Ed's offer. Head of Security."

"I better go." He looked around the room. "Wish I could have said good-bye to them."

*And asked him about any stuff they've seen. The burnt buildings on the cliff.*

"Lot of perks with the job, Jack."

She emphasized his name. *Ja . . . ck.* As if there was something funny about it. Something so amusing about this cat-and-mouse game.

"You could come by my place anytime. Split more wood. Or try some other things."

He felt dizzy. The perfume. The musty air of the living room.

And then before he knew it, something happened. Shana leaned close and kissed Jack hard. Her other arm had circled him, holding him tight. Her lips moving, opening as she kissed.

"Jack, any sign of—"

He had pulled away as soon as he realized it had happened. But not soon enough that Christie, who had entered, didn't see.

"Christ. Oh, God—"

In a second, she was gone.

"Oops," Shana said, releasing him.

"What the hell are you—"

He shook his head, and ran after Christie. But she was moving as fast as she could, heading down to the trails, joining other people making their way to the lodge.

He was about to run after her. Bolt, stop her and explain.

Even as he wondered: *Did I want that to happen? That kiss? Am I crazy?*

He looked up.

High to a nearby pine tree. Way at the top.

And he saw something. A small box. Like a birdhouse. Almost invisible amid the branches.

But clearly there. He looked over at another tree. The view blocked, so he took some steps until he saw a similar box, pointed in a different direction. Pointed. Because now he knew what they were.

Cameras. Right. Security cameras. Missed them way up there. Aimed at the camp. Just like Tom had said.

Maybe it made sense. Make sure the camp was quiet.

But why watch the *guests* so closely? Why the need to follow their moves?

He turned around.

Shana still in the cottage.

*Gotta stay away from her,* he thought.

*Stay away until we leave.*

Thinking that, he knew that time would be soon. Something was wrong here, and the feeling was growing.

It was only when looking back at the cottage that something caught the glimmer of the setting sun about to disappear behind the mountains.

A few steps toward whatever was on the ground, catching the light at just the right angle.

Jack reached down.

And picked up a set of car keys.


He leaned across the dining room table. Christie had picked a seat so she wouldn't sit near Jack, but across. The room buzzed with chatter and eating. Lowe gave Jack a wave and a smile; the happy prospective employer.

The kids were eating the food hungrily, the day's exercise having its effect.

Jack waited until Christie, who had been avoiding his gaze, finally allowed her eyes to land on his.

"Can I explain?"

"What?"

Her voice—the word was like a dull hammer hitting wood.

"I did not do that."

He saw Kate look over, finally catching on to the fact that in the world of her parents something was up.

"You think I'm blind, Jack?" Christie said. Then she, too, noticed Kate, chewing, listening in. "Can we talk on the way out? Please?"

Christie's eyes were stone cold.

Then: "Okay."

They went back to eating.

They walked together. Christie looked over her shoulder.

"Let the kids get ahead," she said.

When they did, Jack explained how it came to be that Shana had kissed him.

Christie walked on, not saying anything, until Jack stopped her, holding her elbow, getting in front of her.

"Look at me. Do you really think I would do anything like that?"

"I don't know what to think."

"Yes, you do. You know it was her. Almost like she knew you'd walk in. I pushed her away as soon I could."

She looked right into his eyes now, then away. But when her gaze came back, he thought that maybe she finally believed him.

"Crazy bitch," she said. Then she laughed.

Jack didn't laugh. He started walking again.

"There's something else, Christie. The alarms."

"Yes. The horns."

"Before we came back, I saw something out there."

He described the burned buildings, the blackened timbers.

"God."

Then: "And I thought I saw a body up there, a skeleton."

She turned to him, and suddenly his fear, his paranoia—was hers.

"How? What do you think happened?"

"I don't know. Don't look anywhere. Just listen to my words. Wait—then look."

"You're scaring me."

"Okay. Stop here. And just ahead—close to the cottages. Check out the trees. Way up. You'll see something. Hidden. But you can tell, whatever they are, they're not part of the tree."

Christie took a quick look. Head moving left and right, then quickly back to Jack.

"I saw something. What are they?"

"Cameras. All around us, cameras. Fixed, tracking those walk-ways, all the cottages." He took a breath. "All the guests."

"Security?" she said.

Nothing. Then: "Right. Sure. Reason I stopped you right here, I didn't see any camera that could pick up this spot." He shook his head. "Could be security. Could be. After all, one bad incident here, and this place could get shut down."

"And you don't believe that?"

"I don't want you afraid. I don't want the kids afraid."

"Tell me."

"Shana was looking for something in the Blairs' cabin. And outside—"

Jack looked around. No one seemed to be watching them talk. No cameras here.

"—I found these."

He pulled out the set of car keys like it was contraband.

His wife said nothing.

"Found them outside the Blairs' cabin. I mean, they could be any-one's. But something feels wrong here."

Jack could feel her fear. Her eyes darting.

Then: "All right." Christie took a breath. "So, now what?"

"For now, tonight—nothing. Place seems to go into lockdown mode at night. Tomorrow morning, I think we leave."

No words back from her this time about the job offer, about the crystalline lake, the clean air.

Christie nodded. "We can play some board games with the kids. Nice and quiet. Get them to bed. Get up early. Go home."

"Right. Listen. It could all be nothing, Christie. We live in a strange world; that makes places, people strange. Maybe it was too much to hope that we could find some place peaceful. Some place to escape."

She turned and looked down to the lake. Getting dark. Kids skipping stones, a small fire.

"Say nothing to the kids, okay?" he said. "For now."

"Of course. Maybe we'll feel differently in the morning."

"Could be."

They started back. She grabbed and held his hand.

Holding it, giving it a squeeze every now and then, letting him know that they were together in this.

the last day

# 32

## 12:55 A.M.

He might have dozed off.

But each time sleep came close, Jack would pull himself back to alertness. He listened to Christie's breathing, always the gentlest of sleepers. While she complained that he, on the other hand, snored like a bear through the night.

She had been asleep for a while. But he wanted to wait.

Let that sleep deepen.

Let other people in Paterville go to sleep.

Let it get as quiet as it can.

He looked at the glowing face of the travel alarm clock. Nearly

1:00 A.M. He pulled off the sheet and thin blanket. He slowly swung his legs out and moved his feet to the floor.

The pain immediate. A Vicodin would be so good.

But not now. Not tonight.

He walked over to the dresser. He had thrown his pants there. He grabbed them, and then slowly opened the drawer to recover the flashlight and his small .44.

Now that he knew how well Paterville's security worked, he wouldn't go anywhere on this property without a gun.

He went out to the living room, taking care to quietly shut the bedroom door behind him. Not closed so tight that there would be a telltale click. Just enough so that any noises he made would be masked. He didn't put on a light.

He put on his running shoes.

He was ready.

Jack looked out the front window.

He could see guards out there. Back on duty. Watching all the good sleeping vacationers.

He knew that going out the front door was out of the question. Before he had gone to bed with Christie, he had checked out another possibility.

First, though, he picked up the car keys he had found off the coffee table.

He walked to the small bathroom at the back of the cabin.

Straight to the window. Open now, assorted bugs mashed up against the screen. Might just be big enough.

The toilet right next to the window.

That would give him enough height. But could he fit?

The screen—an old-fashioned piece of mesh held in place by primitive metal clips—had to be removed. Jack would need to pop it out and let it fall to the ground.

Jack put down the toilet cover and stood on it. The bowl wobbled, bolts in need of tightening.

He steadied himself on the bowl.

Then he pushed two clips on the side of the screen, and then one at the bottom. The three released, sending the screen falling back and away from the window.

It made noise hitting the brush outside.

Jack hesitated.

Not much of a noise. Not a bad noise, he thought. Not anything that could attract attention.

Now the hard part.

He brought his arms up and wedged them on either side of the open window.

Pressure to either side. He'd need to pull himself up, then somehow through the window.

Then pressure. A curl from the biceps, lifting his dead weight up and off the toilet, into the air. Now with a combination of the lift from his arms and wriggling his chest, he was able to get his upper torso part of the way through the window.

He unlocked his arms and reached outside the frame to the walls on either side. Grabbing there, palms against the wood, while he squirmed more, pressing his feet against the inner wall of the bathroom.

No purchase there, but the rubbery toes of his running shoes got some traction.

Had to be done in one move, he knew. And no grunts. No sounds.

One smooth move to slide out.

His landing would make noise. Nothing he could do about that.

He started pressing with his hands as he pushed with his sneakers, attempting to use the wall. And all the time, he wriggled from side to side.

*Like being born*, he thought.

But it worked. He slid through the hole. The frame scraped his chest, then his stomach, maybe drawing blood. It would at least leave nasty bruises. His right knee banged the inner wall, kicking, squirming.

He kept on going. This was the only way out.

*And I'm getting out.*

One last push with his hands against the wall, and finally gravity did its work and he tumbled, headfirst, down into the brush, the sound of his landing seeming so loud.

For a few seconds, he just lay there.

Listening to see if his maneuver had aroused any attention.

Nothing.

He got to his knees and then, urged by pain, quickly stood up.

He double-checked his gun. Secure in its ankle holster. A pat to the pocket to guarantee that he still had the keys.

He headed into the woods behind the cabins, away from any paths, away from any light, away from any guards.

Deep into a stand of pines, Jack went off the path and navigated around the side of the camp, away from the lake and the lodge.

At one point, the strip of woods narrowed and he came close to the fence.

He moved slowly there.

A thought: What if they have motion detectors out here?

But how could they? Every small rodent would trigger it.

Once he heard voices—guards patrolling the nearby fence.

But then the woods opened up again, and Jack quickly moved away from the fence, curling well behind the Great Lodge, behind the field and the cabin where Shana had so effectively split wood.

The woods ran behind the lodge, close to the parking lot before merging with a sloping hill dotted with pine trees and the dead trunks of deciduous trees.

His eyes adjusted to the darkness. He reached a secluded spot near the lot.

Jack crouched down and left the safety of the trees for the maze of cars filling the lot.

So many cars.

He could have used the electronic key, but the flash of lights would advertise that someone was there.

Instead, he tried the car key in the one thing he thought would not produce a light.

The trunk.

Moving from car to car, crouching the way he imagined soldiers did in some godforsaken city filled with snipers.

How long before a guard on his rounds spotted him? Called for some help to see who the hell was down there.

Then what? Jack making up some bullshit story about how he got out of his cabin? And what the hell was he doing?

So many cars.

He came finally to one near the back of the lot, the car pointed at the hill leading up to the service camp.

Parked that way, Jack would be totally exposed as he went to the trunk.

He used his fingers to find the lock on the trunk. Then, keeping his fingers there, he slid the key in.

It fit.

He turned it.

A click, then the trunk attempting to fly open.

But Jack held it open a crack, the trunk light squelched by the lid being held low.

*Got the keys—and now I got the car.*

*A fucking match.*

He slid to the left of the car, finally out of sight of anyone who might look down at the lot.

He couldn't enter the car. The inside would light up. And like most cars, the interior light would stay on for a good few minutes.

He brought his head up slowly to look inside. Just at the level of the door lock. Another inch, so he could look inside.

On the dashboard—a picture magnet. The frame looked like a palm tree.

A picture in the frame.

Too damn dark to see.

He looked over his shoulder.

He'd have to risk a quick flash.

It would have to be so goddamn fast.

He dug out the flashlight.

He held the compact light next to his eyes. He aimed the light as if it was a weapon.

Targeting the small frame stuck just to the side of the radio.

It was possible that the frame held nothing.

Some knickknack that someone bought along. Empty. Useless

He held the light close to his face, breathing steadily. One quick flash.

Three, he thought.

Two.

One.

Now.

His thumb flicked the light on, then off.

To anyone looking, it might have seemed like an illusion. A flash of light? A lightning bug? Maybe nothing.

But Jack's eyes had been locked on the small magnetic frame.

The light had missed its target by an inch or more, but there was enough of a glow around the core ray to hit the frame.

For Jack—whose eyes were locked on that frame—to see:

Tom Blair. His wife, Sharon. The two boys.

Then the image was gone.

Jack fell back, falling onto the ground.

He felt sick. He could throw up. The fear so real now. *This* was Tom Blair's car. They hadn't gone anywhere.

And only after sitting there for what seemed like such a long time did Jack look up.

To see a glow on the car's front windshield.

A glow, picking up a reflection from the hill, from the service area up on that hill, up that road.

Something fiery, streaming up, way above the treetops, dissipating into a plume of smoke.

The reflection danced on the windshield of Tom Blair's car. Something happening up there so late at night.

This night wasn't over.

Not yet.

Again, Jack got into the painful crouching position.

He knew where he had to go.

He started a slow careful climb up the small hill.

# 33

## 1:41 A.M.

Christie turned in the bed and let her arm reach out, a chill in the air making her seek warmth.

Instead, her arm touched nothing. The years of sleeping with another person by her side, just right *there*, made her awaken.

She looked at the empty space.

And immediately she sat up.

"Jack?" she said quietly.

Thinking he'd gone to bathroom. That he was somewhere outside. Again: "Jack?"

But there was no answer and even before she slipped out of bed, feeling how cool the night had become, she knew he wasn't here.

She stood in the middle of the living room. Then she went to the window. She saw Paterville guards standing outside by the lampposts at the end of the path leading from their cabin area.

Did he leave, just walk past them?

And where did he go?

But she knew. She knew as strongly as she knew anything. As much as she might have wished that Jack left work, his cop mind back in New York.

It was impossible. He wasn't wired that way.

And if those keys . . . if they *really* were Tom Blair's keys—

*God, what would that mean . . .*

Then he would have to find out.

And if they were, what would he do?

No—what would *they* do?

Because she also knew that Jack would talk to her. Tell her everything. He may have slipped out somehow. But when he came back, he would talk.

For now there was nothing she could do but sit down on the couch, in the darkness, and wait.

She grabbed a throw blanket filled with woven images of a summer mountain holiday from the nineteenth century, people with parasols and top hats.

Times change . . .

She draped it over her, then pulled her legs up, tucking them under the blanket.


Every step that Jack made brought the possibility of a noise that would catch someone's attention.

He took care to bring his weight down slowly, testing the underbrush.

Near the top of the small hill, he stepped on a twisted piece of dried branch. The crack of the wood sounded like a gunshot.

Jack immediately looked up, eyes scanning the nearby woods for any movement, any response to that cracking sound.

Nothing.

He thought of his face, so pale, probably catching any light.

If there had been a moon, he'd easily stand out. But all there was were the flames from a chimney ahead, the dancing fiery embers floating up with the smoke.

The closer he got, the more light would fall on him.

*Steady,* he told himself. *No rushing.*

Another few minutes at a crawling speed, and he was at the top of the hill.

Closer to where the woods ended.

He finally saw where the service road led.

And for a minute, all he could do was look.

Cabins. Lots of them. People lived up here. Way too many for just the workers and the guards. The cabins looked bigger, like homes. Not the rustic summer-only places down below.

And other buildings, one nearly the size of the Great Lodge. A central meeting place maybe. Other buildings nearby. Mostly all dark.

He saw the building with the chimney, the smoke, the flames licking the sky.

The thought, standing there in the chilly darkness, *It's a town. This is a fucking town.*

Something hidden from the guests.

Back to the big building with the chimney off to his left. What happened there? What were they doing there in the middle of the night?

He thought of something stupid.

*They're baking bread. Making tomorrow's gruel. Cooking the soy crap, whatever the hell the cook used for soy.*

Mighty big flames.

He had to get closer to this hidden town. But more important, to this one building that seemed to be operating at full steam.

Jack hugged the apron of the woods to get closer to the big building.

He also passed the cabins, dark as those below. Some with cars parked out front.

*Because people live here,* Jack thought.

This town also had guards—two stationed where the service road ended, both holding rifles.

And behind the town, above the woods, a turret like those by the main gate. No telling if it was manned; no lights.

*Of course it's manned,* he thought.

*They'd have a good look at the whole service area.*

*Got to remember that.*

*And cameras.*

*Got to have cameras here as well, not that I'd be able to make them out.*

The odds of not getting spotted seemed slim.

But he had no choice.

He felt like an animal, step after careful step, moving closer to the big building.

And still well away from it, he caught the first breeze that carried the building's smell.

It filled his nostrils. His stomach tightened. A stench that he couldn't identify. He opened his mouth to breathe and then he kept moving.


Alongside the building. Crouched in the bushes.

Jack looked at the building's few windows. But they had all been glazed with a whitewash. No way he could see anything inside.

The back of the building was closest to where he crouched. A front entrance faced the cabins and other buildings.

This building—well away from the others.

No cabin, no workshop, was even close to it.

That was good.

He needed to get in.

He looked up at the turret. It stood far away from this area, near another exit out of Paterville. They could get a look at him if he left his cover, but only if they happened to be looking at this spot at the right time.

And while Jack looked around, immobilized by his analysis of what he was going to do . . .

Two back doors to the building flew open.

The cook, Dunphy, walked out, a dark shadow in his apron and sleeveless T-shirt. He laughed. Two other men, one on either side, walked beside him.

The two men were half the cook's size. The cook a monster. Obese. But having seen him in the kitchen, Jack knew he was also a monster with arms as thick as most men's thighs. No neck, just that bowling-ball head that melted into a barrel of a body.

The three of them passed a bottle back and forth. Cook's moonshine, Jack thought. More laughter, the words blurred but the tone lewd, drunken.

They walked to the side of the building, Dunphy fumbling at his pants. Moments later, Jack heard the sound of the cook's piss hitting the ground.

*C'mon*, Jack thought. *Go walk somewhere else. Let me look inside.*

Then, as if hearing Jack's thoughts, the three walked around to the front of the building. Cool night. Maybe it was hot inside.

Jack waited.

A few more steps, and the three of them stood near the front, out in the open. The laughter faint now. The bottle still being passed.

He took a breath.

Struggling to remain in the crouch, he hurried to the two open doors at the back of the building.

———

*Charnel house.*

That's what he thought going in. Huge bubbling pots, the floor filled with blood.

A big oven under the chimney had massive black pans and pots bubbling away. On the other side, a walk-in freezer. The biggest walk-in freezer Jack had ever seen.

The walls, lined with saws, bolt guns, butcher knives.

The image so powerful he didn't move, even though Dunphy could walk back and find him any minute.

And how would that go down? Jack thought.

Not too well.

He moved to a table to the right, a solid block of thick wood. He crouched down just in case the cook returned. On the floor something glistened. A curved butcher knife that must have fallen off the table.

Across the way, the entrance to the freezer. He crouch-walked his way to the double doors of the freezer.

He moved behind what had to be a twelve-foot-long table as if he was a soldier moving up on a target.

He looked around as he moved.

This kitchen, this insane place with its smells and cooking pots, could all be seen from here.

He saw something on a table across the way.

His attention first drawn there by the steady drip, drip, drip of blood running off the table.

His first thought: *They're going to eat the Can Heads.*

Like when desperate cattle ranchers fed their steers the dead offal of other creatures . . . anything to try and make some money.

*Is this their food?* Jack wondered. *Is this where they get it from?*

Who'd be crazy enough to eat Can Heads, knowing that whatever threw a switch turning them into feral animals could be within them, ready to infect whoever ate it?

He slowly stood up, keeping his ears cocked for the sound of Dunphy and his laughing companions.

When he stood he could see the table, and what was on it. A body. First thought: They are dismembering the Can Heads and using them for food. For the chili, for the stews, for whatever the hell they served and ate.

But after a glance at the open back doors, Jack took a step toward the table, then another. Expecting to see some crazed Can Head face on the table.

The face, smeared with blood, but intact. Though already, its legs had been removed. One arm left.

He fought the gag reflex.

Until the angle was about right and he could really see the face.

*Tom Blair.*

Jack realized that he had been pushing that thought away the whole time.

Still no sounds from outside. It had only been minutes. They could stay out there for awhile, letting these pots bubble away.

He turned away from the big wooden table. Next to it, the freezer.

He hobbled his way over.

Hand on the freezer door. It had a latch that could be thrown over the handle and a place for a massive lock. But the latch wasn't flipped, and there was no lock in sight.

He grabbed the handle. Important to pull it gently, he told himself. Don't want a telltale click that cuts through the night sounds.

He pulled back so slowly.

He felt the latch disengage, the large freezer door ready to swing open.

When it was free, he pulled on the door smoothly now. A cloud of frost rushed out.

He saw metallic shelves loaded with covered plastic trays—so many, stretching to the full height of the freezer, which was nearly as high as this charnel house itself.

And deep. The freezer went back and to the side, easily half the length of the whole building.

When Jack walked in few more steps and the frost settled, he saw the hooks.

A row of fifteen metal hooks. Things hanging from them.

Different sizes.

His brain screamed at him: *Leave. Don't look. You've seen enough. Leave!*

More steps into the freezer, his strides kicking up icy clouds as the humid air from outside also entered the freezer.

He saw the bodies hanging from the hooks.

God. The bodies.

Still dressed. Different sizes, because some were adults.

Some were—

Children.

He was close enough that he could touch the nearest, a woman. His hand felt the frozen, crinkly material of the skirt. The body twisted a bit, the head hanging down, gaping right at Jack because the hook had to be embedded in the back.

Sharon Blair's eyes wide open.

Her dead, dull face for once registering something.

Horror.

His mind repeating dully:

*Leave. Now.*

*There are things to be done.*

Things that had to be done. He had seen enough. He knew enough.

He limped out of the freezer. As carefully as he had opened it, he shut it.

He went over to his hiding place, near the fallen knife. His journey from there seeming to have started a lifetime earlier.

Before he knew—really knew—*everything*.

Crouching down. Listening. So quiet.

# 34

2:28 A.M.

He heard the laughter.

Dunphy the cook, his helpers—shit, they were coming back. The laughter louder. No way now to get out before they returned.

He stayed crouched.

The only guide to what was happening now were the sounds. The steps outside. The cook's loud drunken voice. The others, the human hyenas at his side, laughing at anything, everything.

The voices passed close by, and the cook's tone shifted.

"Chuck, go give the damn oven a look. Got to be cooked down soon. And Willy, let's finish breaking this fucker down. I wanna get some goddamn sleep tonight."

Everyone getting back to their assigned tasks.

The human butchery getting back in operation.

But Jack hadn't heard them shut the doors.

He edged as close as he could to the way out. There was an open space of six or seven feet before he could slip away.

If anyone looked, they'd see him. They'd be all over him.

*No,* he thought. *That can't happen.*

*I have things to do. Things that must be done.*

Like a simple—what did his wife call it?—a mantra.

*I have to get my family out of here.*

He gave them a few minutes to get to their places, two men hacking at what was left of Tom Blair, the other at the stove. Possibly all of them looking away when Jack started to move.

Which he did.

Staying low, nearly crawling to the open doors. The blessed outside air hitting his nostrils. Step after awkward step. Not so fast that the footfalls made any sound, not with all the bubbling, and now the hacking, the chopping, the sawing.

*Whack, whack, whack.*

He finally got outside and moved like some insect, a hunted bug, a wounded cockroach hurrying as fast as he could to the safety of the dark woods, miles away, an eternity away as he sucked in each breath with every step.

Then deeper into the woods, still refusing to stop, though clearly sheltered by the darkness now.

Until, so deep, he felt he *could* stop and he fell forward.

His face catching a thorny bush, the prickers tearing at his face. He felt so happy, so goddamned happy that he had escaped, that he nearly cried with joy.

He had escaped.

He could get his family out of here.

He gave himself a few minutes to recover.

Such a small rest before he started moving again.

———

Christie sat on the couch, the throw blanket tight on her lap, when she heard the sound from the back.

She had seen the open bathroom window and realized how Jack had left. She looked in that direction and waited.

She heard a grunt. Then the sound of the window being shut, sluggish from humidity.

Jack's steps told her he was limping.

*Welcome to our vacation*, she thought.

He walked into the room. He might have passed right by her.

"Jack," she said quietly, not wanting to startle him in the darkness.

He stopped.

"You're awake," he said.

"I woke up. You were gone." A pause. Then: "Where were you?"

He tossed the keys onto the coffee table.

Even in the dark room, the keys caught some light.

"I had to know," he said. "About those keys."

"I figured that, when I woke up and you were gone. Guess I know you."

She looked up at him standing there like her young son would if caught doing something he shouldn't.

"Sit down."

Jack maneuvered around the coffee table and sat down beside her, falling into the couch. His right arm brushed hers, and she felt the cooling sweat on it. Close now, she saw his face covered with sweat, and then the scratches.

"What happened?"

He looked away.

"Jack?"

When those eyes turned back to her, she knew he'd tell her everything.

The room felt frigid. Christie had her hands locked together.

She looked at Jack as he told her about the car, how the Blairs never left, then described what he saw inside the building with the smoking chimney.

He hesitated then. He couldn't go on. But then without any prompting, he finally finished his tale.

And when he described going into the freezer and touching Sharon Blair's body, Christie's hands untwisted and went to her face.

Did she sob? Or was it merely a gasp that she needed to muffle? Was her heaving all from the fear?

She didn't know. The feelings overwhelmed her. She felt Jack put his arm around her. Somehow that brought no sense of comfort.

Finally, she brought her hands away from her face. She felt wet trails on her cheeks, drying now. She had been sobbing as quietly as possible. But that was done.

"God, Jack." Her voice a whisper.

She looked in the direction of the bedroom, the kids. "Jack. What are we going to do?"

Thinking all the time, *he has to have some idea.* He was her rock. He was someone who faces fear and death and madness every night. Surely he had to have a plan here.

His voice low. "We have to get out of here."

"Now? Right now?"

He shook his head.

"No. You've seen the guards out there. And I can only guess what the roads outside are like at night. No, it'll have to be in the daytime."

She looked right at him.

"W-will they let us?"

He took one of her hands. "I wasn't seen. I got into their cook-house, whatever the hell that place is, and no one saw me."

"And the car? The Blairs' car?"

"No one saw me get the keys. The parking lot was dark." He took a breath. "I wasn't seen."

Which Christie took to mean, *I hope I wasn't seen.*

After all, hadn't Jack shown her all the cameras?

Then the details.

"How will we do it?"

And those details rolled out, showing that Jack had indeed thought about it.

"Leave everything. We split up and—"

"No. We can't—"

A squeeze to her hand.

"Listen."

"We can't split—"

"Christie, *please*. We have to split up. If we march to the car together, then they'll know something's up."

He didn't add the obvious.

*Then we would never get out of here.*

"I'll take Simon. You, Kate. Maybe you go by the lake. I'll go near the game room. Then we go right to the car."

"I'm scared."

"We get in. We drive toward the gate. If they don't suspect anything, they won't have a plan to stop us. We'll get out."

She shook her head. "It sounds crazy."

A harder squeeze. "Listen, Christie. It's what we have to do. There are things we have to do over the next few hours. Do you understand?"

More words not said.

*If we want to get out of here.*

*If we want our kids to get out of here.*

*If we want them to stay alive.*

Quiet for a few minutes. An old-fashioned wall clock with a luminous dial showed a little after four. Dawn wasn't far away. Everything that Jack talked about would be happening in the next few hours.

"What do we tell the kids?"

Already she was imagining walking with Kate to the car. Her questions. Her reluctance to go all the way to the parking lot. For . . . what?

Then getting them both into the car, fast, when every second might count.

He said, "We have to tell them."

"No." She shook her head. Almost moaned. "We can't."

"We have to. Who knows what they'll see. What we might face."

"They'll be so scared."

"Yes. But, listen. We get them to the car. We leave."

She nodded at Jack's words. Then, as if she had to be part of this plan: "Right. No discussion, no debate. You and I tell them we need to get into the car *now*. That this is a bad place. And we have to leave *now*."

Jack looked right at her, realizing the bridge she had crossed.

Christie thought of her daughter, more obstinate and self-absorbed each week that she got older.

But she also knew that Kate still had one foot in the world of a little girl.

"I know Kate will understand. And Simon will follow her. We just have to do this fast."

"Yes." Jack took another deep breath. "We can do this."

She didn't say anything. Then:

"Do we wake them early?" she said.

"First light."

She saw Jack look at the door, the front windows of the cabin.

"Right. First bit of light." She choked on the words, feeling this close to sobbing.

Instead, she raised a hand to his face. "You're badly cut."

"Scratches. A bush."

She felt the thin lines of dried blood.

"You should wash them."

"And you should sleep."

She curled her legs up and rested against him.

"I don't think I can do that."

Neither moved as the black night sky outside slowly began to lighten.

escape

## 35

### 6:07 A.M.

Morning. Jack tried to force himself to stop pacing.

Christie led the kids out in their PJs, Simon's with the Avengers battling a bad guy, Kate in a purple T with matching pajama bottoms.

He wanted to tell them before they got dressed. Give it a few minutes to sink in.

*Get dressed, because we have something to do.*

Simon flipped the pages of one of his comics while he sat down by his sister.

"Why are we up so early?" Kate said. "Some vacation."

Christie didn't say anything but sat down beside her daughter.

Jack would give every dime he had for the mindless sound of a TV in the living room, blaring cartoons, news, infomercials—any god-damn thing.

And as he waited, walking from the living room to the bedroom for absolutely nothing, he checked the windows.

The guards had gone.

That was good.

No daytime guards watching over all the Paterville campers.

Things getting back to normal.

He turned to Simon, then Kate. Their faces finally registering that something was wrong with their father.

"We have to leave—"

"Leave?" Simon said. "But I like—"

Jack crouched down close to Simon, giving Kate a look as well.

"We have to leave, Si. There are bad people here. We have to go."

Neither of the kids said anything.

Then Kate, in a small voice, said. "Bad people. You mean . . ."

He shot a glance at Christie, who gave Kate's hand a squeeze. Then amazingly, miraculously, Kate understood. Don't ask that question. Not with Simon sitting so close. The squeeze signaling, *Be strong if you can be.*

Outside, the sky had lightened some more.

It was time to go.

Instead, they all heard a knock on their door.

There was time for just one more look at Christie before he went to answer it.

Shana stood there.

"Morning, Jack."

Christie had come up behind him. He saw Shana keep her smile as she looked from Jack to his wife lurking just behind him.

"Um . . . morning. Really early. Anything wrong?"

Her eyes went wide. "Wrong? Don't think so. Ed just asked me if I could hustle down here first thing and see if you had a minute to chat with him." Another big smile. "I just do what the big boss says."

Jack gestured back at the interior of the cabin. "I was about to take my daughter to the game room."

"How nice. Dad and daughter."

He wanted to say no. No way was he going up to the lodge.

But would that be normal? Kate was not ready yet. The request seemed innocuous. He turned to Christie to see what she might say.

"If it's only a minute."

As if that decided it, Shana turned, and started to lead the way.

Jack said quietly, "I'll be right back."

"Okay."

He followed Shana.

"You okay, Jack? Seem a little tense . . ."

Shana walked close, almost sliding into him as they walked to the lodge.

*Why this escort?* he wondered. Another opportunity for Shana to play with him?

"How come he didn't come down to see me?"

"Ed? I imagine he had something that you needed to see. I don't know. State troopers coming soon. Another sideways glance. "You seem a little tense, Jack. A little *tight.*"

"Yeah. Well, I didn't bargain on dealing with a Can Head attack when I came here."

"Oh, that was rare. Trust me. Never happens. *Ne-ver.* Almost like it was something special."

She stopped at the bottom of the steps to the lodge.

"Just for you . . ."

"What?"

*Special?*

*Just for you?*

"Gotta run. Lot of repairs we're doing today. And we're down a few people."

She started away.

Jack walked up the steps.

"Have a seat, Jack."

"I'm good. Look—"

"I know. You want to get back to your family. I get that. But listen."

Lowe stood up and walked close to Jack. His gut strained against his pants and his plaid shirt.

The closeness of Lowe, the size of the room, all made Jack feel dizzy.

"Have you thought more about what we talked about? Last night?"

"No."

A big Ed Lowe smile. "Wish you would, my friend. You could be great here. Your family. Plenty to eat."

"We do okay."

"And tell me, do you really want them to be outside, those gorgeous kids of yours?"

*Small bodies behind Sharon Blair, swinging on meat hooks.*

*Gorgeous kids.*

"I take care of them."

"But you think this is all over? That it will all end soon? More and more Can Heads every day, Jack. *Every damn day!* They're winning. And soon, places like Paterville will be the only refuge. A last stand. And trust me, Jack. We are ready."

*A last stand? Can Heads on the outside, and Can Heads inside. Except here, they can smile, talk. As if they had made a choice what side they were on.*

"You forget. My job is stopping them."

A bigger smile from Lowe.

"Jack, do you know what did this? What changed the world?"

"The drought. That, or all the strange playing with DNA, the weird genetics."

"Pick a theory, Jack. What's your favorite? 'Cause, you see, it doesn't much matter. It is whatever the hell it is. This is the world. I'm afraid if people like you don't get that, then you can join the dinosaurs."

"We done here?"

"Stay, Jack. Your wife can enjoy the lake. Kids, the clean air. We're just beginning our little experiment here."

Experiment? Lowe didn't even bother to use the word "camp."

Did Lowe know something? The air grew thicker as if filled with an unbreathable dust.

He had to fight the urge to say anything.

Lowe laughed. "Your final answer, Jack? No?"

"You got it. Just want to enjoy the rest of my vacation . . ."

Did the lie pass?

". . . then go back to the real world."

Lowe's smile faded. "*This* is the real world, Jack."

"Right."

Jack turned, and gasping for air, left Lowe's office, hurrying down the hallway filled with offices, all with closed doors, to the reception area of the lodge.

Was everyone looking at him?

Or did he just feel like everyone was?


Jack walked into his cabin and Shana stood there, waiting for them.

He stopped and looked around, finally calling out. "Christie, kids?"

"They're not here."

He went up to Shana and wrapped a hand around her upper arm, squeezing. "Where the hell are they? Where'd they go?"

"Oh, *now* you want to get physical?"

He squeezed harder.

"Starting to pinch, Jack."

"Where the fuck is my family?"

"Not here, obviously. Wish you had accepted Ed's offer. You could have such a good time here with us. Life, as they say, can be good."

Jack's other hand went to her throat. "I will ask you one more time, bitch—where is my *family*?"

Her eyes moved slightly to the side. Jack sensed movement, then realized that she wasn't alone in the room.

A stupid mistake on his part.

He released her arm, ready to grab the gun from his ankle holster, when a needle jabbed into the back of his neck.

"What?"

He spun around. A guard backing away, lowering his gun.

But already the syringe started to work.

Jack's hand went to the back of his head, feeling the needle still sticking in there like a dart.

Looking forward, Shana turned blurry. No longer smiling. Her mouth open.

*No*, he thought. *Christ, no.*

His last thought as he fell to the floor, and everything went black.

## 36

## 4:47 P.M.

Voices.

"Fuck it. We can eat, then come back and get to him. If Lowe lets us."

Jack remembered the smell. He knew where he was. The charnel house, the cookery.

He wanted to open his eyes, but then those voices around him would know that he was conscious.

So he kept his head down, locked in the same position, his brain throbbing from whatever cocktail they had stuck into him.

One voice—the cook's.

"C'mon, just leave that shit for now."

Another voice, closer. "Think we can do it when we get back? Lowe won't—"

Dunphy laughed. "Best not fucking guess what Lowe will or won't do. Best you just shut up and cut when I say cut. *Capiche?*"

"Yeah. I . . . er . . . whatever you say."

Another booming laugh from the cook.

Two of them. Leaving from the sound of it.

Jack tried to get a sense of what his situation was without any discernible movement.

On a hard back chair.

Hands tied tightly to the back. Another rope wrapped tightly around his chest. His feet pulled tight, each one tied to a chair leg.

Tied up, trussed, and ready to go.

He knew that the freezer was nearby.

He thought of Christie. The kids.

*No,* he begged.

*No. They can't be in there.*

If they were . . . if they *were*—he'd slaughter every person, every human animal that lived here.

*They have to be alive.*

Otherwise, he'd be dead already.

*They want me to stay here, to help them.*

Lowe wouldn't kill his only bargaining chip.

That's what he told himself. The logic of it clear. But then other thoughts, a voice that said, does logic work here? Does logic and reason and empathy—does any of that human shit work in this hell?

"C'mon, asshole," Dunphy barked one last time.

The sound of a door. A bit of air, then the air cut off. The door closing.

Jack sat there, head down. And waited.

Counting. To one thousand, so he would force himself not to rush. *998 . . . 999 . . . 1000.*

Slowly, Jack opened his eyes, keeping his head in the same position.
The cookery came into view, his eyelids a slowly raising curtain.
Seeing it made the smells seem more intense.

Now to raise his head.

He did that slowly as well.

Until he had his head up and could look around at the place, turn his head and see the tables, now with fresh carcasses on them.

*Please*, he begged. *Please.*

The angle bad. But one table had a larger body, an adult. The other, someone smaller.

Almost crying with the pitiful thought now. *Please.*

He kept staring at the inert, partially dismembered bodies.

The adult. A woman. The shape round. Someone not too big, someone round.

Not Christie.

He thanked whatever had granted him his pleading wish.

Only then did he look over to the other table. A small body. Impossible to tell anything more than that.

Impossible from this chair.

*I have to get out of this chair.*

For the next few seconds, his entire being focused on that one task, one that he refused to admit was impossible.

The chair stood near the table that had been his hiding place the night before.

A time that seemed weeks, months, a lifetime away.

He faced out, toward the main area of the cookery, facing the freezer.

He couldn't turn and see behind him.

But he remembered crouching near here, and seeing the butcher's knife on the floor.

Somehow a knife had slipped off the table and no one had seen it. Not in their alcohol haze, not with so many blades and saws arrayed on the walls of the room.

What's one knife on the floor?

Would it still be there? No way to tell. Impossible for him to see.

He tried to think if he had other possibilities.

He had been tugging and wrenching at the ropes around his wrists. But they were tight; whoever had tied him up was competent. And the same went for the lashing of his feet to the chair legs.

Some kind of strong elastic band went around his midsection, knotted behind him.

How long would Dunphy be gone to the lodge, to check on the food being served, grab a plate himself?

Something nice and meaty tonight.

How fucking long?

He came back to the only possibility. That knife, if it was still there. That was the chance. No other possibility at all.

Jack started rocking his body back and forth.

The chair would rise a bit at the front, steady, then lift up from the back. Jack had no control other than to make his body move, to get enough momentum so that the chair would tip and eventually fall to the ground.

But how would it tip? Could it leave him pinned in a weird way, unable to move, a pointless maneuver?

*My only chance,* he thought, ignoring all the mental pictures that had him trapped, an upside-down horseshoe crab, waiting for the fat cook to return, and maybe start to work on him right there.

Back and forth, the movements so small. But he found a rhythm; he could build some momentum. The lifts of the front, then the back legs. Higher each time.

Until he knew he was close.

More rocking, using the scant movement all the ropes and lashings gave him.

And then he felt it.

The chair starting to fall over, not to the front or the back, but a strange sideways slip. All he could do was let it happen as the chair banged against the table, his head smacking hard against the edge, then slipping down to the cookery's floor.

He looked left. Fresh blood spatters. He realized after a moment that they were his own.

The chair had landed on its side. Jack looked around to the right, trying to see a side wall of the building.

*Please be there*, he thought.

Straining as much as possible, he saw it. The beautiful shining silver of the blade, the dull black of the handle.

His right leg on the floor, his weight on it.

The foot was nearly immobilized, but there was some room for movement in the leg. Again, only inches.

He heard voices.

Outside.

Dunphy back?

But the voices moved on.

He couldn't have much time.

The leg kicked. More pathetic miniscule movements.

Kick. Kick. Kick

Over and over. Gaining mere inches. But he kept doing it, barely aware that this was his fucked-up leg. Barely aware of anything but this need to contract, relax, using this pathetic kicking movement to move the chair inches closer to the knife, the chair that seemed to weigh a ton.

He paid no attention to the progress he made. As though the only thing in the universe that could bring him pleasure was each small kick, giddy with ecstasy every time he came closer to the knife.

His sole obsession: to kick, to move.

He saw the blade near his head. That made him only kick more. He had to get past the blade, yes . . . get it closer to his hands.

Taking so long. Too long. No way he'd make it.

*Fuck that idea*, he thought.

*I'll make it.*

He couldn't get his head in position to see if he was close enough. It would be a guess, an estimate of how far he had come.

He might have only one chance.

He stopped.

Was the knife close in line with his tied hands?

*Because,* he thought, *while my wrists are lashed tight to the chair . . . my fingers, my palm—they are goddamned free.*

He looked around and saw the other end of the table nearby, a foot away.

An estimate.

He guessed he was close to the knife.

Now, more rocking, leaning left and right, needing to get the chair's back to edge closer to where he thought the knife was. Then, more inaccurate kicking, using his weight, his legs.

Fingers scratched desperately against the floor, feeling nothing.

Again, more rocking, more crazy grasping with his fingers.

Then, a different sensation. Metal.

Another kick, and his right hand briefly grasped the blade, felt the sharp metal dig into the soft skin of his fingertips.

No matter; he was close.

One hand would have to hold the knife. By the handle or by the blade—it didn't matter—then slowly saw the rope. Ignoring the metal if it slid past the rope and bit into his hand, his wrist.

Another crazed grasp and his right hand locked around the knife, partly around the handle, partly around the blade.

Now his fingers had to perform a weird fumbling, knowing that the knife could simply slip away. More guesses as he positioned it, hoping he had the knife tip resting against rope.

His palm and fingers could make the blade go back and forth with only the smallest movements.

His new obsession now, and he thought of nothing else but this movement.

Once he felt the tip of the blade dip, burying itself in skin.

*If I hit a vein, this will all be for nothing.*

He slowed a bit, taking more care with his strange sawing at such a difficult angle.

He felt the rope actually loosen.

Loose, and that meant he could make bigger slicing movements, now almost a mad butcher himself.

Looser still.

His tied wrists now had some space.

He forced himself not to rush. One wrong move here could fuck it up.

Slowly, slowly, as that beautiful distance between the two wrists opened even more. He felt he could slide a hand out, maybe both. But he kept at it.

The need to be absolutely sure *that* important.

Then . . . as if they had never been tied at all . . . his wrists were free.

His hands, free.

Now, with a mad speed, he cut the band around his chest. Not bothering to sit up, he sliced the ropes at his legs and ankles.

He was untied. Still on the floor, still in the same odd position that he had landed in.

Then, a creak. The cookery door opening. Early evening air from outside.

Dunphy's voice.

"Willy, want another hit? You want—"

The voice stopped.

Jack didn't move.

He realized . . .

*They think I'm gone.*

# 37

Jack heard a clanking noise, the sound of metal. Dunphy and his helper had stopped talking.

The sound of them grabbing blades. The clang of metal.

Jack still held the knife that had freed him. But then he heard a sound like a lawn mower. The smoky smell of gas.

There was no time to wait anymore.

Jack crawled to the far end of the table, deeper into the building. There was no point in escaping with these two alive.

He stood up, and clocked the position of the two of them. Dunphy holding some kind of gas-powered saw, something for chewing through bones, cutting up carcasses.

The cook's helper held a cleaver in one hand and a long curved blade in the other.

"Just stop right there, buddy," the cook said, "and nobody has to get fucking hurt." Dunphy grinned, his bowling-ball face one leering smile. "After all, if we *had* wanted to hurt you, that would have happened hours ago, right?"

The helper had taken a few tentative steps closer to Jack.

Jack acted as though he didn't notice.

There was no point talking to these two.

More steps from the helper.

Now the cook began to walk away from the far wall, the saw spitting out smoke, the chained blades grunting as they cut through the air. Dunphy's massive arms held the saw with ease.

Obviously given it a lot of use.

Could Jack depend on his leg?

The two men had moved so each was at the limit of Jack's peripheral vision.

Jack started to lower his knife.

Sharp enough to cut through rope, but how would it do with skin and bone?

He was about to find out.

Lower still.

The cook's smile broadened even as he moved toward Jack, the saw held at chest height, blade pointing forward like the barrel of a bizarre gun.

Then Jack moved.

He turned to the helper. Smaller, he was probably faster. He looked scared, while the cook didn't.

The smaller man immediately stuck out his two blades, a classic and bad move by someone who wasn't used to fighting with a knife.

Jack held his blade close, maximizing his ability to send it jutting out and back.

Sticking it out . . . that just wasted seconds.

Jack took painful steps toward the man and when close enough, he did just that—jabbing his right hand with the blade out. He nailed the man's arm holding the cleaver. The man screamed as he released it and it fell to the floor.

From the sound of the saw, Dunphy had started moving toward Jack.

Only seconds.

The helper now slashed wildly from left and right with the thin blade, a mini-sword ending in a fine pointy tip.

Jack tilted to the left, dodging one wild swing, then another dodge as it came swinging back. He held back on his second strike until that wild arc had been completed.

And when that had happened, the man's midsection lay wide open to an attack.

Another jab, this one straight at the man's guts, then a violent pull up. The whirr of the gas-powered saw right behind Jack.

He left the blade buried.

Saving a precious second or two.

He spun around, the move agony now. Dunphy marched toward him like a human tank, stepping on and over his partner.

Dunphy kept jabbing with the saw. A stupid grin still filled his face. He wasn't scared. He was fucking enjoying this.

Blades all over the room, but Jack was cut off from them.

But the saw was heavy despite the strength in the cook's meaty arms.

"Come on, you dumb bastard!" the cook yelled. His mouth a dark hole.

As much a Can Head as any Can Head Jack had ever faced.

Nothing human about this monster at all.

Close, and Jack was forced against the wall.

But there was a table right in front of him, covered in blood, bone, skin.

Jack did a diving roll onto the table, spinning around on the bone and flesh that had been left there. The smell of decay covering him.

The roll worked. Dunphy spun around, marching around to the other side, his saw sputtering. The smile had vanished.

*But*, Jack thought, *I'm not going anywhere yet.*

He backed against another table. A massive pot sat on it. Jack glanced into it. Filled with milky water and dotted with whitish chunks on the top.

Bones, boiled down.

He grabbed an edge of the pot with his right hand, ignoring the burn, and pushed it forward, sending the bones and the slimy water crashing to the floor. The slimy soup hit the spot where the cook took his next step.

He moved forward, oblivious.

That was a mistake. Because the fat cook wobbled, and the saw flew up as he struggled for balance.

Dunphy even looked wide-eyed at the saw as if it might angle around and bite into him.

Jack—now close to a wall of knives and cleavers and saws.

But he saw something on the table that looked like a gun. A butcher's tool, with a barrel. Sitting right there.

He picked it up just as Dunphy regained his footing.

Jack came close to the cook now, and before the man even knew what was happening, Jack pressed the bolt gun against Dunphy's side and pulled the trigger.

It made a dull thudding sound. No bullet inside. But the fat barrel had shot *something* out.

When Jack pulled away, he could see the smooth hole in the cook's chest. What the hell was it—something to kill people before Dunphy started to work on them? A quick shot to the brain, and it would be all over?

Like steer in the slaughterhouse back in the old days.

This was a human slaughterhouse.

But Jack needed the cook alive.

Jack fired another, now at Dunphy's throat. Another smooth hole opened. Blood gushed forth. The chain saw fell from his hands, and Jack had to step back to dodge it, coughing from the smoke, the chain spinning, still running.

Dunphy fell backward. A beached whale, shooting blood out of the blow hole in his throat.

Jack went to him, crouched down.

"Where are they?"

The cook shook his head. He grabbed at his throat as if he could close the hole.

"Where the hell is my family?"

He pressed the bolt gun against the cook's head.

Dunphy shook his head again.

But he was spraying blood like a geyser. No way he could stay alive for long.

"Tell me. Tell me, you fat fuck, or I'll fill your head with holes."

The cook's mouth opened. More blood dribbled out. There was no way he could talk, Jack could see.

But the lips *moved*.

Once, then repeating the same word, unintelligible.

Dunphy now had two hands around his neck, attempting to stem the flow. Jack pressed the bolt gun against his head, right behind the left eye, and pulled the trigger. A dull thud.

Dunphy's hands fell away from his throat.

Jack let the bolt gun fall from his hands.

He stood up, covered in blood from the butchering tables and cook, and—

Saw the freezer.

Dread building in him with each step, his hand shaking when he finally reached out to unlatch, and then open the freezer.

He knew what he saw there the night before.

He thought of the blood that covered him. The great boiling pan of bones.

*No,* he begged.

The door popped open. The frost snaked out. That made it hard to see for a moment, but then it cleared as Jack walked in.

His superheated body, sweaty, steaming from the fight, created more fog.

Now he walked down the length of the freezer.

He looked at the first body. One of the Blair kids. Then, another, a man he had never seen.

More bodies behind him.

None he recognized.

The joy—immense.

*My family isn't here.*

*My family is somewhere else, alive.*

He turned and started out of the deep freeze.

He had to get the hell out of here. Maybe no one would come looking for a while.

Couldn't be a place people like to come.

*It's not dark yet. I just . . . I just have to get the hell out of here and find my family.*

Over and over. The same thought.

He moved as fast as he could to the back doors of this slaughter-house.

# 38

## 7:50 P.M.

Christie walked over to her two children, sitting so quietly on the bed of this small room.

She stood there, and then paced. Simon had fallen asleep as if some protective mechanism had kicked in during the day. And Kate, sweet Kate, had even put her arm around her younger brother.

Her daughter hadn't slept, but lay in the bed, near catatonic.

The fear of the first hours had changed into this terrible expanse of waiting.

Christie would sit. But only for a few minutes before she'd have to get up.

A guard with a gun outside made sure they didn't go anywhere.

Ed Lowe had explained it like it was some glitch that had to be fixed.

"You see, Mrs. Murphy, kids . . ."

Christie loathed that this man would even talk to her kids.

She imagined doing things to him . . . things that she had never imagined before.

"You'll see," Lowe had said. "Your husband will come around. Sure. You and your kids can be safe. We can use your husband. And he'll *see* Paterville can be a good place for you as well."

Christie had said nothing.

Jack would never agree to live with these people.

Were they any better than the Can Heads? Were they a new strain of monster that could pretend to be human?

Lowe had food brought to them. No one ate any.

With darkness coming, her worry grew. Where was Jack? He'd never agree to be part of this.

And when Ed Lowe figured that out, what would happen to them?

She started walking back and forth again.


Jack sat curled in bushes, waiting for darkness. No alarms. Maybe no one had been in the kitchen yet.

The dark took forever to come.

Each little bit of deepening gloom arriving torturously slow.

But while he sat there like a wounded animal, he had time to think and plan, looking at all the possibilities.

None of them good.

But one had to be selected.

He looked up at the sky, the last bit of light fading.

---

Now, night fallen, Jack made his way through the brambles, ignoring scratching thorn bushes and jagged branches.

He had expected someone to be at his car, guarding it.

But no.

They must have had confidence in Dunphy and how tied up Jack had been.

He crawled down to the car. This time when he opened up the back, he'd have to kill the interior light as quickly as possible. A switch on the roof. Still, it would glow for seconds. Someone could see.

He looked around, but in the gloom he couldn't tell if anyone was watching.

Nothing to do but take a breath and open the door.

He unlocked a back door and as fast as possible he slid in and reached up to the ceiling switch. Bright light filled the Explorer's cabin. And then it went dark.

A moment, waiting.

He shut the door quietly and moved to the back. He opened the rear door. Lifted the rug of the luggage area. Fiddled to get the key into the hole. Opened it. So practiced with that move by now.

No light, so he had to feel, pulling out his other guns—a .44, a Glock. His rifle was gone. Nothing he could do about that. He filled his pockets with shells, making them bulge.

No holster, so he stuck the .44 under the front of his belt, the Glock under his belt at the back.

Then—one other item. One of the explosive devices. A timed C4 charge, a doorbuster. He slipped one in his back pocket.

He shut the tailgate door and started making his way around the camp, through the woods.


A few times, he passed close to a guard. But he'd stop, let them move on, then continue on his way.

There was a narrow point where he'd have to walk out, exposed.

An open area leading from the woods on one side of the property near the lake to the woods behind the cabins.

Best just to stand up and walk.

People still here, maybe even some ordinary guests—like the Blairs were, or Jack's family.

If Lowe felt confident he had things in hand, scaring Jack in the kitchen, all trussed up, then maybe Jack had time.

He stood up and walked from one piece of woods to another, stepping across a bit of camp road. Until he got close to the other wooded section, and then he moved into it.

*Just taking a leak . . .*

And kept walking, deeper into the woods, until he stopped, crouched, waited.

No sign of having been discovered.

Crouching made the gun muzzles dig into him. Despite the pain, so good to know they were there.

He started circling around, to the open field, and farther . . . to Shana's cabin with its split sections of wood laying outside.


Jack waited, watching the cabin as he saw Shana moving around. At one point, she came out and he thought she might leave.

But she simply stood in the open doorway, smoking, and then went back inside.

He moved from his secluded cover. Again, he'd have to cross an open stretch of ground. And the clock had to be ticking. Sooner or later, someone had to come to the kitchen and find the dead cooks.

At the end of the woods, he stood up, then ran up to her cabin as best he could. He pulled out the Glock, and threw open the door.

He didn't see Shana. And then she came out of a back room. With luck, what she was smoking wasn't just tobacco.

She looked up, confused.

"Stop right there," Jack said.

She stopped moving.

"Thought you had . . . another engagement. All tied up."

A laugh. She was stoned.

"Sit the fuck down."

But even stoned, Shana turned and grabbed an arm weight off a back table and threw it awkwardly at Jack. He dodged it but she immediately leaped at him like an animal springing.

Her weight sent them both falling back. And too quickly she had landed on top and was able to grab her ax leaning near the front door.

Her right knee had pinned Jack's arm holding the gun. She quickly smashed the butt of the ax into Jack's jaw, once, then whipped it the other way for another hard smack.

Stoned or not, she had gotten the advantage quickly.

Who the hell trained her? She'd mentioned the army, but he'd never met a soldier who could be *this* efficient half-baked.

"Want to play, Jack? Too bad it's this—there are better games."

She rammed the ax into his midsection. Knocking all the wind out, and then she changed the angle.

*She's going to use that ax on me.*

*And I know how good she is with an ax.*

The gun useless. But Jack could slide his other arm free. Shana brought the ax back, her glassy eyes trained on him, perhaps picturing how she was about to split him like a tree trunk.

His right hand shot up and wrestled for control of the ax handle against her strong two-handed grasp.

He locked his arm, forcing her to twist the ax left and right in an attempt to free it.

Forgetting the important job her right leg did in holding down his left arm.

She had allowed enough room for that arm to slide free, and

with it, the gun. He didn't want to fire. A shot would end all his chances.

But the muzzle made a nice piece of metal to jab into her side.

Which he did, ramming it hard into her midsection.

The ax slipped backward, still held by her but now being pushed away by his arm.

He could sit up, and as he did that, he wrestled the ax away from her.

He twisted the ax around and before she could recover her wind and mobility, he brought the end of the handle flying across her face.

Just as she had done to him. Once, then again, and again, enjoying the blood, the stupefied look, and knowing that he could easily keep doing this until she was dead.

But when she had almost become immobile, a beaten thing on the floor of the cabin, he pointed the gun at her, and lowered the ax.

"Where is my family?"

He knocked her chin, a hard tap with the blunt end of the head of the ax.

She spit out some blood.

"I don't know . . . where the hell . . . your family is."

Another knock to the head with the ax, not to draw blood but letting the heavy metal smack her head back, hard against the floor.

He did it a few times. Because he had no time.

He needed an answer.

"*Where are they?*"

"I don't know. Lowe didn't tell me. Just that they were under guard." Another great cough of spit and blood.

Could be true, Jack thought. Could be fucking true.

Which meant that there was only one person who could tell him where they were.

"Okay. Listen. Let me tell you what's going to happen. And if it doesn't happen *exactly* the way I tell you, then I will, in my own amateur way, cut your fucking head off your fucking body. Understand?"

The smallest of nods.

"Sit up."


"Ed, can you come down here? I need to talk. Something private."

Jack listened as she talked to Lowe.

"No. Ed. Best we talk where no one can see."

He waited. Would Lowe tell her to come up and see him, security be damned?

Did he like to play with Shana? Was that one of the perks?

That might influence his decision.

"Good. I'll see you."

She put down the camp phone.

"He's coming."

"Good."


Lowe walked into the cabin.

Jack smashed the handle end of the ax into one knee, and Lowe collapsed into a crouch. Then his other knee, and Lowe was praying on the floor.

Jack had Shana stand near the back of the cabin.

"What the—"

Now a smack right across the face, and Lowe's lips bloodied.

"Sit in that chair. Go on, get the hell up."

Lowe could see the gun now and knew that getting beaten by the ax might be the least of his troubles.

He struggled to get to his feet, and stumbled over to the chair.

"Tie him up. Tight as you can. And I know tight, so don't fuck around."

Shana tied Lowe exactly as Jack had been tied. Had she been the one who trussed him up in the kitchen?

In seconds, Lowe was firmly strapped to the chair.

"Back away," he said to Shana.

He walked over to Lowe, stood in front of him.

Jack used the flat head of the ax now like a pendulum, and smacking one knee, then the other. Lowe howled.

"Next one hits your face, Lowe. Nice and hard."

"You're dead."

"Okay."

Jack used the ax like a baseball bat, tilting the sharp edge away, and smashed it into Lowe's face. The blow hard enough to make the chair rock back.

"Where is my family, you sick fuck?"

Lowe opened his mouth as if about to challenge Jack again. Jack saw his eyes look back to Shana, but Jack's gun in his other hand kept her pinned to the wall.

"No answer?"

He brought the ax back again.

"All right, all right! I'll tell you. They're fine. They're okay."

"Where are they?"

He brought the ax head close to Lowe's face.

"A cabin up near the service camp." He looked right at Jack. "You've been up there."

"Lot of cabins. Which one?"

"Toward the back. Away from the center. All by itself. Has a number out front, Cabin 12."

"Are they guarded?"

Lowe nodded.

"How many."

"Just one guy. They're okay."

"You said that already."

"You could stay with us Jack. You still could—"

"As if."

Lowe deserved another metal smack on the face.

Was he telling the truth? No way to know until Jack got to that cabin.

"Let me tell you something"—a look at Shana—"and you, too. If they aren't there, you are both going to feel so much pain, you'll wish this place was crawling with Can Heads. You'll wish they were ripping you apart."

"They're *there*," Lowe said quietly.

Jack realized that he just told them both that they'd be allowed to live.

Insurance, to be sure. With them alive, his threat might actually mean something.

He turned to Shana. Be quicker to kill her. Make her kneel and chop into her, kill the animal that she had become.

But then, would he be any different than them?

There were lines in his job—to cross, to not cross. Decisions, judgment calls. Ethics.

Some guys on the job just let it go.

"Kneel down, facing the wall," he said to Shana.

When she had done so, he put the gun and ax by his side.

"Move, and your brains will be on the wall in front of you."

He tied her up, half expecting her to try something. But he guessed that she, too, wanted to live.

He rushed; but in minutes, she was also tied up tight.

He left the cabin, thinking . . .

*I'm close. I'm going to do this.*

Over and over.

And wishing that he really believed it.

# 39

## Cabin 12

He saw the cabin. Had to be. Larger than the other cabins. More rooms, and off by itself, exactly where Lowe said it would be.

Jack couldn't be sure unless he could see the number in the front. But no way that could happen. He'd have to find a way in through a window. He spotted a side door off one end.

There was that way in, and the front, or maybe a window, and, and—

All of them sucked. All of them so exposed.

He spent a few minutes watching the area past the cabin, studying the workers, the people who lived here, these "civilized" people who ate humans and pretended to be different from the Can Heads.

He turned away from the cabin.

Too much activity all around it, people coming out, enjoying the summer night, socializing.

*Hey, neighbor, how are you tonight, and my—wasn't that a good dinner?*

He had one shot at this.

*I can't just run in there.*

He turned back to the woods and started making his way to the great fence that circled the property.

Jack saw the shining mesh of the double fence, and blackness beyond it.

But he also saw a metal box with shelled tubes and wires snaking in and out. Something to control the electricity that ran through the outer fence, keeping Paterville safe from the hordes outside.

*Not anymore,* he thought.

He pulled out the small explosive. Smaller than a grenade, it didn't have a lot of kick. Kick a door in, clear a room—that was about it.

But Jack imagined that it could also do damage to that electrical transformer. Did it need a direct hit? Would it do enough damage?

Only one way to find out.

The digital timer gave off a slight glow, not so much to attract attention, but enough for him to set it.

How much time. A minute, perhaps? Enough time for him to get away.

He had set it for sixty-eight seconds. Then he slid a latch to the right, exposing a single button. One punch and the countdown began.

He pressed the button and then, eyes locked on the transformer, lobbed it. The small explosive landed short of the transformer. A few good feet.

*Fuck,* Jack thought.

Was it close enough?

The seconds melted away. He could go for it, or start running.

Still frozen, looking.

"God *damn* it," he said and he scurried toward the fence. Probably all on camera.

He scooped up the explosive and pressed the button. He had blown his protective cover. He quickly added more time to the explosive, which had dwindled to twenty-three seconds.

Then he placed the device right at the base of the fence, right under the transformer, and pressed the button again, turned and ran.

Surely on camera.

Being watched by the guards, who were already calling Ed Lowe, who somehow wouldn't answer.

Maybe waking up other guards.

The whole night going wrong.

Running through the woods, fast as he could.

Then—the explosion.

Seconds later, the alarm sound, the horns blaring from everywhere and nowhere, filling the camp.

Back to Cabin 12.

Everyone running like ants when their underground home had been exposed. People ran all over. Jack joined them with no one noticing anything.

Good. That part fucking worked.

That alarm meant only one thing: Can Heads could be breaking in.

Would they? Jack wondered. Were they always lurking out there, waiting to stream into the camp whenever something went wrong with the fence?

*I sure as hell hope so.*

No hesitation now. Straight up the steps of the cabin. Into the living room. A guard spinning around.

Not recognizing Jack. Confused by the alarm. Maybe scared. All alone.

"What happened?"

*Doesn't even know who the hell I am*, Jack thought.

Then, a flash of recognition on the guard's face, perhaps seeing Jack covered with blood, his body and clothes becoming a map of this night.

"Wait a fuck—" the guard said, his rifle muzzle lowering toward Jack.

Jack shot him. A clean shot to the head. He heard screams from a room in the cabin.

Jack grabbed the guard's rifle, then grabbed a tablecloth from the dining room and threw it over the body.

Then he turned to the screams, to the room, unlocking it with the key in the door.

Opening the door. To see them. God, to see them, screaming, crying, but alive.

# 40

## The Plan

Christie ran to Jack, ignoring everything that covered him. Kate went around to his side, saying over and over, *Daddy, Daddy, Daddy.*

Simon silently hugged him as tight as he could. Shivering with fear, locked on his father as though there was nothing else left in the world.

But then Jack pulled them away, and looked just at Christie.

"Listen," he said to her. "We have to leave."

She nodded. Of course they had to leave.

"Let's go. C'mon kids—" she started.

He grabbed her arms and held them fast, the strength of his grip nearly pinching.

"No. Before we go . . ."

She saw him look down, aware that the two terrified kids still stood there, looking up.

Jack turned around and picked up the two .44s. He gave one to Christie, whose hand seemed to close over it reluctantly.

His wife let the gun rest in her lap.

Then he took Kate's hand and closed it over the other gun.

He had taken her to the range one day. She had shot a gun before. "This is the safety. You leave it on until we leave here. And you hold it pointed down. Unless . . . unless you have to—"

"Shoot something," she said.

Her eyes glistened as she fought back the fear and tears. He smiled. A nod.

Then, heartbreaking, unexpected . . .

"Dad." He turned back to Simon. "Dad, do I get a gun, too?"

He leaned close and gave Simon a hug. Both Christie and Kate looking at Jack, seeing that his eyes had turned watery. He blinked, the cabin living room suddenly blurry.

"Simon. Son. You have to do something really important, you hear me?"

He felt the boy nod. "You hold your mom's free hand tight. Got that? Tight as you can. Don't let her go. And the other one, you hold your sister's hand. You hold onto them, Simon. Can you do that for me?"

Another nod.

Then, as if it was the hardest thing he ever did, Jack finally pulled away.

They walked out. He leaned close to Christie.

"I have a plan."

She watched him force a smile.

His eyes, still glistening, told her something more than his words.

There was no time for him to explain things to her privately, what would happen, what they would do.

She'd have to hear his words even as the kids followed and they, too, listened. And she'd have to somehow understand what he was really saying.

"Okay," she said, letting him know that she understood.

His eyes wet, tearing up with gratitude that she understood things.

She couldn't imagine what he had been through.

Her heart felt like it could explode at the thoughts of the agony, the madness that he'd had to face. That he still had yet to face.

He told her what would happen, pulling the kids alongside him through the brush even as the branches tried to trip them and rip at their bare arms.

The camp filled with the sound of alarms and gunfire.

"Did you—did you do that?"

"Yeah. Keeps them busy."

His pace relentless, even though his one good leg was doing the work of two he marched them through the woods.

Telling her the details of the plan, all said within earshot of the kids.

So they heard, too.

But did they understand?

God, did they understand?

Jack stopped them.

A quick finger to his lips, barely visible in the dark.

Something moved through the woods ahead. Jack trying to see what was there. Some movement. Maybe this was a bad way to go.

Then a scream from behind. He wheeled around just in time to see a Can Head grab Christie and yank her away from the two kids. Then another Can Head picked up Simon, like a sack of food, tucking the boy under his arm and turning away.

Like a feral creature racing away with its prize.

Not even seconds to think about what to do, no time to weigh options.

Jack had already raised his gun, but a shot could go wrong so easily.

And there was movement to the left, where Kate was, coming from behind her even as his terrified girl raised her gun, wobbling.

Such a stupid idea, that she could shoot, could protect herself.

No time to think.

Jack leaped forward as fast as he could, giant steps, his free hand reaching out, grasping—

Closing on the Can Head's maggoty hair. Tightening, and yanking the thing back like a caught fish.

Pulling the head close to his other hand, the gun barrel pressed right against the head. One clear blast, and the thing dropped Simon, screaming.

Not able to tell the boy he needed to be quiet. The noise would only bring more.

Turning, Kate being dragged away as she kicked at the thing holding her, its blood-smeared face and teeth inches away from hers.

No other option here, and he raised his gun and fired at the thing.

For a stunned second, the Can Head froze as if not sure what was wrong.

There was no way to prevent the blood from dripping onto his beautiful daughter.

But in that second of blood-spattered madness, he saw her raise her gun, turning left and right. She was ready now.

Another Can Head leaped out of the bushes, right at Kate.

Kate held her gun steady.

He had trained her. Took her to the range. God, had he trained her enough?

All Jack could do was watch as she fired.

The thing fell at her feet.

Jack, thinking: *good girl, such a—*

Then—to Christie.

She had fired a shot. Wounding the thing holding her. And again, with so much kicking and movement, Jack didn't have a shot.

But he was the last one. Christie fighting against the Can Head had slowed down its attempt to pull her away.

Jack went to it and whipped the gun at its head just as it was about to bite down on Christie's shoulder.

Then again, and again.

Then a hard smack to the elbow of the thing, a crack at just the right spot, and the arm holding Christie became useless.

Until the creature's head was far enough away from Christie so Jack could come behind it, close its neck in an arm lock, cutting off air.

'Cause the goddamn things still had to breathe.

Christie, herself nearly choked, staggered away, immediately looking to the kids.

She raised her gun to the Can Head. Jack held tight.

And with Jack not even believing what he was seeing . . .

She fired. Right at its skull.

And when it fell away—

—when it slipped down from Jack's hold—

—when it was quiet and there were no more gunshots, no more here at least—

—he stood in the woods and saw his family looking at him.

As if seeing him, really seeing him for the first time.

He saw Simon take Christie's hand, then Kate's.

*My boy. . . .*

"C'mon," he said.

Jack and his family started moving again.

Racing, running now . . . so much that both Simon and Kate took turns tripping, rolling on the brambles.

*But so beautiful, my beautiful children*, he thought. *They didn't give out even a yelp.*

No matter what stuck them, what pricked them in the thick brush, they were silent.

It took all of his willpower to not cry.

Then—they were there—the parking lot. A sea of cars, far removed from the gunfire, the racing guards, the panic behind them.

Jack didn't stop as they left the shadows and went down to that sea.

# 41

# The Gate

Jack turned around and looked at the brown blanket that now covered the backseat. Someone looking could see that there was something hidden back there.

If they got close.

*Something back there.*

The cab light had not gone on, the ceiling switch still thrown.

Now that no one could see him, he reached down under the steering column and felt for the switch. The double-switch he had installed so long ago.

He felt its shape. He could reach it in an instant.

Back to the key in the ignition. A twist, and the Explorer started.

Jack had feared they might have ripped the guts out of the SUV, but the engine sounded fine.

He kept the headlights off, and then, aware that he could be seen, he backed up and eased the Explorer slowly around to the road that led to the center of the camp.

Even with the windows down, he could hear the sporadic sound of distant gunfire. The alarms blaring. Good, they were still dealing with the Can Heads.

Or perhaps what this *really* was: Can Heads fighting Can Heads.

*Let them fucking eat each other.*

As he came to the small rise from the lot, the road that veered near the lodge, he saw a group of people—Paterville residents and guards, those the Can Heads from outside hadn't gotten.

Standing in a cluster, guns ready, bunched up and looking all around, scared.

A few looked at Jack as he drove past them.

They had guns. They could shoot.

But they simply watched him sail past, one lanky man's face having a what-the-fuck look, wondering where the hell this guy could be going.

If someone looked in the back, all they would see was the shape, the blanket.

Would word be passed? A different kind of alarm?

Jack picked up speed as he passed the cabin area, and started down the road past the lake and on the way to the main gate.

He wondered if he had made a mistake.

If he could get out this easy, had he made a fucking mistake? His plan all wrong?

He felt like stopping. Going back. Was there time to change his mind?

Instead, he kept driving. The plan. This was the plan, the way to get his family out.

He pressed harder on the accelerator, passing the fifteen-mile speed limit posted along the road. Twenty, twenty-five . . . thirty.

And more, until the heavy-duty wheels of the SUV began kicking up a steady stream of pebbles and dirt behind it.

A curve, another straight section, then—if his memory was correct—one more curve.

He noticed something. The alarms had ended.

Was the power still out?

Could they have fixed the power to the fence in such a short amount of time?

Another curve, and now a clear straight run to the main gate.

Bright lights ahead, two high beams on the turret at the side of the gate, one at road level.

The turret lights pointed out into the woods, probably hunting for any signs of Can Heads.

Faster. Thinking he was so close.

The two lights on the top of the turret swung around. Almost as if it had been planned.

The guards hadn't been looking for stray Can Heads at all.

The lights swung around and pointed down at the roadway, at the SUV, at Jack racing to the gate.

A bunch of guards on the road, waiting for Jack.

With Ed Lowe at their head.

He didn't brake.

*So, they see me. They'll shoot. The Explorer can take some hits.*

But then, despite the blinding glare of the giant lights, he could see above them, the gate . . . so close.

Faster—and then the group parted.

And Jack saw the trap.

A massive felled tree lay right across the road. The SUV slammed into it.

And backlit, the people waiting there. Guns sticking out like pins in black pincushions, the crowd all shadows.

They waited for him while the front of the car crumpled against the tree, tires exploding, windows shattering.

Jack's head hit the steering wheel. He immediately tasted blood from the gash.

Then, as the shadows moved closer, Jack, blinking—blood in his eyes, too—he saw the struggling figure of Ed Lowe, laboring to walk, but walking.

His camp. His place.

Behind him, a bloodied Shana.

Someone had found them, freed them.

Lowe knew that there was an even worse danger to Paterville than the Can Heads outside.

*Exposure.*

Exposure would destroy the camp.

Jack looked at the seat next to him.

*My gun.*

He reached to the side but felt nothing.

The crowd only steps away. Some moving ahead of Lowe now, eager, perhaps forgetting that he ran the place. Maybe Lowe had had his day.

As they suddenly started racing toward the vehicle, Shana raised her ax. Other women were there too, rocks in their hands.

*Everyone invited.*

He heard Lowe's voice as if coming from miles away.

"Jack! Jack, it's over. We got you, got your family!"

As the crowd gathered close, Jack could only shoot one quick glance at the back.

Lowe stuck his head through a shattered opening in the driver's-side window, his jowly neck catching some of the cracked glass.

"We're going to rip you all into pieces!"

Jack turned. His hand again reached to the seat beside him.

The gun. Fallen to the floor?

He popped open the glove compartment.

A knife there. Used to be there.

His hand closed on it.

A jagged knife for fishing. Probably rusty.

Jack spoke as loud as he could.

"You're right! It *is* over!"

He jabbed the blade into Lowe's neck and twisted it left and right before leaving it buried in Lowe's gullet.

But the action only seemed to embolden the others, now reaching in through the smashed windshield, the side windows, into the back.

No way forward, no way out.

More glass being smashed, pried away. Like opening a can. To get at what was inside.

Jack sat there.

He could see the clock on the dash. The digital clock. The time.

"Now," he whispered.

*Jesus, now . . .*

A rock smashed into the front window, then another, until, on all sides, the windows took hits.

The car tilted forward, wheels flat, engine dead, the SUV now rendered completely immobile.

Until one crazed person kept banging at a rear passenger window with a big rock broke through.

Then, like a feeding frenzy, that small opening triggered the horde to clamber on top of the vehicle, banging, shooting, smashing. A few with flashlights, shooting light into the car to see what treasure waited for them.

Jack leaned down, flailed around, feeling the car floor. The gun had to have fallen down here.

Had to be there.

Then he had it.

He started shooting through the jagged openings in the glass as they tried to get at the door latches, some trying to crawl through impossibly small holes in the windows.

*Just Can Heads,* he thought. *That's all you are.*

Shot after shot.

And then hands reaching in from the side to grab at the blanket, and what lay beneath it.

Jack ran out of bullets. He let the pistol fall. Ammo somewhere . . . but why bother?

The Explorer was covered with Can Heads.

All around the sides, on top, reaching into every hole. Ed Lowe, his throat gushing, still battered at Jack's side window, the bloody spittle flying out.

The SUV like a bit of candy dropped in the summer dirt and soon coated with ants as though it was a living thing.

He reached down to the switch.

Not a slow movement. Perhaps he had waited too long already. He thought he heard something inside the car, on top of the blanket.

Jack threw the first safety switch.

The car had enough explosives to make a crater twice the size of the vehicle.

And blow the dozens of monsters on it to pieces.

He threw the second, now-active switch.

He heard a click.

# 42

## Five Minutes Earlier

Christie sat up in Tom Blair's car.

She looked back at the kids.

"Okay. Just stay down."

Nothing.

"You hear me?" she said.

Kate answered first, her body pressed down as close to the floor as she could. "Yes, Mom."

Then Simon, following his sister's model: "Yes."

She turned the key, hands shaking with the thought that the car wouldn't start, even though Jack had tested it.

He had been so clear in his instructions; so precise in his plans.

To watch the time. Because when it was the *right* time she had to pull out of the lot.

If they were expecting them to leave, it would be the front gate. They'd look for the Explorer.

*But maybe,* he had said, *they'll have their hands full.*

She had tried pleading, the kids able to hear.

They had to stay together. They were a family.

She had to watch her words with the kids so close . . . her eyes were wet, trying to hide that from them. Until she didn't care, as she wiped at them.

*I'll get through,* he said. *Somehow. Let them spot me first.*

With the camp under siege, they could get on the roads and get out.

But if they were watching, he had to make them think that this was how they'd escape. Together.

He had put a hand up to her cheek.

*I'll get away.*

He gave her a kiss. He hugged the kids.

Then another kiss.

And words meant for her ears alone.

*If you hear something . . .*

He held her tight.

*You'll know.*

She couldn't let him go. Couldn't let him go.

But he pulled free.

And then he backed away, moving to the Explorer. She did as he instructed. Getting the kids down. Then she crouched down, even though she couldn't see him anymore, couldn't get a look at him inside the car, pulling away.

Only when their car was gone did she get the kids inside the station wagon, with its ordinary glass, its ordinary wheels.

If they were escaping, they'd expect them all to be in the Explorer.

She started the station wagon. Then pulled around to the back of the parking area, and onto the service road.

She remembered his last instructions.

*As fast as you can . . .*

Despite the rutted dirt road, she pressed the accelerator to the floor.

Christie didn't bother looking at what was all around her. People ran around, their fear sending them in all directions.

At one point, someone ran madly across the road that weaved through this upper camp, and rolled right onto the front of the car, then back, over the windshield, onto the roof.

Random Can Heads roamed around. The sound of bullets closer as people tried to spot them running through the upper camp.

That meant—

*Might* mean that the fence was still open, the electricity still down.

She tried to see where the winding road led to—a way out? A road to the other gate?

She drove over a huge rock.

The jolt made Simon yell.

"Mommeee . . ."

"Sorry, baby."

Then she kept repeating, saying it.

*Sorry, baby, sorry, so sorry . . .*

She saw the road curve right, out of this upper camp, the car swerving as she took it fast.

She heard a noise like a hammer hitting the side of the car.

A bullet. Someone shooting.

"Stay down. Kate, Simon, you gotta—"

Another bullet, this one farther back.

*No,* she thought. Over and over.

*No, no, no.*

*Not my babies . . .*

The car careened crazily down the dirt road, bumping up and

down, jostling left and right, feeling like it might fall apart into a jumble of pieces.

She saw lights. A turret. A gate.

As soon as she saw the gate, a bullet cracked the windshield, and now she could only see the whole scene through a fun-house quilt of shattered glass. But the windshield held together.

She had to ram the gate.

And if the electricity was back on?

All she knew was that she had to keep her foot on the accelerator, pressed hard, hands gripping the steering wheel.

Jack didn't need to tell her what the gun beside her might have to be used for.

If she had to stop.

If they stopped her.

Then the gate, meters away. One guard there.

He raised his rifle to fire right at her.

From behind, two Can Heads jumped on him, dragging him to the ground.

She cried. *Yes*, she thought, *yes!*

In those last seconds before the car hit the gate, before it rammed into the metal barrier with enough force to send it flying, she heard it.

The explosion.

Massive. A tremendous boom that she felt in her stomach. So loud, and the bowl shape of the lake and the mountains magnified the explosion into a giant peal of thunder.

Except it wasn't thunder.

The car plowed through the gate.

She thought: *No.*

She begged: *No.*

Metal pieces of gate and fence went flying to either side of the car. Her kids screamed nonstop behind her.

Christie blinked repeatedly to get her damn eyes to clear, to get them to stop crying so she could see the dark road.

*I have to able to see,* she thought.

*I'm out. I got the kids out.*

*Safe.*

*Up to me now,* she told herself. *That's right. Up to me now to keep them that way.*

She turned on the headlights.

The kids sobbed in the back.

It wouldn't be long before she would answer their questions and tell them what had really happened.

For now, all she could do was drive.

epilogue

# 43

## Scooter's Mill

Christie hit the first checkpoint well before dawn. She slowed the car and pulled the gun onto her lap.

The kids sat up in the back.

Neither had fallen asleep, but they had stopped asking her the same question, over and over.

*Where's Dad?*

She slowed the car. While most of the townspeople at the fence stayed back, one older man walked up to her, a lean man with a weathered face and eyes that squinted as he walked into her headlights.

*Looks okay*, she thought.

He came beside her window and signaled for her to roll it down.

Another look at the other men watching the scene.

They looked . . . okay as well. But then again, so did everyone at Paterville. They had all looked just fine, too.

She hit a button and the window started down. She stopped it when it was only about a quarter open.

"Evening," the man said. She saw him look at the windshield, a spidery net of thin cracks.

She nodded.

"Kinda late to be out. With your kids and all."

"Yes."

"Any problem?"

She tried to think: How would Jack handle this? What would he say?

"We're coming from Paterville."

The man nodded. Another look at the kids in the back. Then she saw him glance at the gun in her lap.

"And?"

"There was break-in. Their fence. It failed."

The old man looked back at his companions.

"Can Heads got into the camp?"

She nodded.

"Lots of them. We— I . . . didn't feel safe. So, I got them out."

A pause. The man thinking this over.

"All by yourself?"

*No. No questions like that.*

"Yes. It wasn't—" she tilted her head as if she was explaining something so strange, so unbelievable—"safe. It wasn't safe there."

"Where you headin', ma'am?"

She looked at him. The eyes that looked back, though sunken in that lined and weathered face, so human. *Can he see what we've been through? Is it that obvious?*

"New York City. Home."

The word caught in her throat, her hands still locked on either side of the wheel.

The man nodded.

*What must I look like?* she thought. *The kids* . . .

"Okay. You have a couple more towns you'll have to stop at before you get to the highway. Guess you know that. I'll call ahead."

She raised her head.

"And let them know you're coming."

"Thanks." She looked at him again. Then:

"Listen. Has there been anyone else? From the camp. Anyone else been through here?"

The question so pitiful. The thought so crazy.

The old man took his time shaking his head no.

Then the man turned to the backseat again and smiled.

"You kids take care of your mom, eh?"

The man pulled away from the car, and signaled to the others. They lifted the fence, opening the road. The sky had begun to lighten just a bit.

Before she pulled away, she turned back to Kate first, then to Simon.

"You guys get some sleep. Okay?"

Her two children nodded.

She pulled away from the Scooter's Mill checkpoint.

*We're going home.*

That's what she told herself.

Over and over and over.

*I'm taking my family home.*

# Acknowledgments

This novel would not exist but for the talent and vision of Brendan Deneen and Vince Mitchell. They took my original short story and—with my blessing—created a powerful screenplay based on that story. This novel is certainly indebted to the creativity, ideas, and writing talent they put into that screenplay. Thanks too to the original publisher of the story, Richard Chizmar, publisher of *Cemetery Dance Magazine*, and the subsequent anthology that contained the tale. It was inside that anthology that Brendan and Vince first discovered "Vacation," and then would just never let me forget about it. And as far as Brendan editing this book, every writer should be so lucky. Lastly, it was my wife, Ann, who told me about these guys who called one day and *loved* this story of mine. I think that somehow she always believed that there was more to come from the tale, and thus—so did I. When she believes, you'd be a fool not to . . .